SHORES

An utterly addictive crime thriller full of twists

KERRY BUCHANAN

Harvey & Birch Book 3

Watch out for those
freak waves!
Kerry Buchanan

JOFFE BOOKS

Joffe Books, London
www.joffebooks.com

First published in Great Britain in 2022

Cover art by Nebojsa Zorić

ISBN: 978-1-80405-229-7

PROLOGUE

Another wave lifted the stern of the ketch, twisting her sideways before dropping her into the next trough, leaving her decks awash with saltwater. Rigging groaned in protest and a crash came from down below.

What lunatic had decided that a North Atlantic passage in December was a good idea? The cargo would be bruised and battered by the time they made land in the secluded bay on the northwest coast of Ireland that was their destination.

Clara's knuckles ached from gripping the wheel. The autopilot had failed two days into this hellish voyage, and she'd been hand-steering ever since, and with no electronics to warn her of shipping in the vicinity she'd had to keep a visual watch the whole time. Despite waterproofs and leather sailing boots, she was chilled to the bone. Her saturated gloves were more hindrance than help, but she couldn't afford to lose concentration for one moment, not in these conditions.

Another massive wave, a doubler this time as they entered a stretch of tidal overflows off the headland, tossed *Snow Goose* as if she was light as a cork. Clara's numbed hands lost their grip on the wheel and it spun out of control.

The boat rounded up, bow into the wind, sails cracking like gunfire, and Clara was thrown sideways across the cockpit. Her lifeline brought her up short, hanging over the guardrails. It took all her strength to haul herself to the wheel, wrenching it around, forcing the big rudder to move against the push of the waves until the boat was back on course.

By some miracle, the flogging foresail hadn't become snarled, and as the bows slowly turned back off the wind, it filled with a bang and the boat surged forward. Clara's teeth clattered together, and a sharp pain in her side hinted of injuries that would give her grief later, but she couldn't think about that now.

Her only thoughts were for the cargo. Their wailing cries filled the night like the screams of gulls, praying and cursing in a language Clara didn't understand.

CHAPTER 1

DC Aaron Birch leaned into the wind and driving sleet. It was a wild Christmas Day, all right. Thick, scudding clouds made the streets of Lisburn almost as dark as early evening, and in December early evening began around four o'clock. Still, the dog didn't seem to care. Meg forged ahead, leaning into her collar until she reached the next interesting smell, then she'd pause for a sniff and set off again, a dog on a mission.

Tomorrow, Boxing Day, he'd take another run at the revision notes he'd made for his sergeant's exam. He'd promised Asha before she left that he'd make the effort, but his heart was no longer in the job.

Since last spring, and the discovery of a tiny skeleton that had led to him and Asha blowing open one of the nastiest corruption cases imaginable, it almost seemed as if their chief superintendent, Yvonne Patterson, had been trying to make the job as boring as possible, at least for the two of them. The suspicion that she might be trying to force them both out was one of the few reasons he'd stayed so far. He wouldn't give her the satisfaction.

Aaron rubbed absent-mindedly at the scar in his midriff where a knife wielded by one of his crooked ex-colleagues,

George Aiken, had almost put an end to his life. He'd thought it would all be over when Aiken's boss, retired Chief Inspector Alistair King, had been shot by a sniper, but it really wasn't, because neither Aiken nor Kernaghan, his equally corrupt colleague, had ever been caught.

Perhaps he should be grateful to be kept on desk work, but instead he was becoming increasingly bored. Now it was all training courses and Patterson making a huge show of "running a tight ship" at the same time as hunting everywhere for signs of corruption and irritating everyone by her obsession with tracking down those two bastards. He sighed.

Patterson's attitude had driven DI Asha Harvey out of the Lisburn Road station and up to Bangor in North Down. Despite the confirmation of Asha's promotion to DI, she'd seen all the interesting cases given to other teams while her own followed up petty thefts and suchlike. Even though Bangor saw fewer serious crime cases than Lisburn Road, she'd still be a big fish in a small pond there and would have more responsibility. He was happy for her, he really was, but he missed her quiet, calm ways and her kindness.

And then there were the counselling sessions Patterson kept trying to send him for. She'd put his apathy down to his injuries. But it wasn't that — or not just that, at least. It was the way the station had changed. Since the two rogue peelers, Aiken and Kernaghan, had gone on the run, any of his colleagues who did believe the allegations, and there were still a few that didn't, had been looking sideways at each other, wondering who else might be bent.

The fact that he was practically the only one in the station without a cloud of suspicion hovering over him should have made it better, but it didn't. It made him different. Whispered conversations stopped when he entered the room, and he got suspicious glances, even from people he'd got on with well in the past.

He sighed, and realised he was being observed. At his feet, the intelligent border collie gazed up at him, waiting to see what he'd decide to do.

"What do you think, Meg? A lap of the lake at Duncan's Dam?"

Her tail wagged furiously, taking her entire back end with it.

"All right — but don't think you're getting off the lead. Last time you jumped in Ellie said it took three baths to get rid of the stink."

At the word "bath", the tail lowered a little, then it started its windmill rotation again as soon as he set off along the road that led to the dam.

At the furthest point of their walk, his mobile went off. The name on the screen made him wince. Detective Chief Superintendent Patterson's voice could cut glass.

He held the phone a few inches from his ear. "Yes, ma'am?"

"We've had a tip-off about a potential drugs haul. Apparently, it's on its way up from Newry in a—" The last word was lost to the weather.

"Sorry, ma'am. Could you repeat that? It's really windy, and I can't hear you very well. It's coming up from Newry in a what?"

"Boat. Bravo-Oscar-Alpha-Tango, boat. I'll fill you in when you get here. Come straight up to my office."

Meg whined as he pocketed the phone, her tail tucked between her hind legs as the sleet began to penetrate even her shaggy coat. "You're right, girl. Time to go home. Fancy a jog to warm up?"

He arrived just as his brother Peter was lifting a giant turkey out of the oven.

"Good timing. We're just about to sit down." Then: "No! Meg, no! Get that dog out of here!" as Meg shook her whole body, spraying gritty water all around her.

"Sorry, folks," Aaron said, unclipping Meg's lead, "but work calls. I've got to go." A chorus of wails from his niece and nephew tugged at his conscience. "I know. I'm sorry. I'll try to get back for tonight, but no promises. Have a wonderful Christmas Day. Love you all."

There were times he hated this job. But the thought of a significant drugs haul, and that the chief was finally sending him out on a proper job, sent adrenaline surging through him. He pressed the button in his coat pocket and located his new car by the orange glow of flashing lights, hazy in sleet that was thickening into real snow. At least the kids would be happy if it turned out to be a white Christmas, even if the bookies weren't.

Sinking into the sports seat of the Golf, he closed his eyes for a second and breathed in the aroma of new car. It had been worth the wait; worth saving his spare cash over the last few years and living in a dive to be able to afford this.

The automatic wipers dealt with the snow, and his lights adjusted themselves to the conditions. If he had to be out in this weather, at least he was doing it in luxury.

* * *

His feet echoed in the empty corridors of Lisburn Road police station. It was quiet — the officers on shift were either out on the beat or on call as he had been, and the civilian staff were home eating their turkey and pulling crackers, lucky sods. He volunteered for duty on Christmas Day because he was one of the few detectives without a family.

Patterson was on her feet, striding up and down the length of her office as she snarled into her phone at someone.

". . . well, deploy a stinger, then. Or do I need to come down and do your job for you?"

A frightened squawk from the phone.

"This is basic training, Constable. We can't have drunk drivers careering all over the town. Just do it, or you'll be back on the list for driver retraining sooner than you expect." She turned furious eyes on Aaron. "Sit."

With a rueful flashback to his walk with Meg, he pulled out a chair and sat on it. "What have we got, ma'am?"

"The tip-off came from one of my confidential informants, usually a reliable source. Apparently there's a significant haul of cocaine travelling north from Newry, hidden inside a new yacht bound for a boatyard in Bangor. The boat is on the back of a lorry."

Light dawned. "Oh! When you said it was in a boat—"

The corner of Patterson's lip quirked. Maybe the old bat had a sense of humour in there somewhere after all.

"Is that what you were on the phone about? Are we pulling the lorry over?"

Any hint of amusement vanished in a deep scowl. "Certainly not. If we do that, all we'll have is a lorry driver who may not even know about the drugs. This is our chance to follow the chain and arrest some key players. I have an unmarked car trailing it from a safe distance to make sure it doesn't stop on the way. You're going to drive up to Bangor and liaise with Detective Inspector Harvey."

"Ma'am?"

She sighed. "The informant was mine, so you are going along to keep at least part-ownership of this case; the destination is in Bangor's patch, and it so happens Inspector Harvey will be the SIO." She turned away to look at the snow that was now swirling around the building and settling in the corners of the window frame. "You're welcome. Now, get out of here."

* * *

Yvonne Patterson fingered the mobile in her trouser pocket. It was a private satellite phone, so private that no one here knew about it, and no one ever would. Only one person had the number, and she'd hoped he might have phoned her by now. He always called her on Christmas morning. Had for the past score of years. The sound of his voice was the thread that connected her to hope.

As if her thoughts had summoned him, the phone vibrated. She swiftly locked her office door, then answered it in a low voice.

"I thought you'd forgotten."

"Never." In the background, waves roared, and wind howled.

"Are you at sea? Today of all days?"

There was a smile in his voice as he answered. She recognised it even over the noise. His eyes would be crinkling at the corners, and his lips quirking up at one edge in the lopsided way that had captured her heart all those years ago.

"Guess my destination, Von? This year, I deliver your Christmas present in person."

Her heart skipped a beat, then made up for it with a powerful thud, leaving her struggling to breathe. "No! You can't. It's too dangerous. You should stay away."

"Things are coming to a head. I come to tell you that you should think about leaving. Come to my village with me. You will like it there, I think, and they will love my tall Viking maiden."

"I can't. Not yet," she said. It took an effort to form the words because the temptation was strong. "There are . . . complications. There is a new player who has decided to expand his territory into mine and must be stopped. After that—"

"How do you intend to deal with this incursion?"

"I shall crush it," she said simply.

He laughed, that wonderful warm laugh that seemed just for her ears alone. "You personally, or will you have it done for you?"

"When have you ever known me to get my own hands dirty?"

The chuckle was deep and rich this time, laden with innuendo. "On occasion, *min kjære*. On occasion."

When the call ended, she sat at her empty desk, aware that she was smiling but unable to suppress it. He was on his way to her, at last. It had been far too long, but they had both agreed that there must be no traceable contact between them. At the time, it had made sense, but as the years passed, it had become harder and harder to make do with stolen phone conversations.

She still remembered the way he'd made her feel that first time. She'd been eating alone in her favourite restaurant.

She preferred eating alone anyway, but in those days she'd had no friends of either sex with whom she felt comfortable.

Across the room, a group of men shared a meal, easy and relaxed together. They spoke an unfamiliar language that caught her attention, and while she waited for her main course, she studied them from the safety of her shadowy corner. They were all tall, well built, around her own age. They chattered like schoolboys. All except one.

His eyes were on her. The watcher watched. She felt an ugly flush rising up her throat and could do nothing to stop it, but instead of laughing about her with his friends, he raised his glass of red wine to her in a silent toast.

And oh, God, he was gorgeous. A little more mature than the others. Dark hair, well-groomed, a shadow of stubble on his chin, a thick neck that spoke of understated strength, and a pair of commanding eyes. She tried and failed to look away.

A waiter walked between then and broke the spell. He delivered the plate of pasta she'd ordered and grated Parmesan cheese on the top of it without a word. She was a regular, and he knew she didn't enjoy small talk.

All the time, she kept her eyes glued to her plate, even when he'd moved off. The man across the room had been entertaining himself at her expense. He'd be telling his friends, right now, about how he'd made an ugly woman blush with just a look. Her eyes burned with unshed tears, and she thrust his image firmly out of her mind.

Think of the food. It was very good, the pasta cooked al dente, just as she liked it. She shovelled a forkful into her mouth and chewed methodically.

A shadow appeared at the table: the waiter, hovering. What the hell could he want?

She looked up, her frown already in place and a put-down on her lips.

It was the man. He was taller than he'd appeared, now he was on his feet.

"Can I help you?" she asked.

The corners of his eyes crinkled, just a little. Her heart gave a hard thump, but she made sure her face hid her feelings.

"I came to ask how it is that such a beautiful woman eats alone?"

That was really laying it on too thick. She rolled her eyes. "Seriously? Why don't you go and pick on someone less experienced? I'm too old for this sort of prank."

His face changed: puzzlement followed by irritation. Suddenly he didn't seem quite as smooth, but hard and edgy. "What nonsense is this? Have you no mirror that you are unable to see what others see in you?"

His accent was faint, more a clipped edge to his words and a strange syntax than anything she could pin down. Not an accent she recognised.

"That's quite enough," she said, irritated in her turn. "I'd like to finish my meal alone, if it's all right with you." That bite of sarcasm drove most people back as effectively as a flamethrower, but this stranger seemed oblivious.

Instead of fleeing, he slid into the empty chair opposite her and put his wine glass on the table between them. His voice was low and passionate. "Whoever destroyed your self-confidence should be shot." He took a deep breath. "Perhaps we should begin again. My name is Ole Hansen, and I am the skipper of a trawler out of Norway."

So that was his accent? She repeated that single word in her mind. Norway. The way he said it made her think of snow-capped mountains and deep blue fjords.

"I come here with my friends to seek a market for our wares. Little did I expect to discover a jewel hiding itself in the shadows."

And they had talked. His friends forgotten, he'd sat there with her until the manager appeared at his shoulder with a polite cough and the bill. Yvonne had been startled to find that they were the last remaining customers. Chairs were upside down on tables, and the lights were out, except for the ones in their half of the room.

Ole's friends were long gone.

CHAPTER 2

"Sorry again about missing Christmas lunch, Ma," DI Asha Harvey said into the phone. "One of the perils of being on call."

"I understand," her mother said. "Bapu and your brothers ate your share, and now Pratik says he can't move. You'd think they hadn't eaten since Diwali." If her mother was saying that to cheer her up, it was working. "Aunt Harriet sends her regards," she added. Aunt Harriet, really no aunt at all, but her mother's best friend since childhood, would have been there the previous night for their weekly bridge game. That would never be postponed, even at Christmas.

Assistant Chief Constable Miller had been Asha's inspiration for entering the police service, but if she'd expected any advantage from the relationship, she'd have been disappointed. Harriet Miller abhorred anything that might be interpreted as nepotism.

A knock on her door heralded Aaron's arrival. "I have to go, Ma. Give Bapu a hug for me, will you?"

Aaron edged inside, looking about him at her modern office. His raised eyebrows showed that he recognised it as an improvement on the shoebox she'd worked in at Lisburn Road. For a moment, they just looked at each other, then she laughed. "It's good to see you, Aaron." Privately, she thought he looked terrible, pale and haunted, but she wasn't about to tell him that.

"The boat has arrived at its final destination," she went on, retreating to the formality of their work relationship. "Not Bangor, exactly, but a small, private boatyard along the coast between Groomsport and Donaghadee. The boatyard belongs to a local rags-to-riches fella, Richard Steele. He made a packet in cryptocurrency and had the sense to get out while he was ahead. Local rumour paints him as an eccentric multi-millionaire used to getting his own way. He had this boatyard and marina built — God knows how he got planning — from pretty much bare rock. Built a huge breakwater, dredged out a deep basin, put in jetties and lock gates, to protect it from the winter storms."

Aaron shook his head. "Why?"

"He likes sailing," Asha said simply. "And he can afford it. I have an unmarked patrol car doing drive-bys to check on the place. So far, nothing out of the ordinary. The low-loader waited outside the boatyard for about half an hour, then someone turned up in a car — the lads say it's probably the yard manager. He let the lorry in and locked up, then he drove the lorry driver to a hotel and left him there."

Asha hadn't been about to waste too many resources on a vague tip-off from a source the chief wasn't prepared to divulge. It would probably turn out to be a wild goose chase. She might respect Patterson, who had risen through the ranks at a time when it had been harder for women to do so, but she had never warmed to her boss. Being told at every annual review that she ticked all the diversity boxes had been wearing, as if Patterson thought her South Asian heritage was the only reason she'd been promoted, so when the opportunity of a transfer to Bangor had come up, she'd grasped it eagerly. The atmosphere here was better, and for a small station there seemed to be a better attitude both to her sex and to her skin colour. So far, there'd been none of the racist "banter" she'd experience daily at Lisburn Road.

“What do you need me to do?” Aaron asked.

“For now, nothing much. I’m keeping that patrol car on watch to see if we can catch anyone trying to remove the goods. In the morning, I thought we could pop over there and drop in while passing, just out of curiosity. No point setting off alarms if someone at the boatyard is in the smuggling ring. I was thinking that you, being a young and excitable detective, might want a closer peek at the pretty boat on the low-loader.”

He snorted. “Happy to play along, if you think it’ll get us in there.”

Asha had forgotten how easy Aaron was to talk to, just as if he was another of her brothers. They caught up on gossip, and she asked after Sergeant Lonnie Jacob and some of the old crew.

It was about 2 a.m. when the sergeant in the patrol car called in. Asha put it on speaker.

“It may be nothing, ma’am, but Jim thought he saw movement in the boatyard when we drove past. I stopped the car just up the lane, out of sight of the gate, and he walked back down for a look.”

Asha’s pulse quickened. “And?”

“Nothing, ma’am. Gate still had the chain on it, and no sign of anyone inside.” He cleared his throat. “Mind you, it’s blowing a hoolie out here and snowing heavily. If there was an army on manoeuvres, he might not have seen it from the gate.”

“Okay, Tom. Thanks for the report. When are you due to go off duty?”

“Eight o’clock in the morning.”

Asha checked her watch. Those two really had pulled the short straw on Christmas night, but then Sergeant Tom Casey and his best friend, Constable Jim Christie, had decades of service between them, and they were both widowers. Maybe a chilly night in a police car seemed preferable to a night staring at their own four walls and losing themselves in memories?

"Very good. We'll join you a bit before that, maybe just after half past seven, and see if there's any more activity by then."

"Probably a wild animal," Aaron said. "Fox or something." But there was an excitement in his voice that echoed her own instincts.

Why would someone be moving a new boat on Christmas Day in the first place? And Patterson had said the boat had come all the way over from France. Not for the first time, Asha wondered where the chief got her tips from. "Do ferries even operate over the holiday period?"

She hadn't meant to ask that aloud, but Aaron grinned and consulted his phone. "This guy came up from Newry, according to Patterson, so that would be the ferry to Warrenpoint from Heysham."

His finger flew across the phone screen.

"Yes, there's a nine-hour overnight ferry that would have arrived at eight thirty yesterday morning."

Asha checked the map on her laptop. "It's only a couple of hours from Warrenpoint to Steele's boatyard. He arrived there around four in the afternoon, just as it was getting dark. What the heck was he doing the rest of the time?"

"I can ask if Lisburn Road station has anything to add? They had an unmarked car tailing the truck."

"Do it. If Patterson is keeping control of this case, the least she can do is to provide information."

Aaron made the call. While he was talking, Asha made coffee. She put a steaming mug in front of him just as he finished.

"Apparently there was a multi-car pile-up on the A1 south of Banbridge. Traffic was backed up there for ages until the site was cleared. Lorry driver stayed in the truck for the duration."

Asha looked at her watch. "Nothing much else we can do for now. Tom will let me know if there's anything going on at the boatyard, so we may as well try to snatch some sleep for a few hours. You can have the sofa and I'll take the chair."

To her surprise, she fell asleep almost instantly, waking with a stiff neck and a full bladder just after seven. By the time she was back from the toilet, Aaron was up and looking disgustingly alert for someone who'd been wedged into a two-seater sofa for the last four or five hours. He even had a handful of breakfast snacks for them, and paper cups of coffee from the machine.

* * *

Aaron's little car soon warmed up and made short work of the winding route to the boatyard. They drove on past — the gates stood wide open now — until the unmarked car came into view, parked in a farm gateway. Aaron pulled up next to it and Asha lowered her window.

"Morning, Jim, Tom." She introduced Aaron to the uniformed officers. "Anything to report?"

Tom began to speak: "Nothing new—" Then he stopped as a shiny black car shot past, engine growling. Just down the hill it changed gear and slowed as if it was turning in to the boatyard.

"Sounds like action. Time to get down there," Asha said. "We'll go ahead and you two follow, and let me do the talking, okay? We have no legal reason to search as yet, so we'll play this by ear."

Asha couldn't help but be impressed with the way Steele's boatyard was laid out. Boats in cradles were set out in neat rows, some under canvas, some not, but all of them glittering with frost under the security lights.

A cluster of worried men stood around a plastic-wrapped boat that still sat on the back of the low-loader. They turned to stare at the newcomers. There was shock on at least one of the faces and anger on another.

Asha got out of the car and opened up her wallet to show the warrant card to the group. "Morning, gentlemen. Detective Inspector Harvey from Bangor Police."

One of the men looked ready to kill. He was holding on to a flap of the plastic wrapping from the new boat as if he'd been in the act of cutting it open. A second man, dressed in oil-stained jeans and an old sweater, looked as if he expected to be the victim.

A third figure climbed out of the Jaguar that had passed them up the lane and turned towards her with a welcoming smile and outstretched hand. "You have excellent timing, Detective Inspector Harvey. I've just discovered we've had a break-in here at the yard, and possible criminal damage to a boat that was delivered late last night."

He shook her hand as he spoke. His grip was firm, his dry palm warm against hers. He held her hand a little longer than she was comfortable with, yet when he released her, there came a stab of regret.

Richard Steele gestured behind him at the wrapped boat. "Tell me, Inspector, did you have reason to suspect there might be trouble here this morning, or does the local constabulary always send out two cars and a senior detective to greet the arrival of a new boat?"

"One of my constables was passing during the night and he thought he saw movement inside your yard," she said blandly. "He checked the gate and it appeared to be locked, but since the place is so remote, and since there's so much value stored here in the form of boats, they called it in. So, here we are."

It was a terrible explanation, but really, what else could she say? At least it had the merit of being the truth, although admittedly not all of the truth.

"Well, whatever the reason, I admire your sense of timing. Not only was the chain that secures the gate chopped through with bolt cutters, but someone has sliced into the plastic wrapping of this new boat."

Asha's heart sank. If Patterson's tip had been good, and if someone *had* sneaked into the boatyard overnight, it was possible any evidence they'd hoped to find would be long gone by now. She walked towards the boat. "Show me."

CHAPTER 3

Snow drove into Phil Johnston's face as he pedalled up the hill from the boatyard. The backpack on his shoulders swung from side to side with his movement, gradually pulling up his hoodie and the layers beneath. A cold draught made him gasp as a bare strip appeared above his belt, letting in snowflakes that stung like icy missiles.

What the hell was he doing here in the wee small hours of Boxing Day morning? He should be tucked up warm in bed, not gallivanting halfway across North Down on a borrowed bike.

Headlights coming from the direction of the town sent a fuzzy cloud of light up into the sky, silhouetting the brow of the hill. He flung himself off his bike, boots sliding in the mud at the side of the road, shoved the bike up into the scrubby hedge, and dropped down into a crouch on the verge, keeping his head down to hide his face.

The car passed in a spray of slush, drenching him and chilling him even more, if such a thing was possible. Fuck! He glared at the receding red taillights, and scrambled to his feet, yanking the bike back on to the road.

Would this night never end?

By the time he reached Bangor, his chest burned from hard exertion in the freezing air and his hands were frozen closed around the handlebars. He didn't want to think about the state of his balls. That pointy wee saddle must surely have been designed by a woman who hated men.

His feet slipped as he descended the steep ramp to the main jetty that ran along through Bangor Marina. His temporary home was at the far end, far from prying eyes. Just as he liked it to be. Needed it to be, on this miserable Christmas night. Oh, wait. Boxing Day morning.

The key was where it always was, beneath the flowerpot on the roof of the old wooden barge. His frozen fingers fumbled it into the lock, and the opening door let out a smug of woodsmoke, diesel fumes, and damp wood. Closing the door shut out the cold night, but not the worry that ate away at him from the inside.

He hoisted the rucksack on to the table and stooped to throw some more logs on to the stove. He'd been gone longer than he'd intended, and the damn thing was nearly out, but the wood was dry and it soon began to spit and flame. From the table, oozing meltwater all over the varnished surface, the rucksack glared at him balefully, daring him to open it.

He sighed. How had he got himself into this? Well, he should probably check the haul, to make sure he had it all. He tipped the contents of the bag out on to the table, remembering to slip on rubber gloves before handling any of the rectangular bricks.

One of these belonged to him. A sweetener, his contact had said when he'd complained at being given a job on his home ground.

His sweaty palms inside the gloves, and the pounding pulse in his ears, said it wasn't enough. If he was ever caught, it would be here, in Bangor, where everyone knew him.

Eyeing the brick sourly, he wondered what the hell he was expected to do with it. He was no drug dealer. How was he to get rid of the damn thing?

He considered chucking it overboard into the sea, but knowing his luck, it'd float to the surface and bob up next to the barge, a neon sign for all to see, pointing to him and screaming his guilt.

No. He'd have to hold on to it for now. Maybe something would occur to him if he slept on it.

But sleep evaded him for what was left of the night. The blizzard still raged outside, rocking even the heavy old barge on her moorings and throwing wet snow against the porthole by his head.

He gave up at seven in the morning and put the kettle on for a coffee. The old man who owned the barge kept first-class coffee on board, and Phil had grown used to drinking it black because he never remembered to buy milk.

The first scalding sip jolted him awake. His brain had been churning over his problems all night, but he still hadn't come up with a solution. A shadow passed the window and he physically jumped before he realised it was just one of the town marina's staff, doing their early-morning security check.

At least the storm had abated. He threw on a waterproof jacket, one of the old man's expensive sailing oilies, and cautiously stuck his head outside.

It was still dark, and the seaside town was quiet. Only the occasional headlights passed along the front. Boxing Day. Season of goodwill and all that. He checked behind him to make sure his haul was out of sight, then climbed out into the fresh morning. A walk would clear his head and might even enable him to think of a way to escape this mess.

The man on duty at Bangor Marina's office building was on the phone behind his glass screen and didn't notice Phil in the half-light as he left by the side gate. They were good lads, these, and pretty conscientious, but Phil knew every back door, every CCTV camera, and he knew their routines better than they did themselves. When he didn't want to be seen, he was hard to spot.

The streets were empty. He pushed himself up the hill, past closed shops and empty parking spaces, then along and down the next street. The walking had raised his pulse rate and made him breathe deeply. It hadn't helped him solve his problem, though.

Then a figure caught his eye, hurrying away down a side street. Steve bloody White, yard manager for that arrogant prick Richard Steele. Probably trying to avoid a confrontation with him, not that he was going to give the man the satisfaction.

Barred from working in Steele's boatyard, indeed! And for no good reason, either. White was a jumped-up little twat.

Well, he told himself, plenty of people were keen enough to get him to do jobs for them. He didn't need a tiny private boatyard halfway to nowhere. He had enough customers without them. *Yet here I am, squatting in an old barge while Steve White gets given chance after chance. And it's not even as if the bugger is as clean as his name suggests.*

That gave him an idea. He grinned unpleasantly at Steve White's retreating form.

CHAPTER 4

Aaron's door slammed and he scrunched across the icy concrete to take up a position at Asha's shoulder. Tom and Jim did as they'd been told and stayed inside their nice, warm patrol car.

The opening in the plastic sheeting was big enough to admit a person, but the rest of the boat was still tightly wrapped. Shrink-wrapped, she realised, now she was close enough to see it better.

"Is there any damage to the boat?" she asked.

"We won't know until we have the rest of the wrapping off." That was the man with the oil-stained jeans and a face like a basset hound. "Steve White, yard manager. I'm the one who discovered the break-in, but I didn't get time to report it before the boss arrived."

He looked anxious, but in a dull way, as if he expected the worst to happen and was ready for it.

"Did you check the rest of the yard?" Aaron asked. "Any sign of other damage anywhere?"

"I did a quick walk around, but I couldn't see anything else. I'm afraid I didn't notice the cut plastic at first. It was covered with ice and frozen slush, you know? Road spray from the journey, all frozen in a lump. It wasn't until the owner, Mr Mills here, started to cut into the plastic that he discovered the hole."

"Well, perhaps we should stand by while you unwrap the rest of the boat, just in case," she said.

The plastic was thick, heavy-duty stuff and in the cold conditions, it was cumbersome. The yard manager and the boat's owner cursed as they wrestled with it. Finally, the entire boat was revealed.

Despite her lack of nautical experience, Asha was impressed. It was huge. The sides gleamed white, and there were a pair of shiny bronze propellers that looked as if they should have been fitted to a Stena ferry by the size of them.

Dark, tinted windows formed a horizontal line along the side, and the blunt bow looked as if it was dying to fly across the water. There must be stacks of room inside this monster to stash illegal drugs.

The boat's owner was grinning from ear to ear, all his anger forgotten. "Tell me, isn't she a gem? Have you ever seen anything so beautiful?"

Asha smiled. "She is that, Mr Mills. Do you have a name for her yet?"

He pointed at the bow of the boat. The yacht's name was painted there in flowing script: *Dreamweaver*.

Mills was chuckling away to himself. "Made my money in web design," he said. "Like it?"

"Very good," she said, with no clue what the relevance of the name was. "What happens next?"

"Next, we get the crane and lift her on to her cradle," Steve White said. "If we're allowed?"

"Go ahead."

Asha gave Tom and Jim leave to go, since their shift was ending and there was no reason to keep them, but she and Aaron stayed, by mutual consent, watching from between the rows of boats.

"I'd still like to get a look inside that thing," she said quietly. "I'm hoping the owner will invite me. Pity we can't sneak a sniffer dog on board, but we don't have probable cause to do an official search yet."

Aaron agreed. "That's one hell of a yacht. How much do you reckon he paid for it?"

She shook her head helplessly. "More than the value of my house, I expect. More than either you or I could ever dream of, that's for sure."

"Unless we went on the make, like certain ex-colleagues." At her expression, he held his hands out. "Whoa! Only joking. Sorry."

"I'd rather be poor and straight than rich and crooked."

"Yes, me too," he agreed fervently.

"Thus speaks the driver of a brand-new VW Golf."

The crane engine fired up, and after that it was too noisy for conversation, so they just stood and watched as the huge boat was lifted using wide canvas strops that passed beneath the hull, padded with clean cloth so as not to mark the perfect whiteness, then raised above the low-loader.

The lorry driver pulled forward out of the way, and the crane trundled across the concrete, boat dangling inside its massive square structure. An empty frame had been set up ready to receive its new occupant, and the crane lowered the boat gently on to it while the yard manager ran around adjusting the supports. Even the frame was new, all galvanised steel with padding where it would touch the boat.

Once it was in place, the strops were detached, and the crane drove slowly back to the far end of the boatyard.

Richard Steele came over to stand next to her. "What do you think? Like the boat?"

"I know nothing at all about boats like that," she replied. She'd sailed in dinghies with her brothers when they were all children, and canoed on Carlingford Lough, but had never been near a luxury yacht.

"I'll tell you a secret," he said in a low voice, leaning in close to her in a way that was far more personal than she was comfortable with. "Neither do I. I prefer the ones with a big stick and bits of cloth."

She took a sideways step, so she felt less trapped against the hull of the boat next to her. "Do you have a boat here, Mr Steele?"

"Yes indeed." His expression softened. "*Cloud*. She's down there on the water, if you'd like to see her?"

She glanced at Aaron, who appeared highly entertained by her predicament.

"I can stay here, ma'am," he said. "In case Mr Mills finds any damage."

She couldn't even shoot him a dirty look, not with Richard Steele watching her face so closely. Little tick. She'd have words with him later.

"My colleague has been desperate to see inside the new boat," she said. "Boys and their toys, you know?"

Richard called across to the boat's owner, who seemed delighted to have another admirer for his expensive purchase. Aaron trotted off to join him while Asha followed Richard Steele down a steep sloping ramp from the small car park to a floating docking area with rows of empty pontoons and only a few boats still in the water.

The nearest vessel was a workmanlike motorboat, then there was a huge inflatable with a solid hull, but that one was lifted out of the water on some sort of floating cradle. The third boat was a totally different animal: a sailing boat, with long, graceful lines that, even to Asha's uneducated eye, looked sleek and fast.

"It's beautiful," she said. There was something of the supermodel about the shining hull and the way the mast raked slightly backwards. It took pride of place at the end of the main jetty and took up the full length of the pontoon.

"You should see the inside," he said.

She shook her head. She was here to search for drugs, not to allow herself to be seduced by a rich man's toy. His face showed his disappointment, and she felt a stab of guilt. "Maybe another time?"

"I'll hold you to that, you know. Maybe when you're not on duty."

That sounded far too much like a date for Asha's peace of mind, but there was something inevitable about Richard Steele. She'd expected brash and overconfident, but there was vulnerability there, too.

Oh, for God's sake! Catch yourself on.

"I'd better check on my colleague," she said. "Once he starts asking your Mr Mills questions about his boat, I'll probably have to drag him away."

She turned to retrace her steps along the jetty, but Richard Steele's voice brought her up short. "Why are you really here, Detective Inspector Harvey? On a miserable Boxing Day, with full back-up, and showing an intense interest in a new boat delivery? This isn't just about one of your men thinking they might have seen something in the yard, and you weren't *just passing*, were you?"

This man hadn't become a millionaire by being an idiot. Of course he'd be suspicious. She turned around slowly and tried for an amused look.

"I've a strong suspicion you're right, Mr Steele. I think my colleague might have allowed himself to be seduced by the prospect of getting close to the luxury yacht he saw driving through Bangor last night. And it is Christmas, after all. Who am I to deprive him of such an innocent pleasure, as long as the boat's owner is happy to indulge him?"

He winced at the words "Mr Steele". "I wish you'd call me Richard," he said.

She laughed. "All right. I'll call you Richard. Would you like me to record the crime for insurance purposes, or would you prefer to wait until you've had a chance to check the boat for any more damage?" She handed him a card with her contact details on it. He hesitated before taking it from her.

"If I wait, does that mean you'll have to come back out here to get the details, or will you just send a minion in your place?"

She couldn't help laughing. "We'll have to see, won't we?" *Oh God.* Now she sounded as if she was flirting. *Wise up, woman.*

CHAPTER 5

"Be my guest," Mills said expansively. Too expansively. He either knew nothing about any drugs, or he was confident there was no longer anything to find. Aaron suspected the former.

It was easy, searching the boat. The owner was only too happy to show him every secret hidey-hole and hidden cupboard, proud of the design features. Every seat lifted to reveal cupboards; each seat back hinged up to reveal a space behind it; even the carpeted floorboards hid storage areas, as well as a giant freezer. Aaron was beginning to understand why grown men became so excited about boating.

For his sins, the enthusiastic little man took him all over the boatyard, showing him the system they had for storing boats on cradles and all about the big hoist they'd seen in action earlier. He even showed him the shed behind the office where the controls for the lock mechanism were housed.

"Lock? I thought you only found those on canals?" Aaron said.

Mills laughed. "Aye, they're not that common in these parts, but Richard had one installed when he first built the marina. We're prone to a lot of swell on this stretch of coastline, and this means he can raise the lock gate if there's bad weather forecast and keep the worst of the waves out of the marina. It can limit the times boats can enter and leave, but that's a small price to pay for the security of a nice, sheltered harbour, and if the weather's bad enough to close the gates, you'd be mad to go out there anyway."

Aaron found himself strangely fascinated by the whole setup. It was dawning on him that boating could be a complex affair.

"Find anything?" Asha asked as they walked together towards the car.

"No sign of anything suspicious, and believe me, I've seen pretty much everything in the entire yard. Saying that, Mr Mills's new boat could have been designed with smuggling in mind, it has so many secret cupboards." He glanced around. "Where's . . . ?"

"Steele's gone to see if his yard manager's found anything in the CCTV footage from last night."

Aaron lowered his voice, all the same. "I'd swear Mills had nothing to hide, but was that because he knew someone had already removed the evidence?"

Asha sighed. "No. I thought the same. Wild goose chase?"

"I don't know. There *was* a break-in, and that cut plastic. Somebody could have got on to the new boat and retrieved a package. Plus, I trust the chief; don't you?"

"She's sharp, all r—"

"DI Harvey!" They both turned at the shout. Richard waved at them from the office door. "There's something you should see on the security footage."

The boatyard's office, a set of portacabins joined together, was combined with a social room. Sofas lined the walls, and there was a small kitchenette at one end, a *WC and showers* sign pointing down a corridor. Beneath it was a second sign for *Office.*

A small halogen heater spun in a limited arc on the floor by a desk that housed a flatscreen monitor and a keyboard. Steve White perched on the corner of the desk where he could see the screen.

"Hello," Steele said, with eyes only for Asha. "Sorry it's a bit basic in here. Come and see." He pulled the room's only other chair over next to him. It looked as if Aaron would have to stand.

"Watch this one first," Steele said.

The camera gave an oblique view of the approach to the gates. A figure emerged from the snowy interference, male from the way he moved, and stockily built. He wore a light-coloured hoodie and trousers, and carried something long under his arm.

The intruder's shoulders heaved as he brought the pair of long-armed bolt cutters to bear on the chain. He squeezed through the gap, pulled the gate closed behind him, then did something to the chain before walking out of sight.

"Keep watching," Steele said.

The recording played on until another figure appeared at the top of the laneway. It was Jim Christie, hands shoved deep in pockets. He plodded down the path to the gates, looked at the chain without touching it, peered through the mesh for a moment, then dandered back up the hill out of sight.

"Northern Ireland's finest. Well, I suppose I should be grateful he took the time to check, and that he reported it to you, Detective, or I wouldn't have had the pleasure of your company this morning."

"Community policing, sir," Asha said. "But our intruder was clever, putting the chain back like that in case anyone checked."

Richard Steele gave her a wry smile. "Quite right. Let's see it from another angle."

This one was a longer shot, harder to see anything through the blizzard. The hooded figure replaced the chain from the inside, then moved clumsily over to the low-loader. He felt his way along the length of the boat, presumably looking for the best place to cut his way in.

Aaron expected him to produce a knife, but he didn't. He just tugged at the sheeting and a flap came loose. "What the fuck?"

"Yeah, that's what we said when we first saw it. There's more."

The intruder disappeared into the boat, wriggling through the hole in the wrapping, and not reappearing until the time stamp in the corner of the display showed nearly fifteen minutes had passed.

When he did re-emerge, he'd changed shape. He'd been stocky before, but now his pregnant belly had disappeared. Instead, he had a rucksack on his shoulders, stuffed full. He climbed down, then turned back and reached inside, retrieving a couple of packages each about the size of a brick. He put them down on the concrete while he spent some time replacing the plastic sheet, shoving handfuls of snow into the gaps to disguise its edges.

Finally, he reclaimed his packages, tucking them inside the front of his hoodie, and left the boatyard. He secured the gate behind him so it looked as if it hadn't been tampered with.

"Hold on," Steve said. "Go back a bit, would you?"

Steele obligingly reversed the recording.

"Okay. Play now." He leaned in close to the screen and Asha moved back to give him space. "Pause there!"

The figure had jumped down from the boat and was turning back to lift out the last few packages. For that moment, he was caught by the edge of a beam from the floodlighting, revealing the face beneath the hoodie.

"Do you know him?" Asha asked.

Steve didn't answer at first, then he took a deep breath. "Yeah. I think so. I think that's Phil Johnston. Local odd-job man. He does a spot of gardening, takes things to the tip in his van, but he really likes working on boats, because that's where he reckons the money is. He's cheap, always cheerful, can never do enough to help."

Aaron could feel the *but* before it appeared.

"But he's sloppy, doesn't stick to his quotes, and some boatyards won't let him work on their premises. Including this one."

"Is that—" Steele began.

"Yeah. The fella I was telling you about. He's always sniffing around our owners, offering to do cut-price work for them. They're forever telling me he's going to work on their boats, and I have to tell them he's barred from the yard. He buys them drinks in the pub, apparently. Everyone thinks he's a great guy."

"I feel sick at the thought of someone using my yard, and a boat belonging to one of my friends, to smuggle drugs into the country." Steele's hand clenched on the mouse. "I take it that *was* a shipment of illegal drugs?"

Asha cleared her throat. "It's clear this man, Johnston, knew there was something to find on the boat. The likeliest explanation is drug smuggling, but if the evidence has already been removed, it might make it hard to prove." She tilted her head. "How do you think Mr Mills would feel about a sniffer dog?"

Steele leaned back in his chair. "I'm wondering if you already suspected something like this. If there'd been anything on board, I'm certain you—" he nodded to Aaron without taking his eyes off Asha — "would have found it during your oh-so-thorough search." Steve snorted.

Asha laughed. "You're quite right, of course. We had a tip-off that there might be something hidden on the boat, but we weren't prepared to inconvenience you based on a potentially dodgy tip, so we kept an eye on the lorry. The constable thought he saw movement in the yard when he was driving past, but didn't see anything amiss, so he assumed it had been an animal of some sort."

"I'm not at all sure Fred will be happy about a sniffer dog on his new boat. I'll let you ask him, if you can get him to listen."

Fred Mills was, understandably, not at all keen to have a dog "tracking dirt across the carpets", but when Asha showed him the video footage, he soon changed his mind. He emerged with high colour and a blood vessel thrumming at his temple.

"Call all the fecking dogs in. If there's been drugs in that boat, I'm straight on to the builders. She was shrink-wrapped at the factory in France, so the stuff must have been hidden there."

While Asha tried to explain that the plastic had already been sliced open — suggesting the *stuff*, whatever it was, could have been hidden at any point on the boat's long journey — Aaron took the opportunity to touch base with Patterson to tell her the tip-off had likely been correct, but that the cache had been removed overnight. She promised to send a sniffer dog and handler out as soon as she could rake one out of bed.

He ended the call, then noticed that the lorry driver, who had been busy rolling away all his transport straps, was climbing up into his cab. It looked as if he was getting ready to set off.

"Whoa! Stop!" Aaron ran across the yard, feet sliding on patches of ice. The driver seemed oblivious to his shouts. He was fastening his seatbelt and started the engine as Aaron leaped up on to the step and knocked on the window of the cab. "Stop. You can't go yet."

The window came down and a puzzled face stared down at him. "Can't? *Pourquoi?*"

Damnit. He was French, of course. Aaron dredged up his schoolboy lessons. "*Arrêtez-vous,*" he tried. "*Il y a quelque chose dans le bateau. Nous faut chercher le bateau.*" Shit, that wasn't right, was it? But he seemed to have got through to the driver, who switched the engine off and leaned back with his eyes closed, as if he wanted nothing to do with the whole affair.

Very dramatic. Very French. But if the stuff had been hidden during the boat's journey, that made this man a prime suspect.

CHAPTER 6

The dog handler was no happier to be dragged out on a stormy Boxing Day than his dog seemed to be. The springer spaniel cowered at the back of its cage in the small white van, tail vibrating between its hind legs.

"This better not be a false alarm," the handler muttered as he coaxed the dog out and clipped a lead to its collar. "Brandy doesn't like the wet."

"I thought springer spaniels were water dogs?"

"Not this one. He's a dry-land dog, aren't you, mate? Him and me, both."

"Well, we'll get this out of the way as soon as we can and let you get back to your Boxing Day." Although Asha doubted if Patterson had given him any choice in the matter.

She wondered how he'd get the dog up the ladder, but he just unclipped the lead and made an arm gesture towards the boat. "Search, Brandy. Go!"

The dog ran around the base of the cradle, tail beating a rhythm now it was doing the job it had been trained for, nose to the ground. It did a full lap, then tilted its head and whined at the low-loader. "Up, Brandy. Search."

The dog swarmed up the ladder with no apparent difficulty. He ran around a little then stopped at the cabin door, whining and scratching at the frame. Asha was glad she'd persuaded Fred Mills to stay inside the building, to "give the dog room to work".

The handler mounted the ladder and opened the sliding door. Asha followed, keeping her distance.

A muffled yapping came from deep inside the boat. The handler shot her a startled look then followed the sound, down a narrow staircase into the main cabin at the back of the boat, Asha not far behind him. Brandy was pawing at the base of a giant bed that dominated the cabin, whining, tail beating a furious tattoo.

"Hang on, mate." The man lifted a corner of the mattress to reveal a hatch that opened with a finger hole, so a sheet of ply could be lifted to give access to space beneath the bed. He removed the cover with gloved hands, propping up the mattress with his shoulder.

Brandy leaped up and stuck his head inside the hole, then sat back on his haunches and howled.

"Good dog! Good dog, Brandy." The handler made a big fuss of the dog, rubbing his ears and scratching his neck. Then he straightened and turned to Asha, who was hovering in the doorway. "That's definite, ma'am. If Brandy says there were drugs in here, then there were drugs, but they're not here now."

Asha sighed, not sure if she should be relieved or disappointed. "Any idea about the nature of the drugs? Or am I pushing my luck?"

"Well, Brandy's trained to recognise any class A drugs, but knowing him as well as I do, I'd say cocaine."

She must have looked as cynical as she felt, because he flushed. "I know. The other handlers think I'm mad, but honestly, ma'am, he does react differently to different scents. We had a big cocaine haul a year or so ago — that one was in a boat, too, oddly enough — and his reaction was exactly the same as today, but when he found marijuana at the airport last week, he was much more subdued. It wouldn't hold up in any court of law, but if it helps—"

He'd become far friendlier since the dog had reacted so strongly on the boat. Brandy, however, was wriggling and straining at the lead.

"It does." So, Patterson's tip-off had been accurate, by the sound of it. Cocaine in a boat travelling up from Newry. Once again, Asha wondered where on earth the chief got her information. "Thanks again for turning out. I really appreciate it."

Aaron was standing outside the building with Richard Steele, waiting for her. "Any luck?"

"A definite for drugs, and the handler thinks cocaine." She turned slowly, taking in the surroundings. "Phil Johnston, if that's who it was, left on foot. I wonder if there could be any footprints in the mud at the edge of the road?"

Aaron pulled a waterproof jacket from his car boot and eyed Asha's suit jacket dubiously. "I'll go. You'll freeze in that."

"Borrow mine," Richard said. He took it off and handed it over. "I can huddle in a nice warm building."

She shrugged herself into it, trying not to breathe in the smell of aftershave from the collar. Not until she was out of sight, at least.

They trudged up the access lane to where it joined the road. Aaron took the far side of the road, and she took the near side. Cars had used the wider area in the turn as a pull-in, churning up the ground, but a thin double line wove its way across and through the snow-covered ruts. No, two thin lines. Someone had ridden a bike across here and then back out again, and recently.

She scanned the area. *There*. A single footprint, smeared where the wearer had skidded in the mud beneath the slush, but still a recognisable bit of tread from the sole of a heavy-duty work boot. Wheeled, then, not ridden. He'd wheeled the bike across the rough ground before mounting.

She photographed the tracks, and especially the footprint, putting her own shoe next to it for scale, a size six. This was a good few sizes bigger, although it was hard to be certain because of the movement in the print. But at least there was a clear imprint of the tread. She brushed her wet hair back from her face so she could see better, then wondered why her face felt sticky. A glance down at her hand showed that she'd managed to smear mud across her face.

The SOCO team they'd requested arrived shortly afterwards; a pair of dour, middle-aged men who barely said a word except to complain about trying to cast an imprint in these conditions. When they'd finished, they moved on to the yard and started to dust the boat and the edges of the plastic sheeting for fingerprints. Asha and Aaron took shelter inside and watched through the window.

Fred Mills hung around nearby, anxiously watching as his boat was dusted for prints, then he came back in, blowing into his fists and stamping his feet. "They're taking fingerprints from all of us for elimination. I don't think Steve is too happy about it." He nodded out of the window, where Steve White was staring gloomily at his stained fingertips. "They've finished with *Dreamweaver*, anyway," he said, and went back out into the cold again to check his pride and joy.

"What about Mr Steele?" Asha asked. "Do we have his prints?"

"Got him earlier," Aaron said. "In fact, he volunteered. I'm a little surprised he didn't try to avoid it, so you'd have to come back and get his another time."

"Oh, ha-ha. What did you tell the lorry driver?"

"I told him he'd need to stay here a couple more days and I took his passport off him. Steve says he'll drive him over to the same hotel he stayed in last night, but he doesn't think the fella has much money to pay for it. How long do you think we'll need him for?"

"We don't actually have a lot of evidence to prove there's been anything illegal going on here," Asha pointed out.

Aaron opened his mouth to argue, then frowned.

"See what I mean?" Asha continued. "We have a tip-off, we have tampering with the boat's wrapping, and we have a sniffer dog who swears there have been drugs hidden on board. Did you read that article in the newspaper last year about sniffer dogs in airports? Great at finding sausages and cheese, rubbish at finding drugs. What we need is proof, preferably the actual drugs."

"We have the CCTV of that fella carrying packages from the boat."

"Could have been his packed lunch. Sausage and cheese sandwiches. The point is, we can't prove *anything* criminal."

Aaron sighed. "You're right. So, what next?"

"Let's look into this Phil Johnston: confirm his identity if his mug's on file, and then ask him nicely if he happens to be carrying any cocaine."

* * *

Bangor police station was warm and cosy after the wintery day outside. Asha asked one of the duty constables to run the prints from the boatyard and check the lorry driver for any record of criminal activity through the Interpol database.

Only as she shed the heavy waterproof coat did she remember that it belonged to Richard. She hung it up to dry and wondered how long it would be before she'd find an excuse to return it. She pushed the thought aside. He was right at the heart of a criminal case; she couldn't afford to get interested.

"I'll look into Mr Steele," she said to Aaron. "Can you have a dig into Steve White's background? We only have his word that the intruder is Johnston. It could just as easily be Steve himself."

She ran Richard Steele through HOLMES2, then through NICHE, in case he might have had a criminal record within another force's area, and was relieved when the only time his name came up was in connection with a car break-in. He'd had a valuable guitar stolen from the boot of his car when it was parked in Belfast. Out of curiosity, she pulled up the report and skimmed it.

The guitar had been a vintage Martin acoustic from 1937, and Richard had valued it at nearly five thousand pounds. Asha knew less about guitars than she did about boats, but the photograph attached to the file didn't look like five grand's worth of guitar to her eyes. If he'd been any less wealthy, she might have considered insurance fraud.

"Got a hit on our wee yard manager," Aaron said. "Arrested for disorderly behaviour in a public place, and affray. He was chucked out of the pub and then proceeded to throw punches at anyone who came within range, including one unlucky young PC."

"Do we know what triggered that? Perhaps we should ask him about it. When was it?"

"Two years ago, almost to the day, twenty-seventh December. Too much to drink at the office Christmas party?"

"Find out, but I really can't see him in the role of drug dealer, can you?"

Aaron shook his head. "No. Just seems like a bit of a sad man."

"What about our French lorry driver, Serge Durand? Anything from Interpol?"

"Nothing. Not even a traffic offence. He almost seems too clean. I'm trying to find a French speaker to phone his employer, but no success so far."

If the drugs had been placed in the boat at the factory, the last thing they needed was to alert whoever was responsible. "Yes, do that as a priority, and get someone from Uniform to take his phone to be checked. If he is part of this, I don't really want him phoning home and giving them warning the drugs have been discovered. In the meantime, let's pursue the leads we have at this end and see where they take us."

"I have an address for Phil Johnston. He's a funny one. Nothing major on his file, but he's had a couple of cautions."

"Anything online?"

"Well, he's got a couple of Facebook pages — the personal one's a bit laddish, and the work one advertises his services as a 'Man Friday'. He has a lot of posts from satisfied customers on that one saying he's a great all-round fella, but then there's almost an equal number of posts saying he ripped people off. Did a shoddy job, took the money and never finished." He clicked the mouse. "Take this one, from a Swedish sailor who visited the area last summer. He claims Johnston quoted for a new engine control panel for his boat when his broke, and that he paid up-front, but then Johnston fitted a panel that was clearly used, not new, and it failed when he was out at sea in a force six gale, leaving him unable to start his engine. He had to be rescued by the RNLI."

CHAPTER 7

Phil Johnston's landlady had a mind like a grasshopper and couldn't seem to stay on topic for five minutes. Aaron spent far too long trying to elicit information about Johnston's whereabouts from her before he finally managed to learn that she'd thrown Johnston out over a month ago for not paying his rent and had no idea where he was now.

Walking away, he passed an old, beaten-up van with a transfer of a lawnmower on the side and the legend, *Man Friday, You name it, I'll fix it.* He wandered over to it and peered in through the dirty rear window. He had to clean the glass to be certain, but there was a large sports bag inside full of clothes that spilled out across the floor.

He got his mobile out to phone Asha, but it rang before he'd brought her number up. "Detective Constable Birch."

"Err, hi. It's Steve here. Steve White? Yard manager at Steele's boatyard?" He sounded unsure, as if he didn't expect Aaron to remember him. "Sorry to bother you, but I didn't know who else to call."

Aaron's heart sank. They occasionally got these sad blokes who just wanted to chat, and he never had the heart to dismiss them out of hand.

"Yes, Mr White. What can I do for you?"

"Well, I can't be a hundred percent certain, but I think Phil Johnston might have been inside my house. I was having a spot of tea when I heard a noise from upstairs. I went up to have a look, and while I was on the top floor, I heard the front door closing. I didn't see him actually coming out of my house, but a few seconds later, I did see him — I'm pretty sure it was him — crossing the road a wee bit along. He got on a bike and cycled off towards the town."

That frisson of excitement when something developed in a case never grew stale. "Hang on there. I'm on my way over. Don't touch *anything*, especially not the front door."

"All right," Steve White squeaked. He sounded as if this was the most exciting thing that had happened to him in years.

Aaron called Asha to tell her where he was going.

"Do you want me to send a uniform over there to meet you?"

"Could you spare someone to dust for prints? If we can bring yer man in for breaking and entering, it'll give us a cast-iron excuse to question him about what else he's been up to in the last twenty-four hours or so."

"Good thinking, but . . . Aaron?"

"What?"

"I know you're no rookie, but please remember: it isn't breaking and entering unless he's broken a lock or a window to gain access. Be careful to check for that."

"Ma'am."

As he drove the Golf towards Steve White's address, he indulged himself in the train of thought triggered by the word "rookie". There was one particular rookie constable he'd become quite close to over the last couple of months, since Asha had moved up the road to Bangor. PC Faith McAvoy, with her shy, gentle nature and mischievous sense of humour.

The roads were unfamiliar to him and by the time he arrived at Steve White's the SOCO team were already pulling in. He left his car on the side of the road, snapped on a pair of gloves and checked his pockets for evidence bags.

"Who's the CSM?" he asked the SOCOs.

An older man raised a hand. "Martin Paley. What do you need?"

He indicated the front door. "I need the outside and inside of this door dusting, for a start — but let me talk to the householder." He leaned forward and spoke with his face close to the wood. "Mr White? It's Detective Constable Birch. I'll check the outside of the door for signs of damage, then one of the team will check it for prints."

Aaron watched as the team photographed the door handle and the wood around it. There were fine scratches around the mortice lock and more around the Yale lock above it. Was that enough to count as a break-in? Once the team had dusted the door, he heard Martin say, "Okay. You can open the door now."

The Yale lock clicked and the door swung inwards to reveal Steve White's haggard face. "Thank you for coming. I didn't know if I should call or not, but I'm nearly sure he was in here."

"You did the right thing, sir. Can you show me where you think he might have been?"

"Upstairs. I heard a board creak, and I know every sound in this house. I checked the rooms on the next floor and didn't find anyone, so I went up to the top floor. That's when I heard the front door close. That Yale lock clunks. There's no mistaking it. I ran to the window, but it doesn't give a great view of the street. I can show you."

As the rest of the SOCOs worked on the ground floor, Martin and Aaron followed as Steve led the way upstairs, talking as he went. He stopped at the first bedroom door.

"I opened this door, but I didn't go inside. It just felt empty." He moved on. "The bathroom was definitely empty — nowhere to hide in here — and I'm pretty sure there was no one in the main bedroom. I suppose he could have been lying down behind the bed, but it seems unlikely."

Martin Paley scribbled notes on a pad as Steve White indicated each door, Martin's intelligent eyes darting from one spot to another. *Keen to get on with the job*, Aaron thought.

The main bedroom was immaculate, as if it was never used. Odd that, because Steve White didn't strike Aaron as the neat-and-tidy type. There was a feminine touch evident in the choice of curtains and bedspread, and some period features, like a stage set for a TV costume drama. Steve was right. If there'd been someone hiding in here, he'd almost certainly have seen him.

They followed Steve upstairs to the two rooms up in the eaves. As soon as Aaron entered the smaller room, he understood why the main bedroom had appeared so tidy. Clearly, this was Steve's living space.

A single bed, pushed under the eaves, was rumpled as though the sleeper never bothered to straighten the covers. Or wash them, judging by the rank smell. A wooden chair had almost disappeared beneath a pile of clothing, including oil-stained overalls, and a pair of work boots lay on their sides under the bed. A real bachelor pad.

"Your room?" he asked, for the sake of something to say.

"Yeah. I was in here when I heard the front door lock behind him. I knew I couldn't get downstairs fast enough to catch an intruder, so I went into the room next door" — they followed him into another room — "and that's the window I saw him from."

Aaron tried to open it, but it had been painted shut. Steve wouldn't have been able to see straight down, but there was a limited view — past the line of the roof and the wide Victorian guttering — of the other side of the road, and the iron railings that separated it from the steep slope down towards the coastal path and Pickie Park.

"So you don't think he'd got as far as this floor?"

Steve ran his hand through his hair. "I don't know. I don't know if he was already in the house when I came home, or if he came in while I was in the kitchen, heating my soup. I just know he was in here, that's all."

Interesting. He'd gone from suspecting Phil Johnston to being certain he'd been in the house. Witnesses did that, sometimes. The more times they recounted their story, the more changes sneaked in. It was often a sign of an unreliable witness. He'd have to hope the SOCO team found some evidence.

Martin, seeing that this was an end to the tour, went out to call his team upstairs.

"How about we go back downstairs and leave Martin and his team to get on with it?" Aaron suggested. "Do you have any coffee?"

The kitchen was small for the size of the house, a narrow passageway that estate agents would probably call a "galley kitchen" to make it sound romantically nautical. The counters were grubby, and dirty plates and bowls were piled high in the Belfast sink. Steve must be the type of person who only washed up when he ran out of plates. Aaron had shared a student house with someone just like that, and it had driven him up the wall.

"I've got a jar of coffee somewhere," Steve said vaguely. "It's probably at the back of the shelf. I'm a tea drinker, myself."

Aaron located the jar of supermarket's own-brand coffee and gave it a shake. The powder had set to a solid lump in the bottom. "Tea it is," he said, cheerfully.

Steve went back to the sitting room and dabbed disconsolately at his cold soup with a hunk of bread while Aaron sterilised a couple of mugs with boiling water and some washing-up liquid. The tea bags smelled musty, but he tried not to think too hard about mould. Hopefully the boiling water would kill most of the bugs.

"Here you go. I couldn't find any biscuits, but there's half a piece of ginger cake in the fridge. Do you want it?"

Steve perked up a bit. "Oh yeah. I'd forgotten about that. We can share it, if you like?"

"No. Doesn't go with my diet," Aaron lied. At least the milk in the fridge had been fresh. He'd tested it in Steve's cup to make sure it wasn't clotting before adding a splash to his own.

"Nice house," he said, for something to say. "Been here long?"

Steve's long face told him it had been a bad question. "Around ten years. I really need to get around to selling it and move somewhere smaller, but the wife chose it, and I haven't had the heart."

"You lost your wife?"

Steve laughed. "You could call it that, I suppose. She left me two years ago. Divorced me as quick as she could, and now she's marrying some other lucky fella. Git."

The git could have been the absent wife or her prospective husband. Two years ago would have been around the time Steve had been arrested for affray.

"I'm sorry. It must be hard."

"Yeah. I'll get over it." He looked as if he was going to add something else, but a call came from upstairs.

"I'd better see what they want." Aaron was glad of the excuse to leave the room. There was something depressing about Steve, a sort of darkness that threatened to suck in anyone around him.

He took the stairs two at a time. "What have you got?"

A gowned and gloved SOCO officer beckoned him into the main front bedroom. "Thought you'd want to see this, Constable." She pointed towards a corner near the bottom of the bed where the quilted throw had been lifted to reveal the space beneath.

A small, grey brick sat there looking as harmless as a lost sock, but this little brick was wrapped in plastic, and it was about as far from innocent as it was possible to be.

CHAPTER 8

Asha pushed the papers around on her desk disconsolately. This case had an unpleasant feel about it already. The only silver lining was that Aaron was working alongside her once more. And Richard. Did he count as a silver lining or a pitfall?

She yawned and leaned back in her chair, only to sit up sharply when the desk phone rang. Aaron's voice came through clearly, although he was speaking quietly as if he didn't want to be overheard.

"Either our Mr White isn't as clean as his name suggests, or Phil Johnston has tried to incriminate him. I'm not sure which."

"I'm on my way," she said, and put the phone down.

Steve White's three-storey house stood out from the others in his road because it was lit up like a Christmas tree, lights on in every room. The SOCO's small, scruffy van was parked behind Aaron's Golf, so she parked up behind that and said a brief prayer to the god of traffic wardens.

Voices from upstairs drew her in that direction, but as she passed the door into the front room, she glanced in to see Steve White hunched on the sofa while a family quiz show played at low volume on the TV screen in front of him.

"In here," Aaron said as she reached the first-floor landing. He beckoned her into a good-sized bedroom and pointed to the wrapped brick under the corner of the bed. "I thought we should wait for you before I let SOCO take it away. It's been photographed and checked for prints."

She snapped on gloves, then squatted down for a closer look. Hard to be sure, because the film footage had been so poor, but it did look like one of the packages their intruder had taken from the boatyard. "Okay. You can lift it now. Any prints on it?"

"Not a single one," said the suited figure of Martin Paley. "Not even a partial. It's been thoroughly wiped."

"Interesting. Has anyone checked the house for used gloves?"

"There's a pair of Marigolds by the sink," Aaron said.

"Nope. Marigolds have a distinctive pattern on the fingertips. It'd have shown up on the wrapping, and there's nothing there at all," the SOCO assured him. "They're more likely to have been nitrile rubber, or latex, like surgical gloves."

Asha missed the SOCO team she'd worked with at Lisburn Road. Martin was good at his job, but he had none of Jana Wiśniewska's quirky brilliance. "Good thought," she replied, nonetheless. "Let me know if you find any sign of gloves that might have been used."

"Yes, ma'am."

"You can call me Asha," she reminded him, not for the first time.

"Thank you, ma'am."

Oh well. Baby steps. She took Aaron aside. "Bring me up to speed."

"If it was Phil who planted the drugs, he'd have seen the big bedroom and assumed that's where Steve slept. They're not exactly best buddies, so he might not know much about Steve's private life."

"Before I came over here, I got a couple of officers checking traffic cameras between here and the town centre in case they picked up Phil and his bike. They're already checking footage from the other direction, from out at the boatyard and coming into town."

"That's good. I wonder where he's staying."

Asha's phone rang, a number she didn't recognise. "Hello? Detective Inspector Harvey."

"Hi there. Richard Steele here. Just wondering if you had time to come over and review a little more CCTV footage. I was talking to a friend who owns an eatery overlooking Bangor Marina. I told him about our intruder, and he thought I might be interested in something he'd picked up on his own CCTV."

"Tell me more."

"Easier if I show you. I think you need to see this." He gave the name of the place and said he'd meet her there.

It was full dark when Asha spotted Richard's Jag parked outside a cafe, reflecting the flashing colours from a Christmas tree in the window. Aaron pushed the door open for her, releasing a warm cloud of noise and garlicky fumes.

Richard was waiting for them at a table near the counter, half-turned so he could watch the door and still speak to the thin, dour-faced individual taking orders, whose expression might curdle the milk.

"Here they are," Richard said, but his smile seemed to be for her alone. "This is Sam. He's given us permission to work away at the CCTV footage." The unsmiling owner gave them a brief nod in between serving customers.

Asha smiled and raised a hand in thanks. "What do you have for us?"

"Follow me." Richard pushed himself off the chair. The movement brought him close to her.

He led them through a door marked *Private* next to the bar, and up a narrow set of stairs covered with carpet that probably dated back to the seventies. He pushed open a door to a small office with a desk, computer, and some rough-and-ready steel shelves with box files on them.

"I left the file open, so you should just need to wiggle the mouse," he said.

The CCTV playback had been paused to show a figure cycling into view from the Donaghadee direction. The time stamp showed it to be around forty minutes after the boat-yard CCTV had shown the intruder leaving.

"This was the middle of the night. What drew your friend's attention to it?" Most people with CCTV only watched the recordings if there'd been an attempted break-in, or suspicious behaviour. Or if they were asked to by the police.

Richard laughed. "His daughter lives in Australia and she's just had a baby. He was up in the wee small hours to chat to her and happened to see our friend wobbling past on the camera. He thought nothing of it until I mentioned the break-in at my place, and that a bike might have been used."

Aaron hit play and the figure moved forward, a bit wobbly in the blizzard. He wore the same backpack and hoodie as in the earlier footage at the boatyard, but with the hood down this time. Asha leaned closer to the screen as if it would bring the figure into sharper focus.

"Wait," Richard said quietly.

The figure put his feet down then swung his leg over the seat to dismount clumsily, as if he didn't often ride a bike. He paused to cross the road leading into Bangor Marina and the public car parks outside it. Headlights from an approaching vehicle lit up the screen just as he turned. His features were spot lit for a long moment, clear as daylight.

"It's him." Aaron had been spending time on Johnston's social media. "That's Johnston, all right."

"Keep watching," Richard said.

Johnston walked the bike across the road and into the marina car park, where he disappeared from the camera's view. Richard clicked the mouse and the frames flashed past, cars moving at impossible speed in and out of the lifting barrier of the marina gate, then another click, and it slowed to normal speed again. The time stamp now showed 17:03.

Johnston reappeared, pushing the bike with one hand and with the backpack dangling from the other. It looked lighter now, flatter, and swung freely as if most of the weight had been removed.

He leaned the bike against the low wall of the car park and pulled something from his pocket. It was hard to be sure what they were seeing until he pulled the pale objects on to his hands. Rubber gloves.

He checked the contents of the bag, then slung it on to his back, mounted the bike, and cycled off towards Pickie Park. Towards Steve White's house.

They watched him wobbling into the distance until he disappeared from the camera's view.

Asha leaned back in her chair and breathed out. She hadn't realised she'd been holding her breath. "Is that it?"

"Almost," Richard said. "He returned about an hour or so ago. Hang on; I'll show you."

The next CCTV footage showed Johnston cycling back. The night was dry now, and clear. A thin, intermittent stream of white came from his mouth as he pedalled, looking pleased with himself.

"He's whistling," Aaron said. "The cat that stole the cream. I think we've got him, ma'am."

"So, he's holed up somewhere in Bangor Marina," she said. "I wonder if we can find out where, exactly."

"I might be able to help with that," Richard said. "The staff all know me. I could ask a few questions." He reached out and touched her hand. She didn't draw back. A jolt like an electric shock robbed her of coherent thought for a moment, then she caught Aaron's quizzical expression. She withdrew her hand reluctantly.

"You've been a great help, Mr Steele, but we'll take it from here. Aaron, can you please ask the owner of the cafe for permission to copy the footage we've just seen? Then we'll go across to Bangor Marina and talk to whoever's on duty."

"Are you sure that's a good idea?" Richard asked, then his face closed as if he'd immediately regretted the words. "I'm sorry. I'm not trying to teach you your business, but they might tell me things they wouldn't tell you."

"You're very kind to offer," Asha said, hating the stiffness in her voice, "but we really can't allow a member of the public to become involved in a police operation." If there was one lesson she'd learned over the last couple of years, it was that civilians were a liability. As soon as you let them poke their noses in, someone got hurt. And the thought of Richard Steele getting hurt was not to be considered.

Richard shrugged. "Okay. But if you need me for anything, I'll make sure I'm available. Here's my number." He handed over a business card.

Aaron cleared his throat. "Thank you, Mr Steele. You've been a great help."

Asha heard Aaron's words as she escaped on to the staircase and out into the cold.

CHAPTER 9

There was only a single light on inside the office building at Bangor Marina. "No sign of a bike," Asha observed.

The outer door was unlocked, but there was a keypad to access the inner door, with an intercom above it. She pressed the button.

"Hello?" a tinny voice answered.

"Detective Inspector Harvey and Detective Constable Birch. Can we come in and ask you a couple of questions?"

There was a pause that went on so long she was beginning to think the intercom might not be working. Then the door buzzed open and they pushed through into a foyer with seating around a low table covered in boat magazines.

The man behind the counter slid open a glass pane and leaned towards them, a little startled. "Detectives? What can I do for you? We haven't had any report of a break-in."

"No." Asha tried to sound reassuring. "It's nothing like that. We're here to ask if you've seen this man this evening?"

Aaron held his phone up to the screen. He had it open at a photo of Johnston from his Facebook page, smiling and sun-tanned with a colourful cocktail raised in his hand.

The man at the desk frowned. "Phil Johnston? Yeah, he comes here a lot, but I haven't seen him tonight. Why? Has something happened to him?"

"How long have you been on duty?" Aaron asked. "Could he have come in before you arrived?"

"It's possible. I started at six this evening, but I leave the building every couple of hours to do a walk around the jetties, making sure everything's safe. And even if he did come in, he doesn't need to come inside the building to get into the marina. There's a side gate. Most of the boat owners use that unless they need the loo on their way in."

"Is he a boat owner?" Asha asked.

The man flushed and looked away. "Not exactly, but he's friends with quite a few of our owners, and I think they might sometimes lend him a key fob." He coughed, his embarrassment clear. "He does work on boats for people, you see."

"Can you tell us which boat he's likely to be working on at the moment?"

"No idea. Sorry."

"Would we be allowed to go on to the marina and have a walk around?" Aaron asked.

"Err . . ."

"We could come back with a warrant," Aaron said blandly, "but it would be much easier and cause less fuss if we just had a quick look now."

"I'll have to phone the manager," the beleaguered staff member said. "It'll only take a moment."

"We can wait here."

He closed the glass sliding window while he phoned, but Asha could still hear some of his words. When he put the phone down, his attitude had changed. "Boss says that's fine. Would you like me to walk with you, show you around?"

"Thank you."

He came out from behind his counter through a door that was away off to the side, then pulled on a lifejacket before holding his hand out. "Mike Gibson."

He led the way out of the building through a different door.

The first thing Asha saw was a mountain bike, propped in a bike rack. The wheels and frame were splattered with mud, and it looked very like the mud out on the coast road, where she'd found the bike tracks. Aaron stooped in close, then straightened up and nodded at her.

"Whose bike is that?" she asked Mike.

"It belongs to a fella who lives aboard all year round. He doesn't have a car, so he uses this to cycle up to town to do his shopping. Heavy old thing, but he says the exercise does him good."

Now he'd been told to be helpful, Mike Gibson couldn't do enough for them, it seemed.

A steep ramp led down from the main building to the floating jetties, which were lit by low yellowish lights every twenty metres or so on alternate sides. The night was still, but Asha thought she'd hate to have to pass along these floating walkways in a high wind. They were slippery underfoot with the damp, and still sparkling with frost in places, despite the thaw.

Mike led them along a slightly narrower jetty at right angles to the main one. There were fewer boats tied up this far from the main building, and they were bigger than the ones they'd passed earlier. Asha yelped as she walked into something hard and unforgiving.

"Sorry," Mike said. "You've got to watch out for anchors sticking out on these big boys. Some of them overhang the walkway a little."

She reached out and touched the thing she'd walked into. They were halfway between lights, so she hadn't seen the massive lump of stainless steel that had almost certainly left a bruise on her upper arm.

"I usually start at this end of the marina and work my way backwards," Mike said cheerfully. "The guy who owns the bike you were asking about lives on this boat at the end, on the hammerhead, but he's away at the moment, staying with his son for Christmas."

The boat he pointed out was huge, with two stubby masts and a low, square cabin roof. An old-fashioned barge with a fat body and blunt bow.

"Okay," Asha said quietly. "So, if the owner is away, why is there a light on in the cabin?"

Mike shook his head. "Maybe he leaves it on for security?"

"Have you noticed him doing that before?"

"No, but then I hadn't noticed this time, until you pointed it out."

Asha turned to Aaron. "Go and see if it's Johnston, would you? Quietly."

He nodded and disappeared along the jetty, flitting from shadow to shadow until she could no longer see him. Only when he'd gone did it occur to her that Aaron might have some qualms about moving around in a marina at night after he'd nearly drowned in one a couple of years ago.

She thought about Johnston's stocky build. If he was on that boat, they'd be foolish to take him on without back-up. She'd call for a couple of uniforms to make the arrest. Both she and Aaron had had enough of cold water and it wasn't worth the risk of a physical altercation here in the dark, where their target knew the lie of the land better than they did.

In a moment, Aaron was back with her again. "I think he's there. There's someone wearing clothes like his, sleeping on the sofa, and there's a half-empty bottle of something on the table."

"Good. Back to the marina building, I think, then we call the cavalry."

Mike Gibson started. "Cavalry? What exactly does that mean?"

"Sorry, sir. Figure of speech. It means I call a couple of uniforms down here and we arrest Mr Johnston. He's a person of interest in a case we're investigating."

"I'll need to phone the manager," he blustered, well above the whisper they'd all been using until then. "I don't think he'll be happy to hear about an arrest being made on marina property!"

"It's all right," she said. "I'll call him myself and explain. I'm sure he'll want to be here to see what's going on, so if we could possibly use your office while we wait?"

As she spoke, she shepherded him and his loud voice back along the jetty, away from the boat that held their one and only real suspect.

The marina manager, Ian Nicholson, was keen to help and already on his way over, judging by the background rise and fall of a car engine passing rapidly through the gears.

He was a slim man who looked to be barely out of his thirties, but he brought with him an air of efficiency that Asha found promising.

"How do you want to handle this?" he asked.

Asha smiled, warmed by his co-operation. "We have a couple of uniforms on their way, sir, but I think the key is to keep it as quiet and low-key as possible." She had a thought. Aaron had seen Johnston, but his identification hadn't been certain. This was tricky territory: with a clear sighting of the suspect on board, they needed no warrant, but maybe she should cover her bases to be safe. "What about accessing the boat Mr Johnston is on? Do I need to try to chase up a warrant, or can you grant us permission to enter?"

He frowned, as if he was thinking it through, and Asha liked him for that. He wasn't one to rush in with promises he couldn't keep. Then his face cleared. "Give me one minute. I'll call the boat's owner and check if he's okay with it. I'm pretty sure he will be. He's a sensible guy."

He quickly found the number from a file that Mike already had open on the desk and made the call.

"He's furious," Ian Nicholson said, when he hung up. "Apparently, Johnston got halfway through servicing the cabin heater on that boat, but then he upped tools and disappeared, leaving everything in a mess and with some essential parts missing completely. He hasn't been answering calls since, so Roy sacked him by text and told him never to go near the boat again, or he'd call the police. He's all in favour of you arresting him and unreservedly grants permission to board and search his boat."

That made everything easier. "Good. Now we just need to wait for—"

Mike Gibson interrupted her. He was peering out of the big front windows of the marina building into the patchy darkness out on the jetties. "He's on the move."

Asha strained to see, catching only glimpses of movement as Johnston flitted along the jetties, hidden intermittently by boats as he passed. He kept pausing as if he was searching for something.

"Is there any way he can leave the marina without having to pass us here?"

Nicholson had raised a pair of binoculars to his eyes and was watching the jetty through them. "There's the side gate, but we'd see him approaching from here. It's only useful to him if we're behind the counter. Otherwise, only by sea."

Then the distant figure disappeared, but a couple of masts swayed as if a wave had passed beneath the boats. He couldn't have jumped in, could he? The water would be near freezing. No, he must have jumped on to one of them.

Nicholson cursed and set off at a sprint, Mike and Aaron a heartbeat behind him. Asha was ready to follow but a flash of yellow caught her eye. The two uniforms she called for were at the outside door.

She let them in. "There's been a development. Our man might be trying to escape by boat. I'm going to phone the coastguard, but you two get down there after DC Birch and see if there's anything you can do to help."

They nodded and lumbered off towards the action while Asha tapped 999 into her phone and asked for the coastguard. There was probably a direct-dial number, but she didn't have it. This way was as quick as calling via her own dispatcher.

In the distance, a small, sleek powerboat began edging out of its berth, turning and motoring between the rows of boats. Aaron and the other two men were running along the jetty, but they were going to be too late. The motorboat was already clear and accelerating.

"Belfast Coastguard."

She forced calm into her voice. "Detective Inspector Asha Harvey, Bangor Police. We have a suspected drug smuggler heading out of the marina here in a small powerboat. I don't even know if you guys can respond to a situation like this, but is there any way of intercepting him?"

There was a moment of muffled noise, as if the speaker was turned away and talking to someone else, then the voice came back.

"Yes, Inspector Harvey. I'm actually sitting in the coastguard office here in Bangor, right above the marina buildings. We can see the boat in question from here, both visually and on AIS. It's just crossing the outer harbour, heading towards the open sea. As it happens, we have a routine training exercise going on currently, a joint operation between the Belfast Harbour Police and Lagan Search and Rescue. They have two officers on board, and their ETA is roughly twelve minutes. I've redirected them to intercept your suspect. If you stay on the line, I'll keep you updated."

Once again, Asha heard the rumble of voices in the background. She strained to see, but the little boat had rounded the corner and disappeared. The marina building seemed empty suddenly, and she felt very alone.

Aaron and the others must be on their way back. They'd surely have seen Johnston driving off and know it was too late to intercept him. But they didn't appear.

Instead, a second boat eased out of its berth and turned for the exit. Asha cursed silently, wishing for the binoculars Nicholson had taken with him.

CHAPTER 10

Aaron ran as fast as he dared, heart pounding every time his foot slid on the frozen planks. He concentrated on placing each step, distracting himself from the memory of icy water closing over his head, filling his nose and mouth . . .

The other two slowed and stopped. "He's away," Mike said, breathing heavily.

"We can take the workboat," Nicholson added, panting so hard that his breath plumed in the frosty air. "At least we'll be able to see which way he goes."

Aaron followed them a short way back along the jetty to a fat little boat that looked more like a kid's bath toy than a seaworthy vessel. The others jumped into it, making it rock alarmingly. Mike started to untie various ropes while Ian ducked into the little cabin and emerged with a life jacket for Aaron.

"Crotch straps," he mumbled, and pointed towards his own groin.

Aaron lowered himself carefully down into the boat and put the thing on. It was a heavy dark-coloured tube that draped across his shoulders with clips to hold it in place. The crotch straps were thin webbing straps that went between his legs from the back and then clipped in at the front of the life jacket. They dangled loosely enough until the boat rocked, and he sat down unexpectedly hard on the side bench. That was when the crotch straps lived up to their fetish-like name.

The engine fired up, spewing smoke out of the exhaust and nauseating Aaron with the stench of diesel and oil. Mike hauled the ropes back into the boat, and it bobbed away from the jetty.

What am I doing here? I'm nothing but a liability.

The two uniformed officers arrived as the little boat began to accelerate away.

"Go back to DI Harvey," Aaron shouted. "She'll tell you what to do."

Then he had no room in his mind for anything other than the chase, as the workboat surged forward with surprising speed for such a dumpy craft. He gripped the side and held tight.

The night was still and clear, distant clouds thinning to allow moonlight through. The workboat rounded the harbour wall towards the open sea and spumes of foam flew into his face as they hit the waves. His stomach contracted and he clamped his lips tight, determined not to throw up.

The bow of the boat lifted then crashed down, soaking his clothes and filling his nostrils with the tang of the sea. He sneezed and held on tighter.

Mike pointed and shouted, but Aaron couldn't hear the words over the engine. He followed the finger and spotted a small white dot in the distance, moving rapidly away from them. It was clear even to his watering eyes that there was no way they'd ever catch Johnston in this tub.

"We should head back in," he yelled, but his words seemed to fade to nothing before they left his lips. Besides, the other two were like a pair of schoolboys, caught up in the excitement of the chase. Ian Nicholson stood in the wheelhouse like a modern-day Captain Ahab, swaying to the motion of the boat as she surged through and over the waves.

Mike pointed again, to his left this time. Aaron blinked seawater from his eyes, too afraid of being thrown overboard to spare a hand from its grip, and stared.

A second craft was roaring up the lough from the Belfast direction on an intercept course with the first boat. It was moving incredibly fast.

Ian eased off the throttle on the workboat, and she slowed abruptly, bobbing on the waves like a little, fat cork. He raised the binoculars to his eyes once again.

"Looks like Elsar. Not sure what they're doing this far out."

"Elsar?"

"Lagan Search and Rescue. L-S-A-R. El-sar."

Aaron risked standing so he could see better, moving his death grip from the edge of the boat to the edge of the wheelhouse roof and trying to mimic Ian's casual stance. The new boat was closing fast with the one Johnston had taken, but he couldn't see if they'd caught it or not.

Ian lowered the binoculars. "They've got him. I think he threw something overboard before they caught up with him, but it was hard to tell. Hang on." He put the binoculars to his eyes. "The Elsar boat is circling back. They're fishing out whatever he tried to dump."

After that, it was a matter of following the lifeboat and the little speedboat back into the marina. Although the waves didn't seem as rough in this direction, hitting the boat from behind instead of from the front, they caused a horrible twisting, rolling motion instead. Aaron's stomach roiled miserably until they rounded the big concrete breakwater and reached more sheltered waters.

Asha and the two uniforms were waiting on the jetty when they parked up. She greeted the lifeboat crew with a big grin when their orange-and-black boat surged up to stop at her feet, then she jumped aboard at their invitation.

Aaron clambered on to the jetty and went to join them. A subdued-looking Phil Johnston huddled in the bow of the lifeboat. One of the crew, with a Harbour Police uniform, handed Asha a dripping rucksack.

"He tried chucking this overboard when he saw us coming, but it didn't sink straight away, so we were able to go back for it. We left it for you to open, in case you need it for evidence."

She took it but passed it to Aaron. "The honour is yours."

The bag was soaked, but it had been a good-quality rucksack at some time and the material was mostly still waterproof, which was probably why it hadn't sunk straight away. He pulled on a pair of rubber gloves and undid the zip, opening it wide so Asha could see inside as well.

First out was a plastic-wrapped brick almost identical in size, shape and colour to the one they'd found under the bed in Steve White's house. He handed it to Asha. "There's more like this in here."

She weighed it in her hand, letting the lifeboat crew and the police see, then gave it back. "Keep them all together. We'll bring this and him back to the station." She turned to the Harbour Police. "I take it he hasn't been cautioned yet?"

"No, ma'am. We didn't know what he was wanted for, just that he was a suspect in a case. Thought it better left to you."

Very wise, Aaron thought. If the case fell on its face in court because one of them got the wording wrong, far better it was the detective in charge, not a lowly special constable from the Harbour Police. He'd have done the same, in the man's shoes.

They dragged Johnston out of the lifeboat and Aaron read him his rights, cautioning him that anything he said may be used in evidence. It was most unrewarding. Johnston stood like a deflated balloon, head down, unresponsive. Aaron wondered if he'd been sampling his own wares.

They had him almost as far as the patrol car before he woke up, and it happened so suddenly that the two uniformed officers holding him nearly let him go.

One moment he was hanging between them, dragging his feet as if he was too exhausted to support his own weight; the next he was a raging, struggling maniac. If he hadn't had his hands cuffed behind him he might have done some damage. As it was, he probably hurt himself more than anyone else.

"No! You can't arrest me!" he screamed. "Not me!"

"That's enough," one of the two uniforms said, a little breathless as he struggled to hold on to Johnston's upper arm. "No point in fighting it, mate. Get in the car."

Between them, they managed to stuff him none too gently into the back seat and slam the door. The car rocked as he went on fighting, throwing himself against the window.

"Where did that come from?" Asha asked.

"I don't know, ma'am, but if he goes on like this, we'll need to call for a van to bring him in. It wouldn't be safe to transport him in this state in case he knocks into the driver and puts us off the road. This car has no divider in it — we were on traffic duty when the call came in."

"I agree. We'll leave him in there for now, and I'll call for a van." She shook her head. "Just when I thought this case couldn't get any weirder."

* * *

Faith McAvoy darted a look over her shoulder, but she had the street to herself. No wonder, in this weather. Freezing rain drove into her face as she leaned into the wind, pushing herself forward. He feet slipped in the slushy ice, but she was wearing her DMs and the deep-cut soles saved her.

They couldn't save the package she carried, though. She'd had the supermarket bag clutched to her chest, but when she flailed her arms for balance, it fell into the gutter.

With a little cry of distress, Faith snatched it up and tried to shake the dirt and damp from it. The driving rain prevented her from opening it to check the contents, so she tucked it inside her coat, ignoring the icy wet that seeped through her shirt, and strode on into the weather.

This warren of dingy Belfast side streets was dark enough on a bright summer's day, but in this weather it was lethal. Mother made sure the streetlights didn't last long. Darkness served her customers better than glowing orange light that illuminated their faces.

The door looked like any other in this street of Victorian terraced houses. Most of them were student rentals with tiny front yards filled with rubbish and empty beer cans. The blinds were closed, but then they always were, and the front door was perhaps in better condition than those around it. In daylight, it would be cherry red, but at night it took on a grey hue.

She knocked. Three short, sharp knocks followed by three with a long space between them. A silent count of ten, then she repeated the code.

The door swung open, and Mother stood there on the mat, her face set in its natural expression of dissatisfaction with the world. "You're late."

"Work," Faith said. It was the only excuse she'd be allowed to get away with.

"Did you bring it?"

Faith reached into the outside pocket of her coat and drew out a padded envelope. A rapacious hand whipped it out of her grasp and Mother retreated inside, leaving the door open behind her. Faith slipped in and up the stairs before the old woman discovered how little of the brown powder she'd managed to procure. It was getting harder to steal from the evidence room, and she really couldn't afford to be caught.

There was action in most of the rooms she passed on her way up to the attic. Grunting punctuated by moans of fake pleasure from the women. This had been her future, once, until Patterson had shown her another path.

On a single bed in the small room beneath the eaves, a thin figure hugged blankets around it, rocking and singing a Polish lullaby in a rusty voice.

"*Mumia*?"

The singing stopped, and a thin, pale face turned towards her. "Faith, *moje maleństwo*." My little baby.

"Speak English, *Mumia*. And I'm no longer a baby."

A smile transformed the thin, pale face into a ghost of what she must have been before life and addiction wore her down. "Come here and tell me everything you've been doing." She patted the bed next to her, and Faith obeyed. "I am so proud of you." A thin hand touched her cheek lightly, as if checking she was really there.

Faith leaned in, wrapping an arm around the emaciated shoulders. "I've brought you some soup, *Mumia*. It's hot and spicy and has real meat in it. Will you take some while I talk?" She'd learned that this was the only way to get her mama to eat. She'd sip the nutritious liquid without realising as she listened wide-eyed to her daughter's stories of life in the *policja*.

Before she left, she held both *Mumia*'s hands in her own and looked into those rheumy eyes. "I'm going to get you out of here. You hear me? That's a promise, *Mumia*."

CHAPTER 11

The wind had eased at last, but the sea was still restless, tossing the old boat around as if she were a dinghy as she lay hove-to. Clara ground her teeth in frustration. She just wanted to get this awful job over with so she'd be free.

Her contact was late. If she'd managed to get her boat and cargo across the North Sea through one of the worst December storms she'd ever seen, surely they could manage to drive a truck up here on time?

She raised binoculars again, scanning the edge of the cliff and the track down to the narrow strip of gravel beach at its base.

Movement at the top of the cliff. She focused the lenses. A dark green box-lorry had arrived, towing a trailer. Several men jumped out and began to manhandle the trailer. Hopefully it was a good-quality inflatable, because her own tender would struggle with the rough crossing, endangering her cargo even more.

They managed to haul it down the steep path, then another twenty minutes or so crept by while they tried to launch it in the heavy seas. It was a big, black rigid inflatable boat, the sort she might expect to see in the hands of the SAS on a coastal raid.

But these men were no SAS elite troops. They'd be the dregs of humanity, the desperate, the weak, the easily led. *Just like me.*

It would be over soon, then her life could go back to normal.

The men finally managed to push the boat off into the breaking swell, and white water surged around the stern as the outboard tried to push it through the surf.

They got the timing horribly wrong, almost getting flipped over by a big set of waves. By some miracle they stayed upright. Once they passed beyond the white water, the black shape became invisible against the dark sea and she lowered the binoculars. Time to release the cargo.

When she slid the hatch back, a stench of vomit, piss and shit floated up to her, making her retch. God, it'd be weeks before she'd get the old girl clean again after this.

She lifted out the washboards and put them down against the edge of the cockpit seats where they'd be out of the way.

"All right, ladies. Time for your last wee boat trip, then it gets better. Come on up!"

One by one, her bedraggled cargo made their unsteady way up the steep steps from the cabin, wincing as even the faintest shimmer of moonlight assaulted eyes that had been in the dark for the past few days.

They were a sorry bunch. When they'd come aboard in that tiny fishing harbour away in the west of Norway, they'd all been dressed in their finest, make-up perfect, hair arranged, full of excitement for the new life ahead of them; now they were a bedraggled mess, with soiled clothing, and streaks of mascara running down pale cheeks, looking far younger than she'd realised at first.

Clara's heart ached for them.

"They're not being sold into slavery," Ole had assured her. "Every single one *wants* to go to Ireland. They all have friends or family there. Jobs assured. For them, Ireland is the promised land."

She'd allowed herself to believe him at the time. She'd had no choice in the matter in any case, but his story had allowed her conscience a bit of breathing space. It hadn't lasted past the first rough patch of water, when their wails and cries had twisted her heart inside her.

Without her make-up, the last but one to ascend the steps looked no more than twelve or thirteen. She was followed by another girl who had to be a relative. They shared the same high, slanted cheekbones and almond eyes, and their hair was a similar shade of red-gold — or it had been, when they boarded the boat. Now it hung in lank, greasy strands around their faces, and the younger girl was sporting a bruise on her temple that she'd probably got from being thrown across the cabin in those heavy seas.

The girls huddled together along the cockpit benches, arms around each other, silent, until the black inflatable boat bumped up against *Snow Goose*'s hull. Then they roused themselves to follow the directions of the two men in the boat, shouted in the same harsh, guttural language the girls spoke between themselves.

Clara helped them over the rail and into the hands of the men below. It was a horrible job. Their arms were slimy with vomit and worse, and the girls had been weakened by the long journey. More than one fell the short distance into the inflatable to land in a crumpled heap in the bilges, which were sloshing with water after its near-capsize in the waves.

Finally, all the girls were sitting or crouching in the black boat. The man holding the two boats together with a rope around *Snow Goose*'s stanchions, began to cast off.

Clara caught hold of his arm, almost getting herself pulled over the railings as the inflatable fell with a wave just as her own boat rose. Her battered ribs twanged, and she had to fight down nausea. "Wait! I was here on time. I've done as I was told. Is that it? How will Ole contact me?"

He shook his head as if he didn't understand and replied in the same language the girls spoke, but she'd seen the flash of comprehension in his eyes, and knew he'd understood her perfectly well. He gave her an evil grin and pushed the boat away, wrenching his arm free in the process. In minutes, the shape of it was lost in darkness, and all she had was the familiar creaking and groaning of her own boat's timbers.

And the cabin to clean.

CHAPTER 12

By the time they had Phil Johnston locked up in a cell at Bangor police station, the lack of sleep had caught up with Asha. Her limbs dragged and her head was filled with cotton wool.

"You can stay at mine tonight if you like," she said. "I have a spare room." Aaron's tired face brightened. "And you can cook us both dinner."

"Seriously? It's not a DC you need but a skivvy."

They drove back in his car to the modern three-bedroom semi she rented. He found his way unerringly to her kitchen and opened the fridge.

"Ash, are you sick? Lettuce, fruit, veg, tofu. Tofu? Is that even food? I thought it was some sort of poetic form."

"I'm *trying* to be healthy," she said. "Try the freezer; I think there are a couple of pizzas in there for emergencies."

"Thank God for that," he breathed.

"And you might not have noticed, but there's a bottle of wine chilling."

He grinned. "Oh yes, I noticed that."

It was like old times, sitting cross-legged on the carpet in the living room, sipping wine from glasses with trickles of condensation running down them, and nibbling slices of pizza.

"So," she asked as she licked her fingers. "Have you asked her yet?"

Aaron tried to look as if he didn't know what she meant, but she knew him too well. "Asked who what?"

"Faith McAvoy. Have you asked her out yet?"

He blushed like a teenager. "No, and nor will I. For one thing our shifts would never coincide, so we'd hardly ever see each other. For another, how many relationships between officers can you think of that have lasted?"

"There's Josh and Claire. They've been married for years, and they seem happy enough."

"Only because Claire gave up the job to mind the twins. Before that, they were on tricky ground."

Asha was surprised. She'd worked with Josh the previous year, but never really got to know him well. Aaron must have made a bit more of an effort. Or maybe Josh hadn't wanted to unburden himself to a woman.

"Anyway, I could ask you the same question about Richie Rich. Have you asked him out yet?"

She glanced at the clock. "Jeez, look at the time. I'm for bed. The clock is ticking, and we need to make a start on questioning Phil Johnston. Leaving here at seven okay with you? That'll give us time to go over the notes before we start grilling him." She couldn't meet his eyes because she knew he'd be laughing, so she headed to bed, closing the door behind her with exaggerated care.

* * *

The alarm woke Asha at a quarter past six. She was certain she'd only been asleep a minute or two, but when she looked in the mirror, the crease in the skin on the side of her face where the quilt had been folded against it told a different story.

She felt a little more human after she'd brushed her teeth and tidied her hair. By the time she'd showered and dressed, she was fully refreshed and ready to start the day. The sun hadn't yet risen, but the streetlights made everything almost as bright as day. Down below, her elderly neighbour was putting the wheelie bin out for collection. Asha watched for a moment as the woman navigated it past Aaron's Golf, peeking inside it as she went.

This was far more of a goldfish bowl than her old place had ever been. In Belfast, no one cared what time you crawled in at night, or who you brought with you; here, nearly every window in the street had a curtain twitching.

Aaron was up and spreading jam on toast when she went into the kitchen. "Made us both some coffee in non-spill mugs, and a couple of slices of toast and jam to munch as we work."

She inhaled the coffee. "Such a pity I can't nab you for Bangor. You could lodge here and make me breakfast every morning."

* * *

Phil Johnston had already asked for the duty solicitor by the time they arrived. They were closeted together in one of the interview rooms.

Asha glanced in the small window as she passed and breathed a sigh of relief. It was Dirty Harry, the condemned man's last resort. Harry Reed had let free access to port and brandy at Law Society dinners become a habit, as testified by his red nose, the broken blood vessels on his cheeks, and the slight tremor in his hands.

He'd probably been an okay solicitor once, but these days he was rarely sober enough for good judgement. It was a miracle he hadn't been barred from practice, but somehow, he was still here, still defending lost causes, still losing almost every court battle.

Asha used the time to go over the evidence they'd collected so far with Aaron, ticking off points on her fingers.

"One, we have CCTV footage of someone who looks like Phil Johnston, and who has been tentatively IDed as

Johnston by Steve White. We can see him entering the boat and then leaving it carrying small packages."

"Did your boyfriend give us copies of that footage?"

"He isn't my boyfriend, and yes, he sent them across. Two, we have the boot print and tyre tracks, which the SOCOs are going to compare with the tyres on the bike we have footage of him riding. They should have a report for us later today. Three, there's Steve White's evidence that Johnston was inside his house, followed by the discovery of the package under the bed in the main bedroom."

"Have we got a report back from the lab about that yet?"

Asha checked her emails. "Not yet. Perhaps you can chase it up later this morning?"

"Will do." He made a note.

"Four, we have the CCTV footage from the cafe, showing Phil Johnston quite clearly wheeling a bike into the marina. Then we have him staying illegally on someone's boat, stealing a second boat — can you track down the owner of that speedboat and check that Johnston didn't have permission to use it whenever he wanted? Then get a statement to that effect."

Aaron made another note.

"And lastly, we have the packages we found in his rucksack, which should be on their way to the lab by now. Hopefully they'll be a match to the one from White's house."

"How do you want to play the interview?"

"We need to decide how much we're prepared to reveal at this moment. As far as he knows, we only have the stolen boat and the rucksack, although those are bad enough on their own. We'll keep quiet for now about all the rest, and perhaps bring in some of our other evidence as and when it seems appropriate."

"Okay. I'll follow your lead."

Johnston was a lot more confident than he had been the night before. Despite the wrinkled tracksuit he'd been provided with and his unshaven chin, he managed to look

Asha in the eye when she entered the interview room and introduced herself.

"Can I just confirm that all mobile phones and pagers have been switched off?" She glared at Dirty Harry, who was notorious for forgetting to turn his phone off. He fumbled in his jacket pocket and nodded blearily.

Asha pressed record on the digital equipment and went through the usual introductions. Then she joined her hands together on the desk, over the top of the plain, brown folder that she kept closed, and took a deep breath.

"Mr Johnston, at approximately eight forty-five p.m. last night, you boarded a boat named *Nimrod*, belonging to a Mr and Mrs Blake, proceeded to remove the boat from its berth in Bangor Marina, then drove the boat out to sea. As you were not registered as the owner of this boat, the Belfast Harbour Police and Lagan Search and Rescue were tasked to intercept you and bring you and the boat back to Bangor Marina."

Johnston shot her a dirty look. "I have permission to use the boat whenever I want. The owners are friends of mine."

Asha glanced at Aaron, nodding for him to take over.

"I spoke to Mrs Blake at eight o'clock this morning, and she assured me that no one has permission to take their boat out without them on board. In fact, she believes it to be a condition of their insurance that one of them has to be aboard every time the boat is taken out. She says you certainly do not have permission to use the boat, but that you would probably know where the spare key is kept, because you did some maintenance work on the boat a year or two ago."

"She's lying," Johnston said, but he was sullen now.

"To continue," Asha said, "the lifeboat intercepted *Nimrod* and took you aboard while one of their own crew returned the stolen boat safely to her berth. While fleeing from the Search and Rescue boat, you were witnessed, by the crew and by the two Harbour Police officers on board, throwing something into the sea. This object, a backpack, floated, and was therefore able to be retrieved by the lifeboat crew within minutes of being thrown. Do you have any comment about the contents of this bag?"

"It wasn't mine," he said. "It belongs to a mate of mine, Steve White. He asked me to look after it for him."

"So, you're saying that you have no knowledge of the contents of this rucksack? That you didn't look inside it at any time while it was in your possession?"

He jutted his chin out. "That's right."

"When did Mr White give you this rucksack to keep for him, and what explanation did he give for it?"

"He gave me it yesterday. Don't remember what time. He came to my house and asked me to keep it safe for him. I didn't ask why. Mates don't ask questions."

His house. The place he'd been evicted from over a month ago? Asha let that one pass for now. "Would it surprise you to learn that the rucksack contained a number of brick-sized packages, wrapped up in layers of plastic?"

"Yeah. That would surprise me. What'd Steve want with bricks?"

"You tell me," Asha said.

"Objection," Dirty Harry ventured. "My client has already assured you he had no knowledge of the contents of the bag. Any further pressing on the matter verges on harassment."

This was just Harry trying to sound as if he was doing something, so Asha ignored him.

"The lab has those packages at the moment, and I'm expecting a report in the next hour or so, identifying the contents. It might interest you, Mr Johnston, to hear that they seem similar to another package which was found during a search of Mr White's home last night."

Johnston leaned forward in his chair. "Told you! That slimy little bastard's trying to set me up, but the packages are his. He must have kept one for himself."

"That's one possible interpretation of the facts," Asha agreed. "But the reason Mr White's property was being searched was because he reported an intruder yesterday evening, so an officer responded and found the package while checking the property."

"Yeah, well, he would say that, wouldn't he?"

"You might be interested to know who he reported as having entered his home."

Johnston clamped his lips tight shut and glared.

CHAPTER 13

A uniformed constable entered the room, placed a folded sheet of paper on the desk in front of Asha, and left again. She unfolded the paper, glanced through it, then passed it to Aaron, who whistled softly as he read the note.

"For the recording, I have just been handed a sheet of paper with two telephone messages on it. The first one states that the contents of the package found in Steve White's house, as well as those found in the boat Mr Johnston had been staying in and in the recovered rucksack, were identical. The packages all contained cocaine with a total street value of approximately a million pounds.

"The second message is from the camera operators of the Bangor town CCTV network, to confirm that Mr Johnston was recorded riding a bicycle to and from the direction of Mr White's house at times that coincide with Mr White's report of an intruder." She smiled across at Phil Johnston. "Have you anything further to add to your statement, Mr Johnston, or do you still maintain that the packages are nothing to do with you?"

"Yeah." He shrugged off Dirty Harry's hand. "I'm remembering better now. Steve didn't come to my place; I went to his. Just chatted on the doorstep, like, and he gave me his rucksack then." He nodded to himself, apparently satisfied that he'd explained away the evidence perfectly.

"So you'd never seen the rucksack before?" Asha pressed.

"Never." He leaned back, smirking. He really wasn't very bright.

Asha opened the file in front of her and took out a photograph. She held it up so Johnston couldn't see it, then asked him again. "You're absolutely certain you'd never seen that rucksack before Mr White gave it to you to look after yesterday evening? And you don't own a similar rucksack yourself?"

Harry tried to say something, but Phil spoke over him.

"Positive. I'd never seen it before, and I don't own any rucksack. Never use the bloody things."

Asha turned the photo around so Johnston and his solicitor could both see it.

"I am showing Mr Johnston a still taken from a CCTV camera near Bangor Marina. It shows Mr Johnston wheeling a bike along the pavement from the direction of Donaghadee." His features were clearly recognisable, and on his back was the bulging rucksack. The time stamp showed up clearly on the image. It had been taken in the early hours of the previous morning, just as the blizzard was easing.

"As you can see, Mr Johnston, this shows you carrying a rucksack identical to the one you claim never to have seen prior to being handed it by Mr White on the evening of 26 December. The time stamp on the image is four forty-six a.m. on 26 December. I'd also like to draw to your attention the object that appears to be tied to the luggage rack, an object that sticks out quite a long way beyond the back of the bike. We'll come to that in a minute."

Johnston's mouth hung open. Dirty Harry sighed and shook his head, probably wishing he was anywhere else than in this interview room.

"Have you anything further to add to your statement, Mr Johnston?" Asha asked gently.

"No comment."

She glanced at her watch. "Time for a short break, I think. Recording paused at nine fifty-seven. We will resume at ten fifteen."

She and Aaron left the room, taking the file and photo with them. She nodded to the uniform who was standing outside. "See if Mr Johnston would like a drink, would you, Jim? I don't want him complaining of any mistreatment while he's in our custody."

"Ma'am."

When they went back in, a chastened Phil Johnston slumped in his seat while Dirty Harry's face wore a frown. Asha hoped he'd managed to talk his client into co-operating, and maybe even revealing his contact. Someone other than Johnston must have put the drugs on Fred Mills's boat somewhere between the factory in France and Steele's boatyard here in County Down.

She turned to whisper to Aaron while he was still outside in the corridor. "Check with airports and ferry companies. I'd like to know if our man here has made any trips to France in the last year or so."

Aaron nodded and disappeared down the corridor.

"Well, Mr Johnston, Mr Reed. You've had some time to think. I'll start the recording again and we'll pick up where we left off."

Asha clicked the machine and gave the usual spiel.

"Mr Johnston, now you've had time to think, would you like to add anything else to your statement about having never seen the rucksack before Mr White handed it to you?"

"No comment."

"Oh, come on, Mr Johnston. Don't be shy. You've seen the evidence: a clear photo of you carrying a rucksack identical to the one you tried to throw overboard, hours before you claim to have laid eyes on it for the first time."

He didn't flinch. He'd decided to knuckle down and hide behind silence. Time to give him another little jolt.

"Have you ever visited a place called Steele's boatyard, Mr Johnston? Out on the Donaghadee Road."

"No comment."

"I understand from Mr White, and confirmed by the yard's owner, Mr Steele, that only authorised contractors are permitted access to the premises. Is your name on the list of authorised contractors for Steele's boatyard?"

"No comment."

"All right. I can answer that question for you, because Mr Steele has kindly given me a list of authorised contractors." Asha drew the sheet of paper out of the file and placed it on the desk so both Johnston and Dirty Harry could read it. Only the solicitor bothered. "As you can see, your name is not on this list."

He grunted, not meeting her eyes.

"The boatyard has excellent security measures in place," she went on. "With CCTV cameras operating 24/7, and warning signs advertising that fact. It has a high chain-link fence and gates that are secured with a heavy-duty padlock and chain. I think you'd agree that this makes the yard quite hard to enter without permission. To do so would require, for example, a massive pair of bolt cutters to break the chain."

Johnston picked at a groove in the wooden desk surface with his thumbnail, prising loose a splinter of wood.

"Do you own a pair of bolt cutters, Mr Johnston?"

He met her eye. "No comment."

"Are you aware that bolt cutters, especially used ones, are a bit like bullets? Minute grooves develop in their surface that can be used to identify which pair of cutters were used on any particular chain? Say, the chain on the boatyard gate, for example."

He went back to his excavation of the wood just as the door opened to let Aaron into the room. He gave her a folded sheet of paper.

Johnston doesn't have a current UK passport. No evidence of travel other than over the border to the South a handful of times a year, based on his car registering on the toll cameras. We're checking to see if he might have an Irish passport, but no luck so far.

Oh well. It would have been nice to have placed Johnston in France, but it wasn't the end of the world.

"Detective Constable Birch has entered the room," she said, for the recording. "I was just explaining to Mr Johnston the way bolt cutters can leave distinctive identifying marks on anything they're used to cut through."

Dirty Harry stirred. "Did you find any bolt cutters on Mr Johnston's person when he was arrested?" He'd clearly decided it was time for him to engage on behalf of his client.

"I'm glad you asked that question, Mr Reed. No, we didn't, but Mr Johnston is known to have been staying without permission on a second boat in Bangor Marina, a wooden barge, and he was seen on board that boat on the night of his arrest. The owner requested that we search the boat on his behalf for any evidence of damage that might have been caused by Mr Johnston, however inadvertently."

Oh God, she was beginning to sound like Patterson now.

"During our legitimate search, we found a pair of heavy-duty bolt cutters, which have been sent off to the lab for microscopic examination. It will be interesting to see if they find a match for the ones used to cut through the chain at Steele's boatyard."

She took out the same photograph she'd showed them earlier, the one of Johnston wheeling the bike, and wearing the rucksack.

"For the recording, I am again showing the defendant the CCTV image of him wheeling a bicycle. Attached to the carrier over the rear wheel there appears to be a long, double-handled device similar to the pair of bolt cutters we found."

"Oh, come now, Detective," Harry said. "There's no way a still from a CCTV camera gives enough detail to identify this object. That wouldn't last two minutes in court."

"No. You're right. It wouldn't, but when added to the fact that the bolt cutters found on the boat were covered with Mr Johnston's fingerprints, it becomes much more telling."

"My client might have handled those cutters at any time these last few months. He was employed by the boat's owner to carry out work on the heater, so he's bound to have lifted and moved things around to gain access. His fingerprints must be everywhere on that boat."

Asha smiled and said nothing. Instead, she pulled out another image, this one from the CCTV camera at Steele's boatyard. The quality was awful, but it showed a hooded figure manipulating a pair of long-handled bolt cutters.

"I am showing a still taken from the CCTV camera covering the gate of Mr Richard Steele's boatyard. The time stamp shows two fifty-seven on the morning of 26 December. I accept the quality of this image is poor, due to the near-blizzard conditions at the time, but the actual CCTV footage is clearer."

"You're not kidding," Harry said. "That could be anyone. You can hardly make out that it's a person at all, never mind who it is or what they're doing. This hardly constitutes proof of wrongdoing by my client."

"You're right, it doesn't. But what we have is more than enough for a warrant for a more thorough investigation into your client's affairs."

She put the photos away. "As soon as we have the final lab results on the bolt cutters, as well as some other evidence we're currently processing, I believe we'll have a strong case against your client, Mr Reed. If you'd like to discuss a plea bargain — a lighter sentence in exchange for information about the supplier of this cocaine — then now is the time. I'll leave you both to talk it over."

She spoke the usual words to mark the end of the interview, then stopped the recording. "I'm not going anywhere, in case you want to talk."

CHAPTER 14

It was a long slog, close-hauled into the wind, but Clara relished the clean salt air in her face and the feel of *Snow Goose* coming alive beneath her. The old girl was terrible on this point of sail, making almost as much leeway as she did forward motion, but days like this made Clara glad to be alive.

A wave creamed along the side decks to break on the edge of the cockpit coaming, drenching her. She threw back her head and laughed for sheer joy of being alive.

Then the laughter froze in her throat and her face stiffened. She wasn't out of the woods yet. Ole had made promises, but she didn't trust him. And she had been instrumental in carrying all those young women to a life of prostitution. However hard she tried to convince herself otherwise, deep down she'd known all along that was where they were heading.

The boat heeled sharply, and Clara had to loosen the mainsheet, spilling wind to prevent broaching. That was something she'd learned at a young age: disaster is only one rogue wave away if let your mind wander when you're helming.

Another couple of hours on this course, then she could put a tack in towards her destination. It felt good to be back in home waters at last, after six months away.

A low flight of guillemots passed her, heading out to sea, and shortly after, a curved fin surfaced a couple of hundred yards to starboard. Then another. A small pod of dolphins. Seeing them usually made her smile, but not today. Not now.

What could she have done differently?

She'd been less than a mile off the Norwegian coast, on her way to the Lofoten Islands, when *Snow Goose*'s engine failed. That stretch of water was littered with submerged rocks and contradictory tidal eddies. It was a sailor's worst nightmare: a lee shore and no method of propulsion. So when a battered fishing trawler emerged from the mist and offered her a tow, she'd felt nothing but relief.

The skipper had seemed so friendly, so helpful. He'd towed *Snow Goose* back to the small harbour he called home, deep in a beautiful fjord, and got his brother to fix the engine. He'd even sent a man to drive all the way to Oslo to collect a part that had to be ordered in.

Perhaps she should have been suspicious the first time Ole refused payment, but she'd been so worried that the bill would come to more than she could afford that when he told her it would cost nothing, she'd been relieved.

Until he'd said those fateful words.

"Fixing an engine is easy. No trouble at all. I do not want money from you, little Clara, but there is something you can do to help me. It is not a big thing, but it would wipe out any debt you might feel lies between us."

Woozy with alcohol, she'd looked into those sea-green eyes of his and said, "Anything, Ole. I'll do anything you ask."

If only she could have called the words back, but they were already out there, hanging in the air between her and the big Norwegian fisherman.

He'd looked deep into her eyes, held her hand, and spoke. "That is one thing I will not ask of you. What I need from you is the use of your boat and your skill as a sailor. I have a package that needs transporting to Ireland, and I was worrying that I could not easily get to there, when what do I find, bobbing helplessly not twenty miles from my home port? I find a little Irish girl with her own boat and the ability to sail these treacherous seas even in the worst weather the gods can throw at her." He'd lifted her hand and kissed it. "Truly, the gods are wise."

That was when the alarm bells began to jangle in Clara's brain. "I can't carry drugs, Ole."

"Little Clara, do you really think I would ask such a thing of you? No, it is not drugs I wish you to carry for me, only some friends of my sister. They cannot afford to fly to Ireland, and in any case, they would have difficulty with visas, but if you could take them on your boat?"

That didn't sound too bad. Her fears were soothed, and he poured her another drink.

It wasn't until the next morning, when she'd tried to remember what she'd agreed to, that the feeling of disquiet began to grow. And when the "friends" turned up in their best clothes, faces made-up as if for a night out, that disquiet exploded into full-blown fear.

But Ole was there again, reassuring her, introducing her to the girls, explaining that they all had jobs to go to in Ireland in hotels and restaurants, but that there was a minor problem, only a minor one, with the papers of two of the girls. They were such close friends that none of the others would go without these two, so they'd all agreed to travel together with Clara in her boat.

She'd have felt happier if she could have spoken to them herself, but not one spoke English, French, Spanish or any of the other languages Clara had a grasp of. Instead, Ole acted as interpreter, translating her questions and telling her what the girls' replies were.

But she couldn't leave until the engine rebuild was finished, and Ole's brother wasn't going to recommission the engine until she'd agreed to take the girls. She was trapped, and she could see no way out except to say yes.

Ole had hugged her. The girls had hugged her, chattering away in excited voices that sounded like something from a Russian film.

"Where are they from?" she asked Ole. "That's not Norwegian they're speaking, is it?"

"No, little Clara. They're from Belarus, and they speak Polish. It sounds completely different to Norwegian."

At last the engine was fixed, the girls boarded, and they took on supplies for the journey. Clara opened each plastic container —she'd refused to allow cardboard boxes, because they'd just turn into a wet mess out at sea in the persistent damp — and checked the contents.

"Ole, you've been far too generous. These supplies will last us weeks."

He gave her a quizzical look. "Trust me, little Clara. You will need them, the route you will be taking."

Just when she'd been feeling warmth towards him, a shadow crept over her as he stood in the winter sunshine, dressed in his fisherman's knitted sweater and canvas trousers tucked into leather seaboots. "What do you mean? I can coast-hop down to Bergen, then restock with supplies for the crossing to Scotland. I'm planning on going through the Caledonian Canal."

He raised a finger and wagged it from side to side in front of her face like an inverted pendulum. "But that's where you're wrong, little Clara. You won't be coast-hopping. Too many people, too many questions. You wouldn't want the trouble of customs and border control looking closely at paperwork, as they would if you pass through the UK on the way to Ireland. Don't forget one of the girls has a small problem with her papers. It would bring trouble down on us all. You must take the sea route, north of Scotland. And you cannot make landfall. It must be done in one journey."

This could not be happening. She'd already planned her route, pencilling it in on her charts. Even coast-hopping, the Norwegian coastline was no playground for sailors, with treacherous currents and unpredictable weather.

"I can't do it, Ole! It'd be, what, two weeks or more of open-ocean sailing in some of the most dangerous seas on the planet, single-handed? And there are submarines and Russian fishing fleets operating in those waters." She glared at the girls, who were sitting in the cockpit and laughing together. "I can't imagine any of your sister's friends standing a watch, not even during the day, never mind at night — even if I could communicate with them, which I can't."

"This is all true, but I picked you for a reason. Your boat has the wind vane steering, so you can take some sleep, and you are used to sailing dangerous waters; after all, you made it this far, to Norway, all on your own."

"That was during the summer! And it took me months to get this far, stopping off on the way for fuel and to rest. I've never sailed these seas in winter, and never such a long journey without stopping."

He regarded her sorrowfully, then drew his wallet out of his pocket, holding it so she couldn't see inside it. "I had hoped I would not have to resort to such unpleasant tactics, but you force my hand." He turned the wallet so she could see a photograph that lay between the folds. It was her brother, smiling in the sunshine. Her heart stuttered, and a rushing noise deafened her for a moment until she forced herself to listen to his soft voice again.

"If you care for your brother, you will find a way, Little Clara. I have faith in you. But if you do not? Well. I have friends everywhere, and some of them have no scruples at all. I have someone right there in his little boatyard. Someone who is an expert with a long gun, and your Richard is in his sights as we speak. It takes only a word from me, and you will be an only child."

Somehow, Clara had managed not to scream or cry. Numb with shock, she listened to her instructions, and the deadline she had to meet to keep her brother alive. It was tight but do-able, if the weather held.

"And just in case you think of radioing ahead to warn him, I have taken the liberty of disabling your radio set and aerials. Your satellite phone is at the bottom of the sea."

So she'd left with the tide, navigating the fjord in the perpetual night that Norway experienced in the winter, with only paper charts, her compass, and years of experience to keep them safe. Belowdecks, the girls slept, undisturbed by the engine's deep rumble.

* * *

She dragged herself back into the present and made an entry in her log. She'd made good time from the rendezvous point, as fast as the old boat could manage, but until she saw Richard with her own eyes, she couldn't rest or push away the dark cloud of despair that had been her constant companion on this hellish voyage. She checked the tides again. It'd be awful to turn up after all this only to discover the lock gate closed against her, but her timing was bang on. About time her luck took a turn for the better.

Would Richard be there? And if he was, would he see the guilt in her eyes? He'd hold her at arm's length and say, "What's all this, Clara? What's this darkness in your soul?"

And if she told him? Would he turn away from her in disgust?

CHAPTER 15

"Will he talk?" Aaron asked as he walked with Asha to her super's office.

It was a good question. Johnston was a slippery character. He'd tried to plant drugs on Steve White, which revealed the depths he'd go to in order to stay out of trouble. "I suppose it depends what he's most scared of: his supplier, or a jail term."

Aaron grunted. "That's a mystery we need to solve. Who did supply the drugs? Where were they loaded on to the boat?"

A frisson of excitement ran up Asha's spine. This was shaping up to be the biggest case she'd worked on, as long as Superintendent Sewell didn't decide to take it off her and hand it to someone more senior.

Sewell was in his office, glued to his computer monitor. He looked up as they entered. "Asha, DC Birch. How's it going? I understand you have someone in custody."

"Yes, sir. Phil Johnston. Local wide boy and odd-job man." She filled him in on what they'd discovered so far and told him about the CCTV evidence.

"Dirty Harry's right, though," Sewell said. "Some of that is pretty vague, especially the CCTV from the boatyard in a blizzard."

"Yes, sir, but I'm hoping he'll crack and tell us who's behind this. Harry Reed probably won't be able to stop him from talking if he makes his mind up." She glanced at Aaron and then said what was really worrying her. "Will we get to keep this case, sir? Now we know there are class A drugs involved, will you be handing it over to the Organised Crime Unit?"

He looked shifty. "*Do* we know? Have we had written confirmation from the labs yet?"

She drew a breath, then swallowed it. "Not in writing, sir, no. Just a verbal report."

"Well," he said. "It's Christmastime, isn't it? I doubt they'll be writing up reports as quickly as they usually do. Until I see the report on my desk, you two can keep this case. I suggest you do what you can with the time available."

They both grinned. "Yes, sir."

She and Aaron went through their notes together until Asha's phone pinged to warn her of an incoming video call from DCS Patterson.

"Morning, ma'am," Asha said. "We have a couple of updates for you on this drug-smuggling case."

Patterson's face wasn't any more photogenic on the webcam than it was in real life. She squinted at the screen, then spoke too loudly as if she was on a poor phone connection.

"I hear you have someone in custody already. Well done. Have you the second man in the cells, too?"

"Second man, ma'am?"

"The one with the drugs under his bed."

"No, ma'am. The evidence we've accumulated so far suggests that those drugs were planted in a clumsy attempt to shift the blame. We believe Mr White was not involved except as an unlucky victim."

"And yet I understand he has a criminal record?"

"Yes, ma'am. For taking a swing at someone in a bar, soon after his wife left him. I'm not seriously considering him as a suspect, although I am obviously still keeping an open mind."

She added the last bit in response to the deepening frown across Patterson's forehead.

"I should hope so, Inspector. Well, I suppose you'd better give me a full verbal report. How is Birch getting on? I'd expected to see a report from him in my inbox this morning."

Aaron leaned forward into the camera's line of sight. "I'm here, ma'am. I'll send you a written report later today, but we thought you'd prefer a verbal report first."

"Events moved so quickly," Asha went on, "we felt it important to get ahead of things, ma'am. Now we have Johnston in custody we'll have more time to type up our findings and get them off to you as soon as possible."

She went on to report what had happened since the French lorry arrived in Bangor, passing the narrative over to Aaron whenever it related to his own investigations.

"I still need those reports," Patterson said. "The documentary evidence must be as contemporaneous as possible, so I need them with my secretary by noon today. Carry on." And the screen went black.

Asha made sure the webcam was disconnected before turning to Aaron. "Has she been on another management course? 'The documentary evidence must be contemporaneous.' Who even talks like that?"

He laughed. "Still, she's right. We'd better get typing. It'll do no harm to let Johnston stew for a while. He can think through how few options he has. We've still plenty of time to hold him."

* * *

Aaron was still tapping away at his keyboard when Asha finished her own report. A walk out in the fresh air would clear her head and prepare her for the next bout of questioning.

She crossed the road outside the station and drifted into Castle Park, boots crunching in snow drifts as she made her way along the line of trees. Leaning her back against a trunk, she closed her eyes and listened to birdsong soaring above the noise of traffic as Bangor returned to normal after the Christmas holidays.

"Hello. Communing with nature?"

Richard Steele's voice yanked her out of her reverie. He'd pulled his car up alongside her, on the wrong side of the road so he could lower his window and speak from a few feet away.

"What are *you* doing here?" she asked. Stupid! Couldn't she think of anything more intelligent to say?

"Looking for you, as it happens. I was about to turn in to the station when I spotted you and thought I'd come to see what you were up to. Sorry if I spoiled your moment." He smiled, awkward and quite endearing. "I can go away and come back another time, if you like?"

She took a deep breath and pushed herself away from the tree trunk. "No. I was getting some fresh air. What can I do for you, Mr Steele?"

He winced. "Richard, please. I thought we'd agreed that already?"

"Yes. Richard. Sorry."

"Thought you might like to know that when Steve opened up the yard this morning the French truck was still there, blocking access to some of the boats. He called the driver, Serge, to ask him to move it but his mobile rang out so he tried the hotel he was staying at, that one there." Richard pointed to the big new hotel across the road. "Apparently he's not answering his room telephone either. Steve thinks he's just being a lazy sod, but your DC did say that I should let you know if anything out of the ordinary happened. It's a real nuisance. Between that and the shock of you lot finding drugs under his bed, Steve's decided to shut up shop until we can get it shifted. I wanted to let the driver know to phone Steve first because if he just turns up out of the blue to collect it, he won't be able to get in."

Asha stared at the hotel. It was quite a big place, and surprisingly popular for a small town like Bangor. "Yes, you're right. I'll get DC Birch, and we can go and investigate." She smiled down at him, not wanting to be too brusque. After all, he'd taken the trouble to drive here to tell her in person instead of phoning. That deserved a smile, didn't it? "Thank you for telling me."

Richard shook his head, laughing. "I'm not that easy to get rid of. I thought I might hang around and maybe take you out for dinner later. We could even try the hotel, unless that's too close to home for you?"

"How kind," she said in a cool voice that reminded her of her mother, when she wanted to put someone down. "But I'll be working, I'm afraid. And I'm not in the habit of dating persons of interest in a case I'm working on."

The hurt in his face almost made her want to call the words back, but not quite. She shoved her hands deep in the pockets of her coat to hide their trembling and marched the short distance to the station without glancing over her shoulder to see if he was still there.

By the time she'd reached her office, she'd cooled down and even felt a little silly. It was that whole chivalry thing that bothered her, the cool assumption that a man can "take" a woman to dinner, as if she were a precious possession that needed looking after. She didn't need some fancy rich man in a fancy new Jag to make her feel her worth.

Or maybe she'd spent so long defending her position at work it had overflowed into her private life. She groaned. Would she ever learn how to behave around attractive men?

Aaron looked up as she came in. "Who rattled the bars on your cage?"

She laughed, letting the tension leak away. "Steele. Cheeky sod asked me out."

He tipped his head and narrowed his eyes at her. "And?"

"And I told him to get lost. But he did have some interesting information for us." She told him about the lorry driver, Serge. "We might as well go over there on foot. The hotel staff are more likely to be helpful with a warrant card shoved in their faces than over a phone."

Whether it was the warrant cards or whether they'd have been helpful anyway, the hotel staff couldn't have been more willing to do everything asked of them. After trying the phone in Serge's room again, without success, the young Chinese duty manager offered to accompany them up there.

The hotel was modern, obviously fairly new. A Do Not Disturb card hung on the door handle. The manager knocked and called out, but when there was no reply, she opened the door then stepped back. Asha peered inside. The double bed looked as if it had been slept in, and a soft holdall spewed its contents out all over the carpet: underwear, jeans and sweatshirts.

"Hello!" Asha called, hovering in the doorway. "Monsieur?" That was the limit of her French. The room had an empty feel to it. She edged inside.

To her right, the door to the bathroom was closed, but a low hum came from the fan. One more step and she could see the entire room. It was empty, and from what she could see of the bed, there'd be no space beneath it for anyone to hide. She opened the wardrobe door. Empty, the standard hotel safe lying open with nothing in it.

Aaron squeezed past her and went to the far end of the room, checking in case Serge was lying ill on the floor over there. He shrugged and shook his head.

The only place left was the bathroom. Asha knocked on the door and put her mouth to the edge. "Hello? Serge? This is Detective Inspector Harvey. I'm coming in."

She half expected the door to be locked, but the handle turned freely, and the door swung inwards until it hit an obstacle. She tried to push it gently, but it wasn't moving.

"Aaron? Some help here?"

Together, they pushed harder.

And that's when the smell hit them.

CHAPTER 16

"You did *what*?" Yvonne Patterson's fist clenched around the receiver. "I said to threaten the man, not kill him."

"Things got a little out of hand," George Aiken said. "He saw Kerny in the bathroom mirror, and the big man hit him harder than he meant to."

Yvonne drew a breath, trying to control her fury. "He wasn't *just* an employee of our rival outfit," she snarled. "He worked for the French police."

"What?"

"He was an informant for them. He will be missed. You were supposed to be sending a message, a *subtle* message, not declaring war."

"Why weren't we told he was an informer?" Almost a whine.

"Because I only just found out. One of my friends in Interpol managed to intercept a reply aimed at those two in Bangor. I've kept it from reaching them for now, but I can't sit on it for ever." Another deep breath. Aiken and Kernaghan were louts, but they were effective louts. It wasn't worth losing them over this. She made herself calm down, relaxing the clenched fingers and dropping her voice a little. "Do you have the keys, at least?"

"Of course. We're heading down there shortly to pick up the lorry. What do you want us to do with it?"

"Hide it for now. Make it hard to find. Once you have everything in place, I'll let a hint leak out. If we make it too easy, the Paki bitch will be suspicious."

"Will do."

"And George?"

"Yes?"

"Low-key this time. No drama. Go in, take the thing, and leave. Is that clear?"

"Clear as glass."

She ended the call, then looked at the satellite phone. The temptation to call Ole was almost overwhelming, but he'd need all his attention for the sea. She'd been watching the weather forecast, and it wasn't good.

A tiny drop of blood fell on the pale pastel silk of her scarf, and she hissed irritation. She'd worked so hard to hide her nervous habit of picking at the skin along the edge of her thumbnail. It was the only remnant of the nail biting and later the razor cuts that had plagued her childhood. She could manage it when others were with her, like a poker player who instinctively hid their tells, but when she was alone, her fingernails worked away without her conscious involvement.

She dabbed at the offending tear with a paper hanky until the bleeding stopped. The spot of blood was fresh, and she got most of it out by rinsing under the cold tap, and the pattern and draping folds of the scarf would hide any remaining signs, but she would always know it was there.

The scarf went into the wastepaper basket next to her desk.

Then it came back out again. What would the cleaner think? She stuffed it into the pocket of her tailored jacket, ruining the lines.

A knock on the door brought her mind back to the job in hand. She only had to carry on this charade for a few more days. She could do that.

"Come."

The black sergeant waddled in with a pile of paperwork that she placed on Yvonne's pristine desk. "Afternoon, ma'am. These came in the interdepartmental package marked urgent."

Yvonne forced a smile to her face. "Thank you, Sergeant Jacob. How are you these days? Any more thoughts about that retirement package?"

Lonnie Jacob's expression didn't change. She rarely looked Yvonne quite in the eye, and today she seemed fascinated by something on the corner of the desk.

"Not a one, ma'am. As long as there's work here for me to do, I'll do it. When there isn't, I'll stop."

Yvonne laughed. "Very healthy attitude. I feel much the same myself. We women need to stick together."

"Yes, ma'am." The words were said in a warm, chummy voice, but Jacob's eyes were as watchful as ever from between the folds of dark skin.

"Well, thank you for bringing these over. I suppose I'd better get stuck in."

"Ma'am."

When the door closed behind the old woman, Yvonne drew a deep breath. The sooner she was out of here, the better. It was becoming harder every day to keep up the pretence. One last load and they'd be free. Until then, everything depended on her holding her nerve.

She turned her attention to the pile of papers. It was the usual bureaucratic rubbish. Salary reviews, equipment audits, promotion applications. She skimmed the last one, hoping to see Aaron Birch's name on the list, but it wasn't there. A sigh. She'd have liked to see him a sergeant before she left, but he didn't seem to have the ambition.

As she put the pile aside to deal with later, she realised what the old sergeant had been staring at. The paper hanky she'd used to mop up the blood sat in full view, soaked crimson in one corner. Worse still, a line of droplets ran across the desk towards her hands.

She looked down and her stomach twisted. The pale green suit jacket had a long smear across the front. All the while she'd been panicking about her silk scarf, this had been hidden by the rise of her breasts until she sat down. Now it glared like a beacon, revealing her secret weakness to the world.

Her hand reached for the satellite phone and her aching thumb hit the speed dial for Ole. Her heart was racing and her palms sweaty. She needed to hear his voice.

The line rang and rang. Blood dripped unheeded on to the desk and her breathing became shallow, fast. Buzzing began in her ears. She couldn't faint. She'd never fainted in her entire life, and she wasn't about to do it now.

A couple of deep breaths helped drive the shadows back, but still Ole didn't pick up.

He'd be in a storm, fighting wind and waves, that would be why he couldn't answer. Maybe he couldn't even hear the phone over the noise?

But one of his crew would, surely?

How long would it ring? The ring tone faltered into a stutter, and she poised ready to ring off and try again, but just as her finger was hovering over the button, his voice came on.

"Von! What is wrong?"

There was background noise, creaking, but none of the howling wind and surging waves she'd imagined. A young voice made a protesting sound, muffled immediately as Ole put his hand over the receiver. One of his crew, it must be, needing his judgement or seamanship.

"I'm fine," she said. And she was, now she'd heard that deep, calm voice. "I was worried about you, that's all. And when you didn't answer . . ." She let the implied question hang in the ether between them.

"My dear little Vonnie. I was in my bunk. A captain off watch must trust his crew while he gets some rest, or he will make mistakes and sink the boat."

An awful image came to mind, of the boat striking a rock and filling with water while Ole tried to struggle up to the surface, water rising all around him until it covered his mouth, and then his nose, and lastly those beautiful grey eyes.

"Please take care, my love."

"Always."

CHAPTER 17

The stench of faeces filled Asha's nostrils as the bathroom door opened. She turned her head away, filled her lungs with relatively fresh air, then put her face around the door. A pair of hairy legs stuck out at an odd angle, the feet bare.

Serge Durand was lying naked on the floor, his body still blocking the door from opening fully. His eyes were half-closed, and a streak of dried blood ran across his shoulder.

Asha left Aaron to secure the scene until the doctor arrived while she escorted the hysterical manager back down to reception and handed her over to an unflappable colleague. Asha explained what had happened, that there'd be a bit of activity for a while, and that they would need to speak to anyone who'd been on duty since Boxing Day morning.

The scene-of-crime officers were efficient. They photographed Serge and bagged his hands, and Asha was given the all-clear to move him. She tipped his head forward with gloved hands and probed his scalp. The hair on the back of his head was matted with dried blood. She looked around to see if there was any sign of blood on any of the bathroom furniture that might have accounted for it. Perhaps he'd slipped on the tiled floor and hit his head on something?

Asha turned to the crime scene manager, an older officer who'd probably seen pretty much everything by now. "Can you do a luminol test, Carol? I need to know if there's anywhere he could have hit his head as he fell."

The woman made a note and nodded.

"And I need a time of death ASAP. I have someone in custody for a crime that could be related to this, so I need to know if he's ruled in or out — if there's any evidence of foul play on the post-mortem, that is."

The CSM flicked through her notebook. "The doctor estimates death occurred no more than eight hours ago, but probably between five and seven hours, judging by the lividity, the temperature and the early onset of rigor in the face. But he said it's a bit tricky to judge — there's underfloor heating here, and the body's also naked."

"Okay, that helps. Eight hours ago, our man was already locked up in a cell. Thanks." She turned to Aaron. "I'd better get back to Johnston again. It's even more important now to find out who's behind all this." She glanced at her watch. "Could you make a start on interviewing hotel employees?"

"I'll get the manager to draw up a list of names," he said. "Can I request some help, do you think? There'll probably be quite a few of them."

"Why don't you ask Patterson if she'll send someone up from Belfast? It'll make her feel more involved, and so far, it's been Bangor's manpower that's getting stretched."

"I can ask," he said doubtfully.

"You do that. Besides, it'll be good experience for you. If you play your cards right, this could go a long way towards your achievement list for promotion."

* * *

Bangor police station felt cool compared to the hotel, although it was a more pleasant place to work than the Lisburn Road station had been. She gathered up her notes, spoke to the custody sergeant to check Johnston was ready to be brought to interview again, then sat at her desk for a moment, trying to straighten out her thoughts.

Maybe the lorry driver's death had been an accident? But her gut told her differently. And if not Johnston, then who? The only other people she was aware of who knew anything about this case were the yard manager, Steve White, the boat's owner, Fred Mills, and then there was Richard Steele. The oh-so-friendly Richard Steele, with his offers of dinner and his smart car.

She went down to the interview room and waited until Dirty Harry had been tracked down again.

"Well?" she asked. "Are you ready to talk to me, Mr Johnston?"

Harry Reed fiddled nervously with a stack of paper on the desk in front of him, turned upside down so only the blank back of the final page showed. "My client wishes me to make a statement on his behalf, but it is dependent upon certain conditions being met."

"We can hardly grant any conditions if we have no idea what information the statement contains," Asha said.

Reed and Johnston shared a look. Johnston nodded slightly.

"My client is prepared to share a certain amount of information with you on condition that he is granted protection." He cleared his throat, and Asha realised he was genuinely nervous. And stone-cold sober. Whatever Johnston had told him under client confidentiality rules had shaken Dirty Harry.

"I'm listening," she said. And so was the recorder. Pity Aaron wasn't present, but he could hear it all later.

"My client is, and has for some time, been afraid for his life," Harry said. "The people he works for are very powerful, and, well, suffice to say that he needs guaranteed protection from them."

Powerful. Dangerous. She'd dealt with those before, but that didn't make it any easier. "This is all very dramatic," she said, "but if we are to provide protection, we need to know who we'd be protecting your client from. Without that information, we're at a stalemate. And if Mr Johnston's employers are as powerful as he claims, I'd say the fact that he's here with us today will already be enough to make them quite annoyed. It seems he might have no choice *but* to share the information with us."

Johnston slumped a little more and Dirty Harry tightened his lips.

"Very well," he said at last. He turned the sheet of paper over and glanced through the typed text that filled it. Then he lifted his head and looked Asha in the eyes. "My client was approached a little under three years ago by someone representing himself as an employee of a well-known French boatbuilding company. He gave my client an offer of regular work on behalf of the company, commissioning new boats that were to be exported to Ireland. This would involve travelling regularly up and down the country, meeting each new boat as it arrived on the back of a lorry, and carrying out certain tasks required to prepare the boat for launching. My client was, naturally, excited by this offer. He asked some questions, was satisfied with the answers, and agreed to take on the work."

He cleared his throat again.

"The first job he was sent on was to a boat arriving in Howth Marina, just outside Dublin. He was driving down the motorway to meet this boat when he received a call from the same man who had offered him the work. He told my client that in addition to commissioning the boat, he had to retrieve a package from the engine room and deliver it to someone who would meet him in the Applegreen services at Castlebellingham on the northbound carriageway of the M1.

"My client was naturally upset by this request, and argued that he wasn't, and I quote, 'a fucking delivery driver'. The man on the phone promised my client a substantial sum of money on top of the original agreed payment, assured my client that the package was harmless, and that this was the only time he'd be asked to do anything other than commission a boat.

"My client agreed reluctantly on the understanding that it was perfume for the man's wife and nothing more sinister than that."

Asha supressed a snort. "Go on."

"When my client found the package, he saw immediately that it was nothing of the sort. In fact, his suspicions were immediately aroused when he located the package, one brick-sized object wrapped in plastic. He didn't know what to do. He panicked. If he left it there, the boat's new owner might well discover it and assume my client had put it there himself, so he lifted the package and put it in his toolbox. As soon as he was on the motorway on his way back up north, he called the man who'd sent him and 'gave off' to him.

"He was informed that his employer had been having him watched, and that there was photo evidence of him handling the package which could be sent to the authorities if my client disobeyed instructions. My client was distraught" — that had to be Dirty Harry's phrase, Asha thought, because Phil Johnston probably didn't know the meaning of the word — "but he couldn't think what else to do. So he did as he was ordered, and handed the package over to another man, a lorry driver, who approached him and identified himself to my client as working for the original man."

This was all becoming very convoluted.

"After the package was off his hands, my client thought that would be the end of it. He tried to call his employer to tell him that was the last time he'd do a job for him, but the phone number was now listed as unobtainable."

Harry reshuffled his papers and took a sip of water from the plastic cup on the desk.

"As I'm sure you've guessed, Inspector, that was not the last time my client was approached by these people. A month or so later he received a picture message of him at the service station handing the package over to the lorry driver, whose back was turned to the camera. This meant my client was clearly identifiable, but the other man was not. The text accompanying the message told him that there would be another job very soon, and that he'd better not argue this time, or the photo would be sent to the authorities.

"My client was trapped, Inspector. He could see no way out of his dilemma, so he kept on doing what he was told. Until this last time, when the boat was being delivered to a boatyard just up the road from where he lived.

"This was a problem for my client for several reasons. Firstly, he was afraid that if he tried to retrieve a package here, so close to home, he was more likely to be caught because boat owners around here tend to chat to him and hang over his shoulder as he works. Secondly, this particular boat was destined for Mr Steele's private boatyard, and my client is not permitted access to that yard, nor is he permitted to carry out work on any of the boats kept there. Mr Steele's yard manager is no friend of my client.

"My client tried to explain all this to his contact, who he knows only as Michael, but the man threatened his life, and the lives of his family members. Then he told him that if he carried out this job, there'd be a sweetener in it for him, one of the packages for his own use. My client was afraid for his own life, as well as for his mother's and sister's lives."

Dirty Harry looked across at Johnston, as if asking permission to go on. Johnston shrugged, then leaned back in his chair and crossed his arms as if the conversation had nothing to do with him.

"My client again felt he had no choice, but he said that this would be the last job he'd ever do, and that they'd need to find, and I quote, 'another eejit to run errands for them from now on.'"

He swallowed. He was no longer reading from the prepared statement.

"His employer agreed to these terms, which came as a pleasant surprise to my client. But when he thought things through, he realised that false promises are easy, and it was unlikely he'd get away from the situation any time soon.

That's when he decided to try to implicate Mr White by planting his own package in Mr White's bedroom. My client is experiencing deep remorse for his actions and would like to point out that his mental health, by this stage, was so poor that he wasn't thinking straight. He feels he wasn't responsible for his own actions."

CHAPTER 18

Aaron slipped in and joined her at the table. He leaned over and whispered in her ear.

"I left PC McAvoy taking statements. What have I missed?"

Asha explained for the recording that DC Birch had joined her, then gave him a quick summary of events. "Would you agree that is accurate, Mr Reed?"

Dirty Harry nodded. "Yes, that's an accurate summary."

"I think my colleague will agree that we welcome your client's decision to tell his story, but I'm afraid he hasn't given us anything useful yet. So far, all he's done is confirm what we'd already deduced from the evidence, including Mr Johnston's regular trips across the border. What we need is a name, or at least a description, of the man who recruited your client."

"I only ever knew him as Michael," Johnston said. "He had an accent from down south. Dublin, maybe?" It was the first time he'd spoken, and his voice sounded hoarse, as if he had a frog in his throat.

"How about a description? And you could start by giving us the photo you mentioned, the one in the service station. Our tech department might be able to get something off it that could be used to help identify the lorry driver."

"Deleted it," Johnston mumbled.

"There was a phone among your possessions when you were arrested," Aaron said. "Is that the one with the photo?"

Johnston nodded.

It might be a long shot, because this was not American TV crime drama, where technicians with a limitless budget could retrieve deleted information from mobile phones with apparent ease, but it was worth a try.

"What about a description of the man who contacted you? Did you ever meet face-to-face?"

Johnston shook his head miserably.

"Aloud, please."

"Nope. Never met him. It was always phone calls, or text messages, or he'd send someone else to meet me, often lorry drivers. I always handed over the packages at a service station, always in the lorry parking area. Different people every time, I think, but I can't be sure. I'm not good with faces."

"Did you keep a record of dates when these meetings occurred?" Asha was thinking of CCTV recordings.

He shrugged. "About every couple of months for the past two or three years. I don't use a diary."

"Did you keep any of the texts or records of the phone numbers used?"

"I tried, but it was a different number every time. I think he must have used burner phones."

Very likely, and not at all helpful to the present case.

A glance at her watch showed they'd spent far longer than she'd intended in this small interview room. Regulations demanded the suspect be given a break of at least fifteen minutes during every two-hour period, and they were pushing the limits already.

"We'll take a break for a while," she said. "Thank you, Mr Johnston, for your co-operation. I think we'll have a few more questions for you later, but that's all for now. Interview ended at sixteen fifty-two." She clicked the stop button on the recorder, then stood up.

After Johnston had been escorted back to the cells, she turned to Aaron. "Any news?"

"I interviewed most of the staff who'd been on duty this morning, including the cleaner responsible for that floor of the hotel. She said she'd left the room alone because of the sign on the door, and that she hadn't seen Serge at all since he'd arrived there. No one else saw or heard anything suspicious."

"You have his passport, right? We need to contact his next of kin."

"I already contacted the police in his local town. They've agreed to break the news to his wife, and they said they'll give her support. They also asked to be kept in touch with the investigation."

"That's fair enough. Since you've made a start on that, can you be liaison for us?"

"Okay. Luckily, they have a fluent English-speaker on their staff, although he struggled a little with my accent."

"Anything turn up in his belongings?"

"No mobile, no wallet, and nothing else that might identify him. It's a good thing I already had his passport, or we'd have been struggling to name him at all. I'm planning to search his truck next, but there's a problem. His keys weren't among his possessions. I'll give Steve White a bell down at Steele's boatyard first thing tomorrow to see if they have them there. Someone has definitely been through his belongings, but they must have worn gloves. If it turns out he didn't die of natural causes, I'd guess it's the same someone who knocked him on the head."

"Speaking of which, I'll chase up the post-mortem tomorrow as well. Where did they take the body?"

"That's where we're in luck. It's gone to Belfast, to our old friend the Prof, and he said he'd get it done this afternoon if possible. He should have a preliminary report for us first thing tomorrow morning."

"Excellent. You should get Johnston's phone down to Bishop now. I'll hold a briefing at nine tomorrow, but I think that'll do for today. I'm exhausted. Say hello to Sergeant Jacob for me, will you, if you see her?"

* * *

The next morning, Asha called Professor Talbot before the briefing. He answered on the third ring, sounding delighted to hear from Asha.

"I'm putting you on speaker, Mark. Aaron Birch is here, too."

"Wonderful! How lovely to hear from you, my dear. I suppose you're chasing up the post-mortem on our French gentleman. I can only give you preliminary findings at present as I'm awaiting some test results."

"I understand."

"Well, I'll cut straight to the chase and say that I believe he was hit on the head from behind by something heavy and blunt. His skull was fractured, with a large degree of bone fragmentation around the injury. The combination of local damage and the concussive effect of the blow have together caused severe damage to extensive areas of the brain. He would have lost consciousness immediately, but death could have taken some time, perhaps anything up to an hour. Several regions demonstrate haemorrhaging to different degrees, suggesting living tissue responding to injury for a prolonged period after the initial assault. He would almost certainly have remained unconscious until he died, so the poor fellow probably never knew what hit him."

"Wow," Asha said. "And you're certain there's no way he could have just fallen and hit his head?"

"Absolutely certain, dearest. This was an aggressive and vicious attack by someone who knew their job well. The spot chosen was in entirely the wrong place for him to have hit it in a fall, and the damage is far too widespread to have been accidental."

"Any thoughts on the weapon used?"

"I'd be looking for some sort of staff, or maybe a heavy flashlight like that one you carry, Asha."

The Maglite. Not that it had done her any good when she'd needed it. She remembered the heft of it in her hand and the courage it had given her as she walked into a trap.

"Anything else?"

"The attacker was quite tall, judging from the position of the injury. The victim was 182cm tall, that's about six foot in old money, so his attacker was probably a little more than that, say six-two or six-three. What is more, I'd be prepared to hazard a guess, off the record, that this is not the first time the killer has done this. It's too practiced, too assured. A first-timer will often pull the punch a little, so to speak, and not put their full force into it. This chap had no such reservations. In, whack, and away again. Job done."

Asha felt a little nauseous, but she trusted the Prof's judgement.

"That last part might not be in the written report, my dear. It's not something tangible that I can back up in court, but I'm fairly sure I'm right. I think you could have a repeat offender on your hands. Mean bastard, too, I'd say." His voice lightened. "Anyway. If you find yourself in Belfast anytime soon, Sue and I would love to see you, you know. And there's always a pint of the black stuff for you in the snug in my local. Just tell Aaron he's not to embarrass us both next time by ordering 'a half of lager, any lager, whatever's cheapest'. I'm still living that one down."

Aaron pulled a face, and she laughed. "I'll take you up on that, Mark. Next time, I'll order his drink for him. Give my love to Sue."

"Will do. Speak soon." The phone clicked as he rang off.

Asha took a deep breath. "Well, that's put the cat among the pigeons. No wonder Phil Johnston is scared."

"Does he know about the driver?"

"Not unless Dirty Harry knows, but that seems unlikely. Has it been on the local news yet?"

"I've asked the staff at the hotel not to speak to any reporters, at least until we've traced his family and informed them. We're keeping everything low-key. As it happens, the place is fairly quiet, with no one in the rooms on either side of the victim, and the only other occupants of that corridor checked out first thing this morning, before all this kicked off."

Asha opened her mouth to speak, but he raised a hand.

"It's okay. I checked, and it was a married couple, aged in their seventies, regular visitors to the hotel and had been there since the twenty-third of December.

"We'll need to draft a press release, I think, once the French police confirm that his family has been informed. I'll need to run it past my super first, but Sewell's usually pretty keen for me to do things myself. Speaking of which, how's the revision going? You really should be taking your sergeant's exams soon."

Aaron broke eye contact and shuffled the files he held. "All good," he said, glancing at his watch. "We're going to be late for this briefing."

Faith McAvoy and another uniform Asha remembered from Belfast were both at the briefing along with her own team from Bangor. She ran through what they knew so far.

"We're hoping Johnston's phone might generate a lead as to the identity of the person behind this group, but we won't have that data until later today. DC Birch will be chasing that up. It's beginning to look as if Johnston is just a pawn in the game, but we only have his word for that. He tried to shift the blame on to Steve White, which doesn't predispose me to trust him very far."

She went on to allocate tasks. "I want more on Johnston's finances, and possibly White's as well. Mr Mills seemed genuinely horrified that his new yacht had been used to smuggle drugs, but we should certainly take a close look at him for elimination purposes, if nothing else."

"What about Richie Rich?" Aaron asked.

She mentally berated herself for not mentioning him herself. "Yes, I think we should look at Mr Steele, too. He has access to boats, so he could be part of a chain shipping drugs internationally."

The morning was already half gone. "Make a start, people. Let me know if you turn anything up."

They dispersed to their tasks until she and Aaron were alone.

"Sorry about that, Ash," he said, "but if we didn't investigate him, too, there might have been questions asked."

"Don't be ridiculous," she snapped, then regretted her tone. "It's not as if I left him out on purpose, but he's pretty low down on the suspects list and I only have limited resources. Speaking of which, you never did answer my question about the sergeant's exams."

He pursed his lips and blew out. "Yeah, about that. I'm not sure it's what I really want."

That came out of the blue. She couldn't find the words to ask, but she didn't need to.

"It's been hard these last few months, since you left . . ." He let the words hang there.

"Is the new DI not working out?"

"It's not that. Collins is okay, but he's old guard. He does everything by the book, and it's driving me insane."

"What does Lonnie think of him?"

"Sergeant Jacob calls him Detective Inspector Collins and is very polite to him."

"That bad, huh? You know, if you get these exams and your promotion, it's possible you'll be posted somewhere else. I'm currently without a sergeant since DS Bailey went off sick, and we heard last week that he's unlikely to come back. He's pretty close to retirement age, and I don't think he was enjoying working with me any more than you're enjoying working with Collins."

He gave her a mock salute that was more like the old Aaron. "Yes, ma'am. I'll maybe make a bit of time for some revision before lunch."

CHAPTER 19

The damn low-loader was still in the way. Steve needed to crane the work boat out for maintenance and they only had a short weather window; plus, they'd already lost half a day after he closed the yard up yesterday. If he didn't get her lifted out today, it could be a couple of weeks before he'd have another shot.

He stared up at the locked cab. The key wasn't in any of the usual places that drivers hid them and kicking the tyre hadn't made him feel any better. Bloody Frenchman: why was he not answering his phone?

"Got a problem?" Mr Steele called impatiently. The boss had been grumpy since he'd got back from town yesterday.

"This thing's in the way of the crane and bloody Serge still isn't picking up."

Steele came over, frowning. "I told the police yesterday that he wasn't answering. I wonder if he's done a runner. I should call Detective Inspector Harvey and see if they've found out anything."

"Ask if they've searched his room in case the keys are in his luggage. I only need to move it about twenty yards to give the crane room to manoeuvre out."

"I'll do that," Steele said, happier.

Just as he disappeared into the office, a police car drove into the yard and parked up near the lorry. Two peelers got out, shifting their utility belts as they stood up. The amount of kit those fellas had to wear always made them look bulky, but the one who'd been sitting in the passenger seat would have been a big man even without the extra baggage, standing well over six foot and broad with it. They eyed up the low-loader as if they owned it.

"Can I help you, fellas?" Steve asked, wiping his hands on a rag.

The tall one gave him a friendly smile. "We've been sent to impound the truck, to bring it down for forensics. It's nothing for you to worry about."

But Steve knew the ropes. "Do you have any paperwork? A warrant, maybe, and a receipt to say where you've taken it and who ordered it?"

The other man narrowed his eyes. "Right little lawyer, aren't you? Well, we do have paperwork, yeah, but my colleague here inadvertently left it on the desk at the station. So, you can either let us take the truck, or you can make us fetch it, thus getting ourselves into trouble with the boss woman. That means that when we do come back with it, we're going to be pretty pissed off. Your choice, mate."

While the fat man was talking, his partner unlocked the lorry cab and climbed up into the driver's seat. If they had the keys, they must be legit, right?

Steve wanted to argue, but when he looked into those hard eyes the words dried up in his throat. He stepped back, with the faintest of nods.

"Thanks, mate," the tall peeler said. "Have a nice day."

The Americanism sounded out of place in that flat, aggressive voice. Steve walked as fast as he could without running, straight to Steele's office. The boss was sifting through piles of paper on his desk. He didn't look up.

"That phone call worked fast," Steve said. "Two peelers just turned up for the truck."

Steele's head snapped up, and a frown creased his forehead. "What? She was in a meeting. I didn't get her. Did they show you their ID?"

Steve shrugged. "It's just a couple of peelers. They're wearing uniform and they're in a police car."

Steele got to his feet and went to the other room where the window overlooked the yard. "I'm phoning Asha again to check. I don't think they'd impound the thing without letting us know. Keep an eye on them and tell me if they start to move the truck."

Steve ran back outside. The roar of the powerful engine split the quiet afternoon, and smoke belched from the exhaust above his head.

Whether the two peelers knew it or not, it would be a couple of minutes before the truck could be moved. The spring parking brakes needed to reach pressure first, and until then it wouldn't be going anywhere. The Frenchman had complained only the other day how long this process took.

The big man had the engine running in the police car. Was he was going to give the lorry an escort?

Steele erupted from the building and raced past Steve. His conversation with Asha, once he'd finally got hold of her, had been very short and to the point. "Stop! Steve, they mustn't take the lorry. We've got to stop them!" He ignored the police car but ran to the driver's side of the truck instead. He jumped up on the step and tried to open the door, but it must have been locked so he hammered on the window. Steve followed, wondering what the boss was playing at.

The driver grinned down at them, and Steve got a brief look at his thin face and hard eyes.

Then the air brakes hissed. The driver threw a mock salute and crashed the gears, throwing the truck into reverse.

"Look out!" Steve yelled.

Steele was flung sideways by the sudden movement. He swung out from the truck, but kept his grip on the door handle, saving himself from falling beneath the wheels.

A gut-churning grinding noise filled the air as the low-loader trailer reversed into a stack of spare boat supports. They fell with a clatter, but one got caught up between the rear wheels so when the truck moved forward, it dragged the metal frame with it.

The lorry built up speed, the driver furiously spinning the wheel, then the cab crashed into the closest in a row of boats on their cradles.

Steve watched in horror as the first boat tilted past its tipping point, the truck still powering forward on full lock, but it wasn't enough to save the cruiser. She toppled sideways into the boat next to her, which in turn fell; it was like the most expensive domino set in the world.

Steve froze. The far side of the cab, the side that had hit the cruiser, was where his boss had been clinging.

Massive lorry tyres smoked as the truck powered towards the gate, dragging the fishtailing trailer in its wake. The tractor unit made it between the gate posts with little room to spare on the driver's side, but the swinging trailer hit the left-hand gatepost with the shriek of metal against metal. Its engine faded, leaving the sound of crashing boats behind and a long smear of green paint from the cab on the concrete post.

And by the gates, a sprawling scarecrow pile of rags that had once been Richard Steele.

Steve covered the distance so fast his chest hurt. He dropped to his knees at Steele's side. A bloodstained arm covered his face, as if he'd thrown it up to protect himself.

A pulse. Check for a pulse. He lifted the limp wrist and poked it with trembling fingertips, but he was shaking so much he couldn't tell which was his own pulse and which the other man's.

Then Steele groaned and one of his legs moved. Blood was beginning to pool under his head.

Steve fumbled in his jeans pocket for his mobile. His hand was sticky with blood, but he finally tugged it free and tapped in 999.

"Emergency. Which service do you require?"

"Ambulance. It's urgent." He almost said, "and police", but then he remembered the two men in uniform, and left the words unspoken.

The ambulance operator was calm, helping him slow his own breathing enough to tell her what he was seeing.

"An ambulance is on its way," she said, and his heart lifted at the words. Then she talked him through how best to keep Richard Steele alive until the professionals got there.

The distant siren was the best sound he'd ever heard. When the two green-clad paramedics took over he stood back, legs shaking, wrapping his arm around one canted gatepost to stay upright.

Steele was still unconscious when he was loaded into the back of the ambulance, his face so pale Steve might have thought he was dead if it hadn't been for the oxygen mask and drip. They didn't waste resources on dead people.

Shock began to set in. What had just happened?

"Mr White? Are you okay?"

It was that detective, the one who'd been sniffing around on Boxing Day. There was a uniformed constable with her, and Steve started to back away, hands raised in defence, until he realised it was a woman, not one of Steele's attackers.

"Come on into the building," the detective said. "You're in shock. Let's get you warm and then you can tell me what happened."

But try as he might, he couldn't find the words. "They had the keys," he told her. He had a feeling he'd said it a few times already.

Someone pushed a mug of tea into one of his hands and a biscuit into the other. The detective was on the phone, talking to the hospital. Steve nibbled and sipped without thought, but as the warm liquid flooded his body, he began to recover.

"I'm sorry," he said to the constable. He drained the tea and plonked the mug down. "I'll do anything to help."

"It's all right, Mr White. You've had quite a shock. The inspector will ask you a few questions when she's finished speaking to the hospital, but is there anyone we can contact first — family or friends who could run you home?"

"I can't go home," he muttered. "The yard's not secure, and there's all those boats damaged. I have to phone the owners, and the insurance company, and I'll need to get someone in to fix the gate, and what about the boss? He was the only one prepared to take a chance on me and give me a job. The least I can do is to—"

"Slow down, Mr White," the constable said. "We'll help you with all that, and one of my colleagues will phone around to find someone to make the place secure."

The inspector ended her call. "You'll be glad to hear that Mr Steele is conscious. He's had a knock to the head, but it sounds as if he's going to be okay."

That's when Steve broke down and cried.

CHAPTER 20

Steve's skin was pasty with shock. "It's all my fault," he said. "If I'd held my ground, he wouldn't have got hurt. I always fuck everything up. Everything."

"It's not your fault," Asha said, "but you can help me catch whoever did this. Take me back to the beginning."

He wiped his face with a grubby sleeve. "Two peelers turned up. Said they'd left the paperwork behind, and they bullied me into letting them take the truck." He turned tortured eyes on her. "Why did I let him run after them? I should have stopped him."

"Can you describe them?"

He shrugged. "They arrived in a police car. Uniforms, those big heavy belts, guns in holsters."

"What about a physical description?"

"I didn't really get a look at the little one, the one that drove the truck, but I did see the big fella."

"Tell me," she said, keeping her voice quiet and calm as if this was all in a day's work.

"Mr Steele might have seen the driver," he said. "He was right up on the step, face-to-face with the bastard. If he's able to talk, he might be able to tell you more. The other was just a big fella, you know? Tall and wide. Black hair, looked as though he liked the drink." He pointed to his own nose.

It could be Kernaghan, which would make the other one Aiken, but surely the two of them wouldn't be that brazen. Would they? "That's really helpful, Mr White. Would you be able to come down to the station as soon as it's convenient to look at some photos? I'd like to build up a gallery and see if you pick anyone out from them."

"Aye, I can do that, but I need to sort this place first. God knows what I'll do about the gate." He wrung his hands together and one leg jiggled as his stress built up again.

"You've been through a tough experience, Mr White. Steve. Isn't there anyone else who could help you? I'd really rather you went home for a rest this evening."

"No. It's just me and the boss at this time of year. In the busy months, you know, spring and autumn when everyone wants their boats lifting in, lifting out, cleaning and polishing, I get a wee lad up from the town." He tipped his head in the vague direction of Bangor. "But he works in the garage on the main road at this time of year, so I couldn't get him even if I wanted. I don't know how I'm going to face Serge. Imagine, having to tell a man his livelihood has been stolen by a couple of peelers!" He got up and wandered over to the mess of toppled boats, scratching his head.

Damn. He still didn't know Serge Durand was dead. This was no time to break the news.

From the privacy of her car, she called the marina in Bangor. Mike was on duty again, and he said he'd ring around a couple of the other lads and see if anyone was free to help Steve out. She wasn't completely sure she'd done the right thing, but if they turned up, surely he'd hardly turn them away?

Richard Steele had been taken to the Ulster Hospital on the outskirts of Belfast, about a twenty-minute drive. In her own mind, she justified a visit as an opportunity to get a description of the driver of the truck, but that wasn't the only reason.

Her phone rang halfway there.

"What did I miss?" Aaron asked. "The gossip here is going mad."

She filled him in, including the description of the two men in uniform.

"You think it's our old friends, Aiken and Kernaghan, don't you?"

"I do. The barefaced cheek of them, too. Still wearing their uniforms and driving the marked car they disappeared with last year. They must have found somewhere really good to lie low."

"Or someone's helping them."

"Someone with enough influence to protect them despite a nationwide manhunt. I just wish I knew who. I need you to coordinate the search for that truck as a priority, please. Something that size can't just disappear into thin air."

"Okay, boss. Will do."

The roads had been fairly quiet, but she couldn't say the same for the hospital. Both car parks had long queues waiting. She drove on past the multistorey until she came to a pull-in area that led to big glass doors. There was a short-term parking area for pick-ups and drop-offs and as she pulled in, a van pulled away from the kerb. Perfect.

She slapped her Officer Attending badge on the dashboard and locked the car, keeping her head down as she passed the smokers huddling around the entrance in pyjamas and dressing gowns.

She'd passed the entrance to A&E as she searched for somewhere to park. It started to rain as she walked back around the hospital, so she pulled her collar up.

The steps up to the A&E entrance held their share of smokers, including an elderly lady in a wheelchair perched precariously at the top of the accessibility access ramp. She had her eyes closed, dragging at the cigarette as if it was oxygen and she was suffocating.

Asha side-stepped her and made it through the doors as they swung closed behind someone coming out, a tall man with his arm in a sling.

She spun on her heel, and almost collided with him as he turned towards her. She tried very hard not to wince at the state of his face.

"It's not as bad as it looks," Richard said lightly. His mouth was too swollen to smile. "Or so they tell me."

"Are they letting you out?" she asked.

"Not really. They wanted to keep me in for observation for the night, because, you know." He pointed to his temple. "Head injury. I discharged myself. Had to virtually sign my life away, but eventually they let me go." He glanced over her shoulder with exaggerated caution. "Maybe we should make a run for it, before they change their minds. You did bring the getaway vehicle?"

She laughed, giddy as a schoolgirl. "I did, but it's a fair walk. If you can find somewhere to hole up, preferably out of range of that CCTV camera that's pointed straight at us, I can run and fetch it?"

"Not worth the risk. By the time you get back, they could have dragged me back in, kicking, screaming and strait-jacketed. Besides, the cold air will help to clear my head."

They walked the way Asha had just come. She kept her pace slow to make allowances for his condition, but despite the fact it was uphill in this direction, the distance felt half what it had on the way down.

"You'd struggle to get into the straitjacket with one arm in a sling. What happened to it?"

"Dislocated shoulder. Old sports injury, so the damn thing pops out at the least excuse."

He folded his tall frame into the passenger seat, grunting as he tried to find a comfortable position, and allowed her to help with the seatbelt. As she leaned across him to click it into place, his breath warmed her cheek.

"So, where am I taking you?" she asked to cover up her reaction.

"Back to the yard." There was no hesitation. "I need to see the damage, and Steve will be having a breakdown."

She wanted to ask if he was sure, but it would have been a rhetorical question, so she closed her mouth instead and just drove, navigating the afternoon traffic until they were clear of the worst of it.

"You're a rare woman, Detective Inspector Asha Harvey," he said, as they drove across the first of Bangor's many roundabouts, out towards the coast road.

She shot him a glance, but he was looking straight ahead, out of the front window. "How do you make that out?"

"You didn't argue, even though you think I'm an idiot to have tackled those two bastards on my own."

"Actually, I assumed you wanted to be driven to the yard because you live in a hovel and are ashamed of it."

He laughed, then he winced and put a hand to his chest. "Ow."

"Sorry."

"No. I deserved that." He shook his head. "What I should be saying is thank you. Thank you for coming to the hospital. Thank you for putting aside whatever duty took you there in the first place in order to drive this fool wherever he wants to go. Thank you for bringing laughter to a godawful day."

She couldn't resist smiling. "You were the duty that took me there in the first place, and what else would I be doing on a rainy December afternoon? Besides, if I hadn't driven you, you'd probably have got a taxi, wouldn't you?"

"Bus," he said. "At least as far as it would take me, then I'd have walked. I hate taxis. They always drive too fast."

So, the man sitting next to her, one of the richest men in the country, wasn't above taking public transport when he found himself without a car? That was enlightening.

But she needed to get a description of his attacker. She took a breath to speak, but he got in first.

"The lorry driver, Serge Durand," Richard said before she could speak. "I had time to think while I was in the hospital, and I was wondering how those two faux peelers got hold of the truck keys. Was Serge working with them? Is that why he wasn't answering his phone?"

Asha let out a breath, forgetting the questions for the moment. "We don't think so. Serge Durand is dead, Richard. We found him in his hotel room."

* * *

Steele's boatyard was a hive of activity. Someone had set up a generator and work lights to augment the security lights as the early darkness of winter crept in. A mobile crane was alongside the boats that had fallen over. Asha had to wait at the top of the approach road while a digger manoeuvred itself into position, a rock hammer dangling from its front arm.

"What the fuck?" Richard breathed. The sight seemed to have shocked him out of the inertia that had held him since she'd broken the news. "What happened here? World War Three?"

"Apparently the yard owner's head was so hard that everything it hit disintegrated."

She stole a glance at him. He was staring out of the front window with his jaw set hard, fists clenched tight on his lap.

"Steve was going to try to tackle all this by himself," she said, "but it looks as though the neighbours have turned out to help."

"Not just the neighbours," he said with a baffled expression. "That digger belongs to a builder who lives up the road from me and the crane might be his, too, but who are all the others?"

"I might be responsible for a couple of them." She'd recognised a face or two among the volunteers, lads from the station, including Sergeant Tom Casey. "And I think Bangor Marina were phoning around their off-duty staff."

"This bloody country never ceases to amaze me. One minute, we're tearing each other apart over religion and politics; the next, you see something like this." He nodded towards the digger driver. "Jack Rae over there is a staunch Unionist. He marches with a bowler hat and sash in front of the bands every July." He pointed to a pair of brawny lads who were pitting their strength against a large boulder the rock hammer had just loosened. "Those two, Sammy and Joe, go to Mass every Sunday down the coast. On a normal day, Jack spits as they pass him, and they let his tyres down if they can get away with it, but just look at them now."

Someone must have spotted Asha's car, probably one of her own people who knew the vehicle, and they were clearing a route through the debris for her.

She parked up in front of the building. Every light blazed. She went to help Richard, but Steve was already helping him out of the car. His eyes gleamed in the artificial lights, and although they were rimmed with red, she recognised joy instead of the anger she'd half expected.

"Mr Steele, have you seen this lot? They all just turned up in ones and twos with offers of help. I've never seen anything like it." Then he remembered that his boss had been carted off in an ambulance. "Are you sure you should be out of hospital? You looked pretty bad when—"

"I'm fine," Richard said impatiently. "Show me the extent of the damage, Steve. Tell me what happened here."

Asha walked away from the noise and lights, down the ramp on to the jetty. The tide was high, so the ramp wasn't as steep as the last time she'd come down here. That felt like weeks ago, but it had only been, what, two days?

The floating jetties creaked as they rocked to the waves, a regular sound that eased some of the tension from her shoulders as she walked along between the pontoons. She went on until she reached the end, stopping by Richard's own boat, the beautiful *Cloud.* If Richard offered again, she'd accept a tour of the boat.

A movement caught her eye, a flash of white above the rocky breakwater that enclosed this man-made harbour. The top of a mast with a triangle of white sail, approaching the entrance. The sail disappeared, but now she knew where to look, Asha could follow the tip of the mast as it grew closer, faint against the starry sky. She walked along the jetty to get a better line of sight for the harbour entrance.

There. A sailing boat, quite big, coming in under engine. It slowed as it passed through the narrow entrance and turned confidently, as if its skipper had been here countless times before, towards the rows of empty berths. Asha hurried her pace to meet it.

There was one person in the cockpit, so wrapped up in waterproofs it was impossible to tell if they were male or female, young or old. The boat finished the turn, lined up perfectly with the edge of the pontoon, then stopped with a surge of engine in reverse. The sailor strolled along the side deck, stooped to pick up two coils of rope, and leaped on to the narrow decking with surprising lightness for such a bulky figure.

Before Asha could open her mouth to offer to help, the stranger had the boat secured front and back. It was a show of casual professionalism that couldn't fail to impress. Some old salt, Asha assumed, wizened from years of squinting at the sun for midday sights, or whatever it was that sailors did.

Then the newcomer turned towards her, flinging back the hood to reveal long wavy hair and a pair of eyes that looked somehow familiar.

CHAPTER 21

For a moment, Clara thought the lone figure standing on the dock might be Richard, out for an evening stroll, and her heart gave a great thump of relief, but as she got closer, she realised it was a woman, a dark-skinned stranger with long black hair tied back in a half ponytail. She took a short breath, bracing herself to act normally in front of a stranger. The woman wasn't dressed like a sailor either, in that long coat and smart trousers. A tourist, at this time of year? It seemed unlikely. Hopefully she wouldn't offer to catch lines. Nothing worse than an amateur hauling on a bow line when you're not expecting it, so you can't get the blasted stern in.

The woman had the sense to stay back out of the way until Clara had the boat secured, then she approached. Clara pulled her hood down and shook her hair free.

"Hi. I'm Clara Steele. Is my brother around? I didn't get a chance to tell him I was coming." To her, the words sounded stiff and unnatural, but the woman didn't seem to react.

The stranger was tall, slim inside her winter coat, and reflected moonlight glinted in her hair. Clara wondered if the colour would be like a raven's wing in daylight, with hints of blue and green where the sun caught it.

Then the woman stretched out a hand and spoke, her accent the soft tones of someone born and bred in South Down. "Richard's up in the yard. I'm Detective Inspector Asha Harvey."

The tension drained, leaving her weak with relief. Richard was all right. Then she wondered if Ole had ratted her out, and this detective was here to ask her about the cargo she'd dropped off in that isolated bay? Clara pushed down the panic and tried to keep smiling. This didn't seem like an arrest, not that she'd know. She tugged off a damp sailing glove and gingerly shook Asha's hand, conscious of how grimy and sweaty her own hand was.

A loud bang came from somewhere out of sight, followed by raised voices. The detective flinched and glanced back over her shoulder. "There's been a lot going on over the last couple of days, so brace yourself for a bit of a shock. Richard's up there now, supervising the repairs."

"Someone have a wild party?" Clara attempted to sound light-hearted.

"Not exactly. Once you've got your boat sorted, I can explain a bit more if you like."

"Look, I've a few things to do on the boat to make her secure." Evidence to destroy. "I can follow you up there in a wee while and maybe you can tell me what he's been up to?"

Detective Inspector Harvey nodded and turned away without another word. Instead of jumping back aboard to check the boat for any sign she might have missed of her recent guests, Clara stood and watched Asha Harvey walk away. There was a freedom in the way she moved, a flexibility that spoke of physical fitness.

Then she caught herself on. Bloody woman probably did yoga, or that other thing housewives did. Zumba, that was it. A policewoman was the last person Clara needed in her life right now, least of all a detective. She'd been at sea too long.

She climbed aboard, then stood in the middle of the cabin floor and spun slowly around, trying to see it as a stranger would, checking for any stray detail that might suggest that she'd carried six girls on board, but there was nothing. Even the head was spotless after her cleaning frenzy.

She climbed out of her wet weather gear and glanced down at herself. Faded canvas trousers tucked into thick fisherman's socks. A polo neck under-layer with a knitted jersey over the top, same clothes she'd been wearing since she left Norway.

Everything she pulled out of the lockers reeked of mould from the constant damp, and there was nothing much better than her current clothes. She settled for pulling her trousers out of her socks and sliding her feet into a pair of leather deck shoes that had stiffened with exposure to salt.

As she climbed the steep companionway steps into the cockpit, she touched the leather sheath that hung to the right of the hatch. It was a superstitious act, a reminder that she had the means to protect herself, or to cut herself free in case of a knock-down. Not that it had been any protection against Ole.

The reality of the yard was worse than her imagination had allowed for. The place looked like a building site. A boat hung in makeshift crane slings while several complete strangers ran around with props to hold it upright. There was a deep gouge out of its hull and the stanchions were bent and twisted.

Clara stood at the edge of the pools of light and searched for Richard. She passed over him at first, but then some familiar mannerism brought her eyes back to the stooped figure leaning on Steve White's arm.

Her mouth went dry. The policewoman hadn't said he'd been hurt. There she was, over by the building, watching Richard with a worried look on her face. A little of the tension eased. She wasn't interested in Clara, just in whatever had been going on here.

She edged down behind the rows of boats until she was close enough to hear his voice.

"Richard?"

He spun around, bringing Steve with him, and his face lit up in a smile that warmed her heart. She wanted to run to him, to throw herself into his arms, but she couldn't. Not with all these men around, and not—

As he turned, the floodlights shone on his battered face. Her breath caught in her throat, and everything blurred with tears. Then she was inside the circle of his good arm, his weight heavy against her so she had to widen her stance, but her nose was buried in his jacket, breathing in his familiar scent and all was well with the world.

Steve left them together and went back to work. He looked happier than Clara remembered seeing him since Tina left, despite the carnage all around.

She and Richard made their way back towards the marina building. "I think this calls for a celebration," he whispered in her ear. "I'm pretty sure I have a bottle of plonk chilling in the fridge in my office."

She shook her head. "Too cold for wine, but I ran out of coffee about a week ago, and I still have the DTs."

"For you, wee Clara, anything."

She must have stiffened at the pet name. Richard stopped and pulled her around in front of him, so he could look down into her face. "What's wrong? DTs that bad, huh?"

"Just tired, I guess. The windvane steering packed up a while back, so I've been on watch for too long, hand steering and heaving-to for a light nap when there were no other boats around."

"Quite the adventurer," he said with a pride that only made her more miserable. "I want to hear every detail as soon as we're home."

They'd almost made it to the building when he noticed the policewoman. "Asha, you must meet my baby sister, Clara. Come on inside and let me make you both coffee."

She smiled at him, and the warmth in her eyes sent a little spasm through Clara.

In the end, Asha made the coffee while Clara curled up on a sofa with Richard's arm around her. The detective didn't seem to be listening to Clara's conversation with her brother, but she would be. Her presence at this precise time brought an edge of danger that made Clara's pulse beat a little faster.

"Tell me what happened to you," she said, brushing the swollen flesh around his eye with gentle fingertips. "Did you get into a fight?"

He glanced at Asha before replying, and that same niggle of jealousy snapped at her, but Asha didn't look his way.

"You could say that. I got into a fight with a truck. Two bastards pretending to be police stole it from the yard, and when I tried to stop them, the driver wiped me off on the gatepost."

She sat up, and he winced at the sudden movement. "A truck did that to you? Richard!"

His eyes crinkled at her, just as they had when they were children together, and he was winding her up.

"Oh, you're pulling my leg. What really happened?"

"God's truth," he said piously. "Scout's honour." He held up three fingers, the wrong three fingers. This was where she'd usually punch him, but not this time. "A French low-loader, driven by a hard-eyed little ginger git, tried to run me over. Apparently, the gatepost came off worse than I did."

That did catch the policewoman's attention. A spoon clattered in the sink. "Did you get a good look at the driver, Richard?"

"I did. We were literally eyeball-to-eyeball for about twenty yards. Little bastard just grinned at me and drove straight for the post." He tilted his head at her. "Why? Does that description sound familiar?"

She looked troubled. "I'm probably just being paranoid. I asked Steve if he'd come down to the station and look at some photos for identification purposes. Would you consider doing the same?"

"Of course. Anything to help catch the sod."

CHAPTER 22

After a fruitless afternoon chasing up ANPR and CCTV cameras in an unfamiliar police station, trying to work out where the hell the truck had gone, Aaron was ready to pack it in. Faith texted to say she was finished and was going to cadge a lift back to Belfast with one of the other constables, unless he happened to be going that way.

He needed no second bidding. What he and Faith had was hardly what you'd call a relationship, not yet anyway. He didn't want to frighten her off, but he wasn't about to look a gift horse in the mouth.

She was waiting for him at the front of the railway station, far away from prying eyes and wagging tongues in the station. She shivered as she slid into the Golf's bucket seat, so he turned up the heat before negotiating his way out on to the main Belfast Road again.

"Find anything in the financials?"

"Nothing that anyone's prepared to let me in on. I'm just a gofer, doing what I'm told. You probably know more about what I found than I do."

He changed lanes, driving on autopilot. This was the first time he'd had her in his car on their own, and her presence was like a neon sign flashing in the corner of his vision.

"Do you have any plans for tonight?" she asked. His stomach clenched. Was this small talk or . . .?

Play it neutral. Don't jump to conclusions. "Nothing except carry-out and a film on Netflix. What about you?"

She smiled. It made her words warm and open. "Same. What sort of carry-out had you in mind?"

He swallowed. "I was thinking Chinese." No response. "Or Indian." Still nothing. "Sometimes I get pizza." He gave up. "What's your favourite?"

"I'm a pizza girl. We could pick something up on the way, if you like?"

"I do like," he said carefully. "There's a Dominos just up the road from me. You could call ahead and order for us. My card is in the glovebox."

Shit, he'd taken it too fast. But she was already rummaging through his wallet. "What would you like, since you're buying? Extra cookies, wedges, stuffed crust?"

"Don't laugh. Plain margherita, large, no stuffed crust."

She did laugh. "So that's a large margherita with anchovies and green chillies then? I'm on it."

"Hey!"

She phoned the order through. Two large margheritas, one with anchovies and green chillies, one plain. He blustered all the way through the call, but she just raised a hand to command silence and kept talking.

How had he ever thought she was shy? She was a minx.

As usual, there was nowhere to park near the pizza place, so he dropped her off and did a lap of the residential side streets before picking her up again, and she sat with the pizzas on her lap, covered with his big waterproof jacket for insulation, until he pulled up outside his flat, double parked.

He handed her the keys. "You'd better go on in and keep the food warm while I try to find a parking space somewhere in the same county. There's wine in the fridge, and beer somewhere, but it might not be chilled." Beer was his brother Peter's drink of choice, so there was always a supply handy just in case.

He held his breath, wondering if this would scare her off. It bloody well ought to. Then she took the flat keys from him.

"Any security or alarm code I need to know about?"

He breathed out. "Nope. Nothing to steal. It's number two, at the top of the stairs."

She flashed him a smile, perfect teeth and laughing eyes. "Don't be long, or I'll have to start without you."

Thank God he'd done his washing before Patterson sent him haring off to Bangor.

He was back at the flat by the river in minutes and took the stairs two at a time. It felt odd, ringing his own doorbell. It was even more odd when no one answered it. He was beginning to fret when the hall light came on and Faith's slim figure appeared as a silhouette against the frosted glass windowpane.

She opened the door, that cheeky grin still in place. She'd shed her uniform coat and was wearing just the white shirt loose over the trousers. Her feet were bare.

"No cold callers," she said, pretending to close the door in his face.

He stuck his foot in the gap like a vacuum cleaner salesman. "Hard to be anything but a cold caller in this weather. Have you left me any anchovies?"

She stepped back to let him in, but not as far as she could have. He brushed against her chest as he pushed past. The contact sent a jolt through him.

She'd laid the table with placemats and napkins — where the hell had she found those? Two wine glasses were set out, and a bottle of Pinot Grigio with a corkscrew next to it.

"Wow." He looked around for the piles of bumf that usually covered the table. They were neatly stacked on the floor by the window.

While Aaron was still wondering if he should fetch cutlery, Faith lifted a giant slice of pizza with her fingers and took a bite out of it, and he relaxed.

"So," she said unintelligibly as she chewed. "Mmph. Tell me all about this case, all the stuff that isn't in the briefings

— I'm sure there's loads that Asha isn't telling us. Was that dead lorry driver a drug mule?"

He chewed his mouthful of margherita, taking his time before swallowing to give himself time to think. If he was to have any sort of relationship with Faith, they had to be able to trust each other, but there also had to be ground rules. *At least in the beginning*, his subconscious whispered. Now was the time to make those rules clear. He built a mental picture of Constable McAvoy in full uniform, and overlaid it on top of Faith McAvoy, munching pizza and sipping wine in his flat, and wearing a thin blouse that allowed her white bra to show against the dark skin beneath. It wasn't easy.

"You must know I can't discuss case details with you unless they're part of the official briefings. Confidentiality is key in these investigations. If you accidentally let slip something you'd learned from me, we'd both be in trouble."

For a moment he thought she was going to burst into tears, but then she gave a watery smile. "I'm sorry, I didn't think. I'm so stupid."

"No, not stupid! Curiosity is a good thing, but there have to be rules." He pushed his plate away. "You see, if this case comes to court, it only takes the smallest slip from any one of the detectives involved for the defence team to find a loophole. We *have* to keep our data secure. It's not personal, just the nature of the job."

"I understand, Aaron. I really do." She looked slyly at his plate. "Do you not want the rest of that pizza?"

She reached out towards the plate, and he brought his hand down instinctively on top of hers, intercepting her before she could steal a piece. His fingers closed, her hand turned over in his, and there they were, holding hands across the table like a cliché from a romantic film.

Her eyes were deep brown, and her lashes were long. While Aaron was losing himself in those inky depths, her free hand snaked out and stole a slice of pizza from his plate.

The moment was broken, and he was left confused. Had there been anything there, or had she just been playing him all along? For a moment, he'd thought . . .

He sighed. "I thought you didn't like plain cheese?"

Her eyes sparkled with merriment as she bit into the stolen pizza. "I'm prepared to slum it occasionally. Besides, food always tastes better when it's filched."

Aaron laughed out loud. "You're a rascal, aren't you, Faith McAvoy? How do you do it? The meek little probationer act, hardly speaking, never putting yourself forward."

Her face smoothed, the lines of laughter disappearing. "Because this job is important to me, Aaron. It's the most important thing in my life."

They were still holding hands, but she squeezed his lightly and let it go, leaning back in her chair as if to increase the distance between them.

"I can understand that," he said, matching her solemn mood. "I've felt the same way myself."

Faith nodded. "It's what I've always wanted, for as long as I can remember. I'm not about to blow it now."

"Me too. Since I was a boy. My mum was addicted to *Columbo*, and I decided, at age five or maybe six, that I wanted to be that scruffy man in the raincoat who always got to the bottom of the crime."

"And you managed it," she said, the mischief back in her eyes. "You're definitely a scruffy man, and I'm sure you've a crumpled raincoat hidden away somewhere in this flat. You've made it!"

"Hey! I'm not scruffy. I'll have you know I take great care with my appearance . . ." But by then she was doubled up with laughter, and he couldn't go on.

CHAPTER 23

Before she went home, Asha sorted out a couple of dozen images of likely-looking men on her tablet, twelve for Aiken and twelve for Kernaghan. She added images of each of her suspects out of uniform.

Patterson had taken it as a personal insult that the two men had managed to escape and she'd been furious when the manhunt had first wound down and then had fizzled out.

"They must have had help," she'd snarled. "There's no way those two could have slipped through the net without someone in the service helping them. We've had every force in the country, including over the water, involved in this manhunt. Someone's hiding the bastards, and when I find out who, they'll not know what's hit them." Patterson would be taking flak from her superiors about how those two had worked in the Lisburn Road station for so many years without suspicion.

Asha glanced at her watch. Time for home.

She drove the short journey on autopilot, exhaustion dragging at her, but somehow made it in one piece. Instead of making toast before bed as she'd intended, she just crawled into a pair of pyjamas and under the covers. She knew nothing more until her watch alarm vibrated on her wrist, dragging her out of a nightmare in which Faith McAvoy was preventing her from arresting George Aiken, throwing herself between them to allow Aiken to escape. She was soaked in sweat and tangled up in her bedsheet, crying with frustration.

A lukewarm shower with zingy lemon-fresh shower gel helped her recover her balance; a mug of strong, dark coffee with sugar and cream finished the job. She knew it had to be a bad day when she needed to spoon sugar into her mug, but it was necessary to combat the bitterness of the Ethiopian beans she'd added in double-quantity to her grinder.

She was halfway to the station when her work mobile rang. Richard.

"Good morning. How are you feeling today?" she asked.

"My head feels as if someone used it as a battering ram against a steel gatepost, and my ribs hurt every time I take a deep breath, but otherwise just fine."

She smiled, the combination of caffeine and his voice making the day seem much brighter.

"I expect you'll be a bit fragile for a while. Are you and Steve still up for that photo ID session? I can come down to the boatyard, if it's easier."

"I've a better idea. Come up to my hovel. The yard is sealed with police tape and closed to the public until the place has been thoroughly checked, and it'll probably remain like that until the insurance companies get in touch. No one will be going in or out for a while. I can get Steve to come up here, too."

"Okay. What time suits you?"

"Would half ten this morning be okay?"

"Yes, that's fine." Plenty of time to hold a briefing and set everyone tasks before she'd need to leave. Hopefully Aaron would be able to come with her, too. A second pair of eyes and ears was always better.

The small group of uniforms and plain clothes that gathered in Bangor's so-called incident room, the former canteen, all looked as sleepy as she'd felt before the coffee had peeled back her eyelids.

Faith was on time, immaculate as ever, but Aaron turned up a couple of minutes late and with his tie slightly askew. He mouthed an apology as he took a free seat near the door.

"Okay, everyone," Asha said. "Thank you for coming. For those of you who haven't heard it on the PSNI grapevine, we had a bit of drama yesterday down at Steele's boatyard. Two men, purporting to be uniformed officers and driving a marked car, turned up to collect the truck. When challenged by the yard manager, they claimed to have left the paperwork behind. They then proceeded to unlock the lorry, and I'll remind those of you who haven't yet joined the dots, that the keys to the lorry had disappeared from our hotel murder victim's room."

She paused to let that sink in.

"They then drove it out of the yard. The owner, Mr Steele, attempted to stop the theft but he was injured as the truck left the boatyard. He discharged himself from hospital yesterday afternoon."

A ripple of whispered comment went around the room, and she let it continue for about ten seconds before bringing them to order.

She turned to the crime scene manager from the hotel. "Carol? What have you got for us?"

The CSM summarised the results of their search. Nothing to suggest the victim had fallen, no blood anywhere in the room, except for a fine spatter on the floor consistent with blood falling from a height in the centre of the room and showing a shadow where the victim's feet had been. This, she concluded, suggested that he'd been standing upright with his back to the door when he'd been hit from behind and had subsequently fallen.

"Thank you," Asha said. "That fits in with the preliminary findings from the post-mortem. The Prof is suggesting a single hard blow to the back of the skull with a heavy blunt object. He also surmises that the victim may have taken a while to die, although he would have been unconscious for the entire time. It's not a lot to celebrate, but at least he probably wasn't aware that he was dying."

She checked her notes and grimaced. "That stolen truck. Have we really not found any trace of it?"

Heads shook, and no one met her eye.

"How can a low-loader capable of carrying a forty-odd-foot boat simply dissolve into thin air? What have we done so far to trace it?"

Apparently, quite a lot. Aaron had checked with the French owners in case it had a tracking system fitted (it didn't) and contacted anyone in a two-mile radius who might have CCTV, but there was no trace of it. If Aiken and Kernaghan had been responsible, they'd managed to disappear not only themselves but also a huge vehicle. And that police car.

"Keep searching. It can't just disappear." She looked around the room. "Tom and Jim, you two were down at the boatyard yesterday evening. I'm aware you were both off duty and volunteered to help, out of public-spirited generosity" — cue taunts from the rest of the room — "and I'm sure Mr White and Mr Steele were very grateful. Anything to report?"

"No, ma'am," Tom said. "We worked alongside some of Mr Steele's neighbours to make the place secure. The general mood was one of shock and outrage at what had happened in such a peaceful rural community. If either of those two fellas show their faces in the area again, they'll be torn limb from limb."

Asha couldn't hold back a smile. Tom and Jim were from farming stock. Typical North Down countrymen who, despite years of experience to the contrary in the service, couldn't seem to understand why anyone would cause deliberate harm to person or property. They were both rock-solid, dependable officers.

Tom raised a hand. "That Mr Steele, he had a visitor last night. His sister, they said. Sounds like she's been away a long time in that boat of hers, maybe a few months. Steve White said he'd not be seeing as much of the boss now she's home. Apparently the brother dotes on the wee lassie and takes her out all over the place. Spoils her rotten, he said."

"Yes, I met the sister last night. Her name's Clara. I don't suppose we have anything on her, do we? I'm just thinking that if she's in the habit of going off sailing for months at a time, she could be another cog in the wheel for these drugs."

"I'll get on to it, ma'am."

"Anyone have anything else to add?"

Everyone shook their heads and mumbled to the negative. She doled out duties and one by one they all trooped out until only Aaron was left, yawning.

"Didn't you sleep last night?"

He gave her a lopsided smile. "No. Not a lot of sleep was had, but I'll be fine once I get some caffeine inside me. At least one of us is bright-eyed and bushy-tailed. Sounds like I missed all the action yesterday. How's our Richie Rich?"

"He'll live. He was lucky, though."

"You still think it's Aiken and Kerny? The descriptions are spot-on. Patterson won't be best pleased if it is them."

"Not unless we can catch them. All we have at the moment is a brief sighting – and the police car and uniforms. And there's no sign of that blasted truck. How can something that size just disappear in Northern Ireland? This isn't the wide-open plains of America with hundreds of square miles of territory to search. We're all twisty roads and little villages. Someone *must* have seen it."

He yawned.

"Go and get some caffeine. You'll be fit for nothing until you do."

"Want me to bring you a cup?"

"Nope. Already had my beans. Probably my monthly allowance, come to think of it, but at least I'm alert for now."

"Until the rebound," he muttered darkly.

"Yes, but by the time I'm coming down, you'll be on your way up. This way, there'll always be one of us awake at any given time."

Aaron dragged himself upstairs to the coffee machine while she went back to her office to collect her tablet. He reappeared with his tie straightened and his hair damp as if he'd stuck his head under the cold tap in the sink then dried it on the paper towels.

"Ready?"

"Ready as I'll ever be. But can you drive this time? I can get my head down for fifteen minutes on the way."

It took a bit more than fifteen minutes to reach the house Richard had built for himself along the coast, out on the North Channel side of the Ards Peninsula. She'd googled it before they left, so she knew what to expect, or at least, she'd thought she did, but the reality was breathtaking.

He'd had an award-winning architect design a carbon-neutral home on a spit of land that jutted out into the sea. It looked like an upturned boat from the road, with the bow pointing towards the wrought-iron gates. Richard must have been watching for them on the CCTV, because the gates began to swing open as soon as she turned into the wide sweep of gravel.

An elbow in Aaron's ribs brought him awake with a grunt.

"Trust me," she said. "You're not going to want to miss this."

He rubbed his eyes and sat up, staring at the edifice as they approached. It had been designed to give the effect of wooden planks but scaled up, so the house looked like a boat from *Gulliver's Travels*, each plank at least four feet high. The illusion was disorienting, but it was even more so as the driveway brought them around the side and the rest of the building came into view.

The section of the house that would have been the flat stern if it had been a real boat was glass from floor to triple-height ceiling, giving a view out to sea from as many rooms as possible. In one of the upper floors, a telescope stood on a tripod mount, and Asha glimpsed soft sofas and armchairs.

A silver hatchback, far from new, was parked on the pristine gravel and there could have been several more vehicles in the long, low garage, built into the side of the hill off to one side of the house.

"I'd like you to take the lead today," she said. That way she could sit back and watch the different reactions as the photos were presented to the two men. She handed Aaron her tablet. "There are two sets of twelve images, one set for men that look like Aiken and the other for men that look like Kernaghan. I'll leave it to you to decide what order you do things in."

Richard was waiting for them in the open doorway. He wore a pastel pink open-necked shirt tucked into cream chinos, clothes that no male of her family or within her friend circle would be seen dead in, yet he managed to make them look good.

"Welcome. I have a pot of coffee on, and I think Clara's been baking already. Chocolate chip cookies, I believe."

"Thank you, but hopefully we won't be here long enough to need refreshments," Asha said.

Beside her, Aaron groaned.

CHAPTER 24

Aaron tried to look as if his mind was on the job, but it really wasn't. It had been well into the wee small hours by the time he dropped Faith home, and she'd asked to be left off at the end of her street for the sake of discretion. He couldn't remember the last time he'd enjoyed an evening so much.

But now Asha needed him, so he'd do his best to be useful, and not think about a pair of dark brown eyes, and tendrils of hair curling around a face . . .

He sighed. Not doing a great job.

Steele ushered them into a hall that could have graced a medieval castle, with a wide staircase that split into two partway up. The main door closed behind them with a soft hush.

The *Belfast Telegraph* had done a double-spread feature on Richie Steele and his carbon-neutral house a couple of years ago. Geothermal underfloor heating, special glass that reflected the heat back inside in winter and kept the sun out in summer, even composting toilets, apparently, although you'd not know it to look at, if the photos in the paper were anything to go by.

What must it be like to have this much money? To be able to take a dream and turn it into reality?

But Steele lived here alone most of the time. The *Tele* had been pretty nosy about his relationships, and he'd made it clear in the interview that there was no significant other in his life. His sister was an occasional resident, but she was off sailing the world at every opportunity, and rarely home.

They followed Steele upstairs into a comfortable open-plan kitchen and seating area. What estate agents usually called a family room, but in this case, there was no family. Several sofas and armchairs had been artfully arranged around a central open fireplace where burning logs spat brightly coloured sparks up a circular brick chimney. Not so eco-friendly that, Aaron thought with satisfaction. Steve White was settled deep in an armchair, his posture relaxed as if he was at home in this space.

"Have a seat," Steele said. "I made coffee, but can I get you anything else?" He was looking at Asha as he spoke, but Aaron answered.

"Did you mention cookies?"

Steele laughed. "I did, but I'll have to fetch the cook. It's more than my life's worth to open the oven before they're ready. Clara will be with us shortly."

Asha took the other armchair and gave him an encouraging look.

Aaron perched at one end of a wide sofa. "Coffee sounds great."

Steele's sister arrived in a flurry of noise and slamming doors. Aaron hadn't met Clara Steele before. He was certain of this, because she had one of the most memorable faces he'd ever seen. Wide brows, wild, curly hair that flew around her head in a soft halo, eyes that sparkled and freckles across a pert nose. She moved with lithe grace as she bent to retrieve her baking from the oven. The combined scents of soap and freshly baked cookies filled the room.

Steele brought over a tray with a pot of coffee, mugs, milk and sugar, and everyone except Asha helped themselves. Clara passed Aaron a cookie and a teaspoon. Fragrant steam rose from a golden surface dotted with melted chocolate chips. He needed the spoon because it hadn't had time to set, but it was the best cookie he'd ever tasted.

"So, where are these photos?" Steele asked as he sank down on to the vacant sofa.

Aaron unlocked the tablet and found the set labelled *Tall dark*. These images were of dark-haired white men in their fifties.

He handed the tablet to Steele, who was closest. "Just scroll through all the images and speak up if any of them look familiar. These are all images that match the description Steve gave of the taller of the two intruders, the one who drove off in the marked car. I have another set of images similar to the description you gave of the driver of the truck."

Steele swiped through the images. His movements were agitated.

He handed the tablet back. "Sorry. I didn't really get a good look at the other man. He was in the car by then, so I only caught a glimpse. Any of those men could have been him."

Aaron offered the tablet to Steve. "Mr White?" Steve took his time, occasionally going back to look again at one of the pictures. When he reached the end, he swiped through to one particular image, then stared at it for maybe a minute before letting out a breath.

"That's him. I'm a hundred percent sure. I stood face-to-face with him and had a conversation. See the way his nose isn't quite straight, as if someone's broken it for him in the past? And the way one eye's wider than the other? That's him. I'd stand up in court and swear to it."

Aaron took the tablet and turned it so Asha could see the image. It was Larry Kernaghan.

She nodded. "That's really helpful. Thank you."

Aaron handed Steele the tablet with the next batch of photos, all of red-haired men. "Maybe you should go first this time, as you got a better look at the other man." He angled his body to shield the screen from Steve, to make sure there was no collusion.

Steele flicked through, hesitating once or twice, but by the end, he looked angry. "Yes. The bastard who tried to kill me is in there. This one."

Steve took even longer this time, spending time with each image as if he was trying to read their secrets from their photographs. Eventually, he swiped back to one photo. "I think this is him, but I can't be sure."

"It's the same man Mr Steele picked."

Steele's mouth was twisted in distaste. "And I *can* be sure. He laughed as he drove that truck at the gatepost. Looked me straight in the eye and laughed."

"Let's see." Asha took the tablet, then she glanced up at Aaron with a bitter smile.

"So, you do know those two," Steele said. "Care to share?"

Asha shook her head. "Sorry. Not until we have this case wrapped up."

The sister had been cleaning up her baking gear in the kitchen, but now she came over. "Can I see the photo?" she asked.

Asha hesitated, then passed it over.

Clara Steele looked at it long and hard before handing it back. "He has hard eyes. A killer's eyes. Is he a killer?"

"I'm afraid I can't comment."

"Hang on," Steele said, clicking his fingers as though it would kick-start his memory. "I've seen that photo before, or one very like it. There was a manhunt — last year, wasn't it? For two rogue policemen. The tabloids ran it, even though the PSNI denied the story. There was talk of inquiries and internal investigations." He looked Asha triumphantly in the face. "I'm right, aren't I? These are the same men."

"I'm sorry, I really can't comment, Mr Steele," Asha said. "Now, I'm afraid we must be going. Thank you for your help, Mr White."

Aaron bolted down the last bit of cookie, sending it on its way with a gulp of coffee. If he'd been on his own, he'd have licked the plate.

* * *

"Okay. So, what's next? We have positive IDs for Aiken and Kernaghan, but we still don't know where they are. We need a lead." They were back in the car, and he could still taste that cookie.

Asha tapped her fingers on the wheel. "Why would they suddenly surface after months of hiding, just to steal an empty truck? And why kill the lorry driver, if that was them? How else would they have got hold of the keys? I'd assumed they'd managed to get themselves false identities and would be sunning themselves on a beach in South America by now."

"We're missing something," Aaron agreed.

"Those two were involved in dealing cocaine for years, under the protection of our old friend, Alistair King. Maybe he wasn't the only one they worked for, or maybe they decided to go on running the operation without the figurehead. I can't forget what he said to me the night he was shot, about there being someone else involved."

Aaron shrugged, frustrated. "They couldn't have stayed under the radar for so long without powerful protection."

"If we can work out who's protecting them, maybe we'll have a chance at finding them. And the truck." She bit her lip. "We need to go over every detail of that case last year and discover what we missed. There must be something that will point us towards who is running those two now."

CHAPTER 25

At just after 4 p.m., the enquiry line Asha had set up finally yielded a result. A householder in a village near the coast reported hearing a heavy truck going through the gears as it passed his house on the night in question. He said he hadn't attached any importance to it until he read in the paper about the attack on Steele's boatyard and the theft of a truck. She relayed the news to Aaron. "Worth a look?"

He looked up from the pile of old files he'd been searching with increasing frustration. "It's all we've got, so yes."

They had a look at the area on the map. Just past the house where the truck had been heard, a lane wound down between two houses — mansions, really — towards the sea. There seemed to be a large rectangle of cleared ground and evidence of heavy machinery at work. It looked like a building site for something massive like a huge barn, or storage facility.

The date stamp at the bottom of the map was from the previous year, so by now the building might be completed.

Aaron gave Asha directions from the map on his phone as she drove. They missed the lane the first time in the fading light, but spotted it the second time. It was almost obscured by a generous growth of evergreen bushes in the gardens either side. Asha wondered if the homeowners had grown the bushes specifically to block their view of the unwelcome development.

Aaron pointed to a fallen branch that someone had kicked to the side. The white wood of its split end stood out from the gloom, showing it had been broken off recently. They both tilted their heads back and Asha saw where it had come from, high up in a tree next to the lane. Something big had passed that way recently.

"This could be it," she said.

"Call it in, would you? Tell them where we are and that we're proceeding with extreme caution."

He did, and received acknowledgement. It was Sergeant Gibson on duty, and he promised to listen out for them.

"He's a good man. Right." She undid her seatbelt. "I think we should leave the car here and go on foot. I hope you're wearing proper country footwear." Aaron pulled a face.

The night air sucked all the warmth from Asha's fingers within minutes of leaving the heated car behind. She blew into her hands, then shoved them deep into the pockets of her trousers.

Aaron slid around on the frozen ground, cursing softly when his foot went through the ice on a muddy puddle with a crack that sounded loud in the still air.

According to the map, the building site was a couple of hundred yards along this track, which curved around behind a clump of trees before widening out.

The trees rustled and creaked in the slight sea breeze, casting writhing shadows across the path in the moonlight. Asha's heavy Maglite torch weighed down her coat pocket, but she didn't want to expose them both by using it unless she had to. Aaron had his clutched in his gloved hands, ready to use, but he had more sense than to switch it on before he needed to.

They drew closer together by mutual consent as they moved into the shadows of the trees. A twig brushed the back of Asha's neck and she physically jumped, stifling a yelp.

Aaron touched her arm and nodded towards another broken branch on the ground ahead of them.

This one was a substantial bit of tree, and it was as fresh as the one in the gateway. Even in the darkness, the end stood out as pale where it had been torn from the tree.

They stepped over it, careful not to tread on any broken twigs, and moved on. Once past the trees, the ground opened up. A long, low building stood in the centre of the open ground, or so it seemed, but as they walked closer Asha realised it wasn't low at all, just very, very big. At one end a row of silos hinted at agricultural use, and a pale concrete apron stretched out in front of the building and around the side nearest to them. They'd be exposed as soon as they walked out on to it.

She tapped Aaron on the arm. "I think we should split up and go around the building in different directions until we meet up at the far side. But stay off the concrete as much as you can, and keep your wits about you."

Asha's path took her across rough grass and frozen ruts where heavy plant machinery had churned grooves through the land. It took all her balance to make her way without stumbling, with the risk of spraining an ankle.

The last stretch, along the far side of the concrete, was even harder going. Bits of machinery had been abandoned here, partially overgrown with bushes that had lost their leaves to winter, but not their thorns. She cracked her shin against some hidden object, bringing tears to her eyes, and her clothes were constantly being snagged by brambles.

Cursing softly, she made her way to the edge of the concrete where it was easier going. She met Aaron two-thirds of the way along. He was breathing heavily and brushing furiously at his clothes.

"If I never see a nettle again, it will be too soon. And don't talk to me about thorns. There's some low-growing bush back there that's made up of nothing but dagger-sharp spikes as long as my thumbnail. Bastard had it in for me, too."

"Sounds like blackthorn," she said, trying to sound sympathetic in a whisper. "You'd better make sure your tetanus jabs are up to date. Nasty things, blackthorns."

"You don't say?" he muttered. "I didn't see anything at all. What about you?"

"Nothing. I'm afraid we're going to have to go closer. I have a bad feeling about this."

He nodded and they set off across the bare concrete, feeling horribly exposed. At the corner of the building, Asha peered around, looking up as well as at eye level. Still no sign of life, and the only sound was her own rapid pulse booming in her ears.

Stepping out in front of the building, where the moonlight turned everything silver, took real courage. A loose stone turned under her foot with a rasping sound that made her pause, but the silence was otherwise unbroken. The front of the building had doors like the sort you might find on an aircraft hangar. They slid along runners that were a good six inches wide.

The doors would be locked, she told herself. They'd have to give up and come back in daylight with a team and a warrant.

There was a massive lock on the doors, so no surprises there, but a smaller entrance had been built into the left-hand door to allow people in and out without having to slide open the big doors.

Asha tried it. The handle moved smoothly, and the door swung inwards without a sound. The inside was black after the moonlight. It would take her night vision a while to adjust, but they couldn't stay out here in the open, exposed to a sniper.

Taking a deep breath, she slipped inside, and along a bit so she wouldn't be silhouetted against the light. Her back was pressed against the cold metal of the main door with its box corrugations, but in a heartbeat, Aaron's warmth touched her left arm, and she knew he was beside her.

They stood like that for a couple of minutes, listening, straining their eyes, trying to pierce the darkness that wrapped itself around them like a muffling blanket.

Was that a faint chink of light, over there in the far corner? As her eyes adjusted, the moonlight flooding in through the open door became a rectangle of pale grey on the floor. The chink of light could be a reflection on something metallic.

The first step was the hardest, dragging her back away from the cold comfort of the steel and moving into the unknown. After that, it was easier. Arms stretched in front of her like a child playing Blind Man's Bluff, she edged her way across the floor towards the faint chink of light.

Behind her, Aaron's soft breathing told her he was close, watching her back as he always did.

She walked into the corner of the truck, still thinking there was open space in front of her. Her nose scrunched into the metal, filling her eyes with stinging tears, and she steadied herself with a hand on the bonnet.

"I'm going to flash my torch beam around for a moment," she whispered. "Turn away and cover your eyes."

She clicked it on for a momentary beam at low power, making sure she was aiming along the front of the truck.

The light flashed on for a fraction of a second, but that was all she needed to recognise the make, colour, and a glimpse of a French registration number. They'd found it.

Which meant they were in as much danger as her gut had been telling her.

"I think there's a camera up in the front corner of the building," Aaron breathed in her ear. "There's a tiny red light."

"We've found the truck. Let's get out of here and report it now."

"Aren't you going to look inside?"

"I am not. Move back towards the door." Still, he hesitated. "Now!"

The sense of danger surrounded them like a cloud of poison, leeching away at her nerves, making her light-headed. She shoved Aaron hard, driving him forward until they were both running towards the rectangle of light.

She expected it to close before they got there, leaving them locked in the darkness, but it didn't. They made it to the door and tumbled out into harsh moonlight that hurt her eyes after the pitch-black warehouse.

"Keep going," she panted. "Run!"

She matched the words, legs pumping, heart pounding, as if the evil inside that barn hunted them on broad wings, swooping after them as their feet thudded across the concrete then rustled through the long grass.

When the blast came, it picked them both up and flung them. It was like a heavy hand shoving her in the back, forcing her face down and holding her there. The low, rumbling boom that followed was so deep it made her bones vibrate.

Something stung her left thigh as debris rained down on her, but she was still pinned down and couldn't move. Showers of soil and stones flew up as bits of truck and barn hit the ground inches from her head.

At last, the weight lifted, and she drew a breath that seared her throat and chest. The night was alive with flaming tree branches and burning debris.

Get up! You're still in danger, her instincts screamed at her. *Get up!*

She tried to obey. Managed to push herself up with her arms, but there was no strength left in them, and she sagged back down.

Someone grabbed her arm and tugged at it. Aaron's face loomed over her, his mouth opening and closing, but she could only hear a terrible, continuous roar.

At the second attempt, she made it to her knees, and Aaron pulled her the rest of the way, holding her up with an arm around her waist.

She hated herself for leaning so heavily on him, but her left leg wouldn't do what her brain asked of it.

Aaron half-dragged, half-carried her all the way to the end of the lane, then he dumped her against the stone gatepost of the house next door, propping her there like a garden spade, while he went through her pockets for the car keys.

Asha dug in the other pocket and came up with her mobile. The screen swam in front of her as a double image, but somehow she unlocked it and managed to call 999. She couldn't hear the answer, so she just kept repeating the same thing over and over into the device in the hope that someone would respond.

"DI Harvey, Bangor Police. Emergency. Officers injured." She couldn't remember the address, but then Aaron took the phone from her and started yelling into it too. Presumably he was making more sense than she had.

He helped her into the passenger seat of her own car, but as she sat down, pain lanced through the back of her thigh and she screamed. The world spun around her and then the lights went out.

CHAPTER 26

Blue flashing lights appeared in the distance before Aaron heard the siren. A moment later, an ambulance careered around the corner into view, unbalanced on the poorly cambered country road.

He stood back to let the paramedics at Asha. "We're police officers," he said as they cut away her trousers. "There's shrapnel in her leg. I tried to stem the bleeding, but—"

He was babbling. One of the paramedics stood up to face him, a small, blonde woman with kind eyes.

"It's okay, son. We've got her now. Sit down before you fall down, and we'll get to you as soon as we can. You've done fine, now leave it to us."

She was right. He was swaying where he stood. He let himself collapse on to the frosty grass, leaned his head against the wall, and began to shiver convulsively. Asha would be okay. She was in the best possible hands.

He must have drifted off, because it took a hand on his shoulder to wake him, and then he tried to scramble to his feet, almost head-butting a uniformed officer in the face as he did so. Asha was being stretchered into the back of the ambulance, a drip hanging above her.

Her eyes flickered open, and she managed a wan smile before doors slammed shut. Then the lights went back on and it sped away in a flying hail of gravel.

"Sir?" a voice said from behind him. "I need to check you over now. Would you come with me, please?"

The diminutive paramedic badgered him into following her past police cars and fire response units to an ambulance car, where she pushed him into the passenger seat, shone lights into his eyes and asked him endless questions.

"How is my friend? Will she be okay?" he interrupted.

"They got the bleeding slowed down enough to move her, and she'll go into surgery as soon as she reaches the hospital."

"Thank you."

She smiled up at him from her position, crouched on the grass verge, and for a moment he was content — until a voice like broken glass cut through his serenity.

"Detective Constable Birch. Report."

The paramedic melted away and instead Patterson swam into focus, wrapped up in a coat with a high fur collar and with a fur hat pulled low on her brow so only her icy glare could be seen.

"We found the truck, ma'am," he said. "It was in a building." He waved vaguely in the direction of the huge barn. "I think it must have been rigged, like that car last year at the hospital." He swallowed, remembering. "Asha saved us both. She knew something was wrong, and she got us both out of there before it went up."

Patterson raised an eyebrow. "Not quite, it seems to me."

"If she hadn't made me run, we'd both be dead, ma'am." The words came out harsher than he'd intended, but he needed her to know that Asha had saved his life.

"Did you see any sign of an incendiary device? Anything at all?"

"No, ma'am." He tried to think back to that huge, dark, empty space. There'd been a light.

"I think there might have been a camera in the building, ma'am. Like CCTV. There was this little red light, up in the corner."

"Well, the Fire Service have taken charge of the scene now. Their fire investigation boys will hopefully be able to tell us exactly what happened."

As if his word wasn't enough.

"As soon as you get the all-clear from your angel in green, I'll have someone run you down to the hospital to see how DI Harvey is doing. A local officer can drive her car back to the station and she can pick it up as soon as she's discharged."

"Ma'am."

Once she'd gone, the paramedic materialised again at his side. She gave him a wink. "Didn't want to argue with that one. Your boss, I take it?"

He nodded, then regretted it as fireworks went off behind his eyes.

* * *

The officer who drove him to the hospital was a taciturn older man who didn't seek or offer conversation, for which Aaron was grateful. He dropped him off at the entrance to A&E and drove off without a backward glance.

He remembered Faith, who'd soon hear about the explosion on the service grapevine. He'd better call her and tell her what had happened before she began to worry. Gossip was like Chinese whispers; by the time they'd finished, Asha would have been killed and he'd be wheelchair bound for life.

She answered on the first ring.

"Thank God! I've been trying to call you this past hour."

He took the phone from his ear and glanced back at the screen. The little call symbol had a red number seven next to it. "Sorry. It's been a bit mad."

"I'm okay, now I can hear your voice. What happened?"

"There was some sort of explosion. Asha and I got caught by the edge of it. I'm fine, just dirty and with the mother of all headaches, but she got some shrapnel in her leg and they're operating now. I'm at the hospital, just about to go in to see if there's any news."

There was silence, then she took a shuddering breath. "I was so worried about you."

"I know. I was pretty worried about myself for a while, but the paramedics have given me the all-clear."

"I'm coming over. Which hospital?"

"The Ulster," he said. "Text me when you get here and I'll tell you where to come."

He flashed his warrant card at the enquiry desk and asked for Asha. The older lady behind the glass directed him to the A&E doctors' station.

A frazzled junior doctor ran his fingers through his hair and checked the computer. "She's still in surgery. I can get a porter to take you up to the waiting area."

A porter walked him along endless corridors through the old and then the new part of the hospital, up lifts and along more corridors until they came to a small, carpeted room with black faux leather sofas, a low table, and a kettle with some basic tea- and coffee-making facilities. "I'll tell them you're here," the man said as he left.

Aaron sank down on to the soft sofa, which turned out to be a recliner, and closed his eyes. Once again he drifted off, but this time he was woken by a nightmare that involved a fire-breathing dragon with eyes the size of truck windscreens, rising up into the air then diving down towards him.

He was sweating, panting, clutching at his chest, and completely disorientated. *Faith*. He checked his phone. Three texts from her. The first said she'd arrived and where should she go?

The second said she was checking at A&E, and the third said she was on her way up. He smiled. She was a resourceful woman, his Faith.

He heard the click of her regulation boots before he saw her through the glass panel in the door. She burrowed into him like a small animal, wrapping her arms around his middle and squeezing until he protested.

"Ouch! Not so rough."

She instantly let go. "Sorry! I didn't think. Any news about Asha?"

"Honestly? I don't know. I just sat down here for a minute and next thing I was out cold. But apparently they know I'm here, so as soon as there's news, someone will come and tell us." He looked at his watch. "It's after nine, so I'd hope she'll be out of surgery by now."

CHAPTER 27

"I'm almost disappointed you use Google, like a normal person," Clara teased. "I'd have thought you'd have your own personal search engine, you know? All private and secretive."

Richard grinned as he scrolled through the results. "This would be easier if I could remember more about the case. Were you here last summer, around June or early July, or gadding about in your boat?"

She yawned and leaned back. "I would probably have been in the middle of the Bay of Biscay. Felt like I was there all summer, getting thrown around and puking my guts up."

"Oh yeah. I remember. You wanted me to send a helicopter to airlift you."

"I did not!" she flared. "I merely told you my position in case the boat took on any more water. The bilge pumps were barely holding their own at one point, I remember. One of those sudden summer storms that come out of nowhere and can't be bothered leaving."

He'd gone quiet. Stopped listening. She sat up and read over his shoulder.

Murder and Mayhem at Millionaire Mansion, the headline read. There was a picture, taken with a long lens, of a body bag being loaded into the back of a dark grey private ambulance. At the bottom of the page was a slightly blurry photo of a man with short-cropped red hair and hard eyes.

Richard zoomed in on the page and she read the legend: *Is George Aiken the man wanted for multiple crimes including murder?*

In the main article, he was referred to as a serving police officer. The article speculated, with little evidence as far as Clara could tell, that Aiken and his colleague, Larry Kernaghan, were expecting to be made fall guys for the PSNI after an operation on the north coast went wrong and a retired officer was shot and killed.

This particular newspaper was always the first to scream oppression of the masses, especially by the police, so their slant wasn't that surprising. Anything that made the PSNI look bad would be headline news for them.

The next article, same newspaper a couple of days later, was slightly less supportive of the two men. The lettering was much smaller, and it was on page six, not the front page.

Cops On Run was the headline, and below were only a few short columns saying that Aiken and Kernaghan were the subject of a manhunt across multiple forces. It still managed to make the PSNI look bad, but this time it was smearing the "rogue cops" as much as their bosses.

"And that's him?" she asked. "The man who tried to kill you?"

"That's him. The picture's flattering, though. He's a lot uglier in real life."

She shuddered. "I'm glad he didn't succeed."

He twisted to laugh into her face. "Because then, who'd pay for all your jaunts around the world, and who'd offer you free berthing, yard facilities, crane—"

"Okay, okay. I get it."

This was the time to tell him what had happened to her in Norway. Now, with just the two of them, in this very private, very secure study. She had his full attention, and he'd understand. She was sure he'd understand that she'd had no choice. He'd hate what she'd done, but he'd hug her and tell her he'd have done the same in the circumstances.

He'd be lying, but she'd still feel better.

The moment passed. He stood up and stretched.

"Fancy a trip to the yard? I've a couple of jobs to do on *Cloud*, and I feel the need to breathe fresh air."

"Okay," she agreed, and her dominant emotion was relief.

It was a good thing his Jaguar was an automatic, as his left arm really wasn't up to gear changes. He drove with his right hand turning the wheel and the fingers of his left hand stabilising it.

The headlights lit up Steve as he was testing the gates, making sure they closed and met correctly after the new post had been finished. He opened them to let the car through and gave them a wave, police tape fluttering in the breeze of the car's passing. She hadn't seen him look so cheerful for ages.

"What's got into Steve? He's smiling."

"I think he's realised that people care. The number of helpers who turned out really surprised him. I'd guess he needed reminding that people can be kind as well as vindictive."

He parked up and they walked down the ramp in companionable silence. It was low tide, so the gradient was steep, and she clung to the handrail, wary of patches of ice. The clear, starlit sky would certainly bring frost with it.

Once on the jetty, they split up. Richard walked towards his own boat, a pretty vessel despite the drawback of being plastic, as she was fond of reminding him, and she turned the other way for *Snow Goose*.

She swung herself aboard using the stays as handholds and felt the familiar movement of the deck beneath her feet. What owners of plastic boats like *Cloud* would never understand was that wooden boats were alive. It was as if the souls of the trees that went to make up her ribs and planks were still inside, keeping her safe.

Clara closed her eyes as she moved along the wide side decks and stepped into the cockpit. Every inch of this boat was as familiar to her as her own face. She'd never miss her footing on board, as if the boat cocooned her, keeping her safe.

Richard called it a dangerous illusion and said that the boat would tip her in the drink one day. It was Richard who'd insisted she add safety lines and clip-in loops to harness herself in on long voyages, and she had to admit, it had saved her life more than once.

She opened the sliding hatch and lifted out the washboards — she never bothered locking up when she was in her home berth — and descended the steep companionway backwards as she always did.

Something about the smell of the cabin warned her; or perhaps it was the way the boat moved, but she spun around in the sure knowledge that she was not alone.

Sitting on the long seat that she used as sea berth, sofa and dining chair was a figure, leaning back so the face was in the shadows. When he leaned forward, she saw that his hair was gingery red in the moonlight. Longer than in the photos she'd seen of him, and a little unkempt, but those hard eyes were unmistakable.

Her breath caught in her throat, but she didn't panic. Instead, she reached behind her for the sailing knife hanging in its sheath by the companionway where she kept it for emergencies. Her fingers grasped the warm leather, but it was too light, too thin.

"You don't think I'd leave a weapon handy for you, do you, love?" And he held her knife out in front of him like a prize. "Don't be stupid. If I'd wanted to harm you, I'd have knocked you on the head as you came down that ladder, all unsuspecting. I'm here to talk."

She swallowed. "What do you want with me?"

His eyes ran up and down her body. "Well now, that's a loaded question if ever there was one. No, lassie, you're pretty enough, but you're not my type. I like a bit of meat on the bones. Not like my mate, Ole. He prefers the skinny ones. He sends his love, by the way, and he says he's got another job for you."

CHAPTER 28

Steve gazed up into the night sky. The clouds had fled, revealing stars like diamonds scattered across a jeweller's black velvet display cloth, and a crescent moon with a haze around it. It was getting late, but he didn't want to lock up until the boss and his sister were finished. Still, life was good.

He began to whistle a tune he'd heard on the radio, adding riffs and trills as his lips remembered their old skills. Tina hadn't liked him whistling, but she'd moved on now, and it was time for him to do the same.

He did his rounds slowly, checking every boat's supports and covers until he reached the new one. The swimming ladder was let down, and he'd definitely tied it up earlier.

He climbed up and stepped on to the open rear deck of the big motor yacht. The entertainment deck, Fred called it. A dark vertical line along the edge of the glass door into the main cabin suggested it was open a crack.

"Hello? Fred, is that you?"

It couldn't be, because Fred's car wasn't in the yard, and the man never walked when he could drive somewhere.

Heart thumping, he slid the door noiselessly open and stepped inside. The velvety silence of deep pile carpet and suede upholstery enveloped him, but then he saw footprints on the pale carpet, muddy boots with a deep tread. His fists clenched, and his good mood evaporated.

He'd have to tell the boss, of course. Breaking the news to Fred Mills was way above his pay grade.

He jumped down and set off towards the jetties. Someone was coming up the ramp towards him, too short to be Richie and too stocky to be Clara. He waited, trying to make out the features, but the face was shadowed beneath a hood.

The stranger must have seen him by now — he'd be silhouetted against the floodlights in the yard — but the man kept coming. Then he lifted his chin and looked straight at Steve.

His heart stuttered. Reflected light gleamed in a pair of hard eyes that he'd seen recently, in a photo. He started to back away, but his legs felt like lead weights and pain began to flare inside his chest, radiating down his left arm. A flicker of movement caught his eye from the side, just the hint of a shadow as someone moved behind him. He tried to dodge, but his attacker was too fast for him.

The blow impacted the back of his head and the world spun like a fairground ride.

He tried to raise an arm to protect himself, but it wouldn't respond. It hung limp and throbbing at his side.

He lashed out with his other arm, but his attacker seemed to sway out of reach. A face leered down at him, laughing. He was heavier than Steve, and taller, too.

Another blow landed, this one on his thigh just above the knee. What the fuck was he being hit with? His leg buckled beneath him and he went down backwards across the tow-bar of the trailer he'd left out for the workboat. Something crunched. No pain, but a sick feeling of damage done. He fell the rest of the way to the floor, then the pain hit, paralysing his breathing and filling his eyes with tears.

When he came round, the first thing he was aware of was a low whimpering, like a lonely puppy on its first night home. Steve listened to the sound for several of his own pounding heartbeats before he realised it was his voice he was hearing. He locked his jaw and closed his lips tight, shutting down the pathetic sound.

He was helpless, lying on the cold concrete in the dark and waiting for someone to kill him, just as they'd killed Serge. Teeth chattering, Steve lost control of his bladder, a hot gush that chilled almost instantly. Then a voice spoke from the darkness.

"Steve? Mate?"

Relief washed through him. "Richie? Thank God it's you. I thought it was that bastard coming back to kill me." At least that's what he tried to say, but it came out as a long moan.

"I'm calling an ambulance. They'll be here soon, Steve. Just hold on."

CHAPTER 29

Asha woke with a thumping head, a dry mouth, and the certainty that she needed to be sick. Someone said soothing words, then propped her up a little and put a straw between her lips. She sucked at it gratefully, letting the cool liquid flood her mouth and unstick her tongue.

"Take it slowly, Asha. Just a little at a time. You're still quite woozy."

Woozy. She hadn't heard the word in a long time. "Mum?"

"Shh, now. You've had an anaesthetic. Try to rest."

Even speaking seemed too much effort, so she did as she was told and closed her eyes.

The next time she awakened she had full control of her senses. Refreshed, alert, and full of questions for which her own memory didn't seem to have answers.

The door opened, and Aaron stuck his head in. His face was wrinkled with worry lines, and he glanced behind him, out into the corridor.

"You're awake," he said, stating the obvious. "Not sure if that's good or bad, but a quick heads-up: Patterson's at the nurses' station, quizzing your doctor. She'll be in here next, giving you the third degree. Thought I should warn you."

"Thanks," she croaked. "Hey, Aaron. Do you have a moment?" He came in, allowing the door to close behind him. He smelled of burnt cloth and sweat, and there was blood ingrained in the folds of skin where his thumb joined his hand. "Are you hurt?"

He smiled. "Not really, thanks to you. If you hadn't got us running when you did, I don't think either of us would be here now to talk about it. You saved both our lives."

Patterson came into the room, and Aaron instantly straightened as if standing to attention.

"Ma'am."

She stood just inside the door, looking down at Asha with a slight frown puckering her brows. Never a pretty woman, Patterson seemed to have become even more heavy-jawed and solid in the last year. She wasn't someone Asha ever wanted to mess with, but when Patterson wore that serious expression, there was trouble brewing.

"How are you feeling?"

"Better," Asha lied. "Ready to get back to work."

Was that a flash of irritation?

"I'm delighted to hear it," Patterson said dryly. "Because there's plenty of work for you to get back to, but I understand you won't be fit for duty for at least another week to ten days. You received a deep wound to your thigh, which has been sutured, but there's a risk of the stitches breaking down if you move around too much on it. Also, I'm told you lost a lot of blood, so you'll be weak for a while."

"Yes, ma'am, but what if I just take it easy?"

"You will most certainly be taking it easy, Inspector. You'll be flat on your back until the doctors say otherwise."

"But ma'am—"

"I'm recommending you for a gallantry award."

The words bounced off Asha's ears like a foreign language. "A what?"

The corner of Patterson's lip twitched. "You heard me. I'm not in the habit of repeating myself."

After she left, Aaron perched on the edge of her bed. "I told her you'd saved us both with your quick reactions." His phone jingled in his pocket. He fished it out and frowned at the screen before answering. "DC Birch."

Asha couldn't hear the other end of the conversation, only the monosyllabic answers Aaron gave. Then he said, "I'm on my way," and ended the call. "Got to go."

"Anything I should know about?"

The hesitation was minute, nothing she would have noticed if she hadn't known him as well as she did.

"Nothing. I'll be back in the morning to check up on you. Try to get some sleep." And then he was gone, the door slowly closing behind him.

* * *

Aaron tapped his fingers on the steering wheel as he drove. Why had the duty sergeant from Bangor called him and not another detective from his own station?

Once again, Steele's boatyard was lit up like a carnival, with flashing blue lights and bright police tape flickering in the floodlights. An ambulance stood with its rear doors open and the paramedics were carrying someone towards it on a spinal board.

It was Steve White on the stretcher, his face only just visible between the arms of a cheek-hugging neck brace. His eyes were open, staring at the sky, and his jaw was clenched against the pain. This wasn't the time to question the poor bugger; he'd have to wait until the doctors had checked him over. He gave instructions for one of the uniformed constables to go with him in the ambulance and not leave his side.

Steele and his sister huddled together near the marina building. The woman had her face buried in her brother's coat, and it looked as if she was crying. Aaron slowed. Maybe not a good time to question them, but he needed to know what the hell was going on.

Then he spotted an SOC officer in a white suit. He jogged across as far as the taped-off area and called out.

The woman turned, and he recognised Carol, the CSM who'd worked the murdered lorry driver's room in the hotel. She nodded to the young constable on duty at the tape to let Aaron through.

He struggled into the suit, gloves and overshoes, and popped a mask in place before joining her. "What's the story?"

"The victim was attacked here, at the head of the ramp. Paramedics say he took a blow to the back of the head that probably stunned him but didn't knock him out because he also has defensive injuries to his arm and leg. He's lucky he didn't go the same way as our Frenchman."

"Will he be okay?"

She shrugged, her suit crinkling as she did so. "Well, he's still alive, so far. He was hit with a heavy, blunt object. Maybe an iron bar or similar. He injured his back as he fell, so you might have to wait until the medics let you near him to ask him questions."

Aaron sighed. Maybe he should have followed the ambulance, after all. "Okay. Let me know if you find anything earth-shattering. I'm going to have a chat with the yard owner."

"He was first on the scene. It's possible he scared off the attacker and potentially saved the victim's life."

When Aaron strode towards them, Steele peeled himself from the building and held out a hand. The man had a firm grip, but there was no challenge in the handshake.

"I expect you're wondering how another intruder got in past all my security?" Steele said.

"Not at all, Mr Steele. I'm sure your security took a battering when they stole that truck."

Steele narrowed his eyes. "Indeed. And it looks like it wasn't the only thing to take a battering. What happened to your face?"

Aaron touched his cheek. It was tender and swollen just beneath his right eye. He really didn't want to go into any of this right here, right now.

"Can you talk me through everything that happened here this evening please, sir? I'll need to take a statement later, but if you could give me the gist now, that would be really helpful."

Steele gestured to the building. "Can we do this inside? My sister's shivering."

Aaron shot her a glance. Clenched jaw, eyes tight shut, hunched shoulders as she leaned into her brother. She looked sick rather than cold, like someone trying to dry out from an addiction, which raised interesting questions.

The darkness outside turned the windows of the prefab building into mirrors, allowing Aaron to keep an eye on Clara Steele while appearing to be giving her brother his full attention. Steele sat on the cheap sofa and his sister snuggled in next to him.

"Clara and I were down on the pontoons, checking the boats," Steele began. "I came up before her and saw two men attacking a third man on the ground. I shouted, I think, then ran towards them waving my torch."

It was the type that took those big, square batteries and would be a hefty weapon. Aaron made a mental note to get it checked for hair and blood. "Did you recognise the men? Was one of them the same man you identified this morning?"

"I've no idea. As soon as they saw me, both men ran off into the night. I went to investigate, found Steve, and called 999. You know the rest." Steele sighed. "We had strangers all over the yard after that truck was stolen. I can go back over the CCTV footage I have, but two of the cameras were damaged when the gate and fence came down. I suppose those two could have come in among the volunteers while no one was paying attention, and hidden until the place was empty, but why would they? And if it was the same men who took the truck, why would they come back?"

"I'd appreciate you reviewing the remaining camera, sir, if it's not too much trouble."

Steele pulled a face. "Nothing is too much trouble if it helps you catch those two bastards. And I can come to the station any time to give a statement."

Aaron still couldn't warm to the man, but he sounded sincere.

"And what about you, Miss Steele? Did you see or hear anything? Anything at all, even if it seems trivial."

She shook her head, still not meeting his eye. "Nothing. I was down on my boat until after it was all over."

"And you didn't see anything suspicious down on the pontoons?"

Another shake, more insistent this time.

There was something going on there, but he couldn't quite put his finger on what it was. Perhaps Asha would manage to pry it out of her once she was well enough for active duty again.

His mobile vibrated in his pocket, and he fished it out. It was a local landline. He mouthed an apology to the Steeles and took the call outside.

"DC Birch."

"Sergeant Gibson here from Bangor PSNI. There's a report in from the fire team about your case and Superintendent Sewell and DI Harvey aren't here."

"Can you give me the gist?"

"Yes. They say it wasn't just the truck in that building that blew up. There was a smaller vehicle, too. They think it's probably the missing patrol car those two gits stole and used to gain access to Steele's boatyard. Both vehicles are completely burnt out, and an explosive device was used that is similar to the one used last year at the Royal Victoria Hospital. You know, the one that was meant for DI Harvey?"

"Yes, Sergeant. I remember." He'd never forget the burnt-out shell. "Any evidence of a timer, or was the device remotely triggered?"

"The chief investigator thinks it probably was remotely triggered. There was a camera in the building, and it's possible the perpetrators had remote access to it, but they won't know for sure for a day or two." There was a crackly pause, then: "I'd just like to say, DC Birch, that you made a few friends here tonight. Word on the grapevine is that if you hadn't acted as you did, DI Harvey might not have made it. She's well liked here in Bangor."

"Thank you, Sergeant, but actually DI Harvey is the reason we're both still alive. She's the one who got us out of there fast enough to escape the worst of the blast. I understand she's being recommended for a gallantry award."

Whoever had set the bomb had known they were there; he was sure of it. Had Aiken or Kernaghan been sitting on his smartphone watching the camera feed, finger hovering over the detonate button? He shuddered.

Back inside, Steele was standing by the front window of the building. "Did I hear that right?" he asked in a low voice. "Did you say there'd been an explosion? Is Asha all right?"

The strength of concern in his voice made Aaron reconsider his impression of the man, at least a little. "I'm sure it's already being reported in the news, sir, so I think I can tell you that there *was* an explosion. Thanks to the rapid actions of DI Harvey, we both got away. She's going to be fine, but she lost quite a bit of blood."

Richard Steele's hand clenched and unclenched, and he took a few steps away, turning his back on Aaron. The reflection in the window showed a harrowed face, and possibly a glint of wetness on the cheek? Interesting.

"Well, Mr Steele, Miss Steele. If there's anything else you think of that you think we should know, please get in touch with me. Anything at all, even if it seems insignificant. The tiniest details sometimes help us build up a picture of what's going on, and these men have to be stopped before they cause any more damage."

He could swear the woman flinched at his words, but her brother nodded. "We will, Detective Constable. I can promise you that."

CHAPTER 30

Clara's strength seemed to have deserted her. She leaned heavily on Richard's arm as he guided her to his car. He helped her to bed, took off her shoes and jeans, and tucked her up beneath the feathery quilt. Then he bent down and kissed her on the forehead.

"Good night, Clara. Sleep well, and everything will look better in the morning."

Only when the sound of his shoes padding lightly along the corridor had faded did she release her fear and shame in hiccupping sobs. Finally, she lay wrung out and with a thumping head in a damp pool of bitter tears.

Poor, poor Steve. A simple man who still mourned his wife and had no life outside the boats he cared for like children — he didn't deserve what had happened to him.

That red-haired man had the cold eyes of a killer, she'd been right about that, but this time she couldn't run to Richard for protection. She'd got herself into this mess, and now she was going to have to get herself out of it again. On her own. It was a bleak thought.

Silence stretched out, the cocooning house keeping the night at bay, but it couldn't protect her from what she'd done. She dragged her hand from under the pillow and glanced at her watch: 2 a.m. She'd been lying there for hours feeling sorry for herself, and now her bladder was making its presence known.

She slipped out of bed, the hard floor warm beneath her feet, and into the en suite bathroom. From here, she could see out into the back garden, where Richard had planted an orchard that wouldn't give fruit for a couple of years yet. He'd told her of his plans to leave a grassy walk between cherry and apple, pear and plum, with a bench at the end overlooking the sea.

She could just about make out the bench now, but — her heart gave a painful thump — there was someone sitting on it.

They were watching her. They had invaded the places she'd always been safe. First *Snow Goose*, now her home. She had only one coherent thought, and that was Richard's strong arms.

She burst into his bedroom. The bed was still made up perfectly, unsullied by his sleeping form. She searched every room, her breath rasping in her throat as panic closed in.

Then the front door opened and a tall figure in a thick winter coat stood in the opening. She ran to him. His arm came around her, strong and warm and comforting, and she buried her face in the cold Gore-Tex, smelling sea air and frost.

"Now, now. What's the matter?" he asked. His voice was tender, but there was a catch in it as if he had a sore throat. She tilted her head to look into his face. It glistened in the faint light.

She raised her hand to touch the wetness. Her brother had never cried in all their years together. When news came of their parents' death, he'd seemed to grow a hard shell — until that detective had been injured.

He took a shuddering breath, and she snaked her arms around his neck, pulling his face into her shoulder in the same way he always did for her when she was upset. He'd done it that day, when their grandmother had taken the phone call from the Spanish police to say that their parents' yacht had been found capsized, the life raft still attached to the stern rail, empty. There had been an ongoing search-and-rescue operation, but the chances were considered slight as the weather was so bad.

That's when seventeen-year-old Richard had taken her in his arms, already so much taller than her, and held her to his chest. She'd smelled his familiar scent of soap powder and starch from his shirt. The unmistakable smell of school, and the scent of fresh air from his walk up from the bus stop at the bottom of the hill.

Now, she rocked with him, murmuring reassurances. He drew an unsteady breath and returned her embrace.

"I'm sorry," he said, muffled because his mouth was pushed against her woollen sweater. "I don't know what's got into me."

"Don't you?"

For a long while, they stayed like that until Richard's breathing steadied and eventually, he straightened up.

"I needed that hug, little Clara."

That name, from his lips, at this time, undid her completely. He was so fucking straight and honest. He'd never understand why she'd done what she'd done. Why she was going to have to do it again.

She tried to gasp, but all the air seemed to have been sucked from her lungs. Her chest ached, then burned.

"What is it?" The concern in his voice broke her all over again.

This time, he held her until the pain subsided. Then he pushed her away, only far enough that he could look down into her face. "Tell me."

So she did, the words spilling from her like mountain streams in the spring thaw, while he held her and listened.

"And then I made for home as fast as I could, still not knowing if he'd hurt you, or . . ." She choked. Took a deep breath. "I just needed to know you were okay. I would never have told you any of this, except—"

"Except?"

"Except that last night, when I went to check on *Snow Goose*, there was a man waiting for me in the saloon. He said he was from Ole and that he had another job for me to do. Richard, it was the man from the photos Inspector Harvey showed you. The red-haired one. He had my knife, and he said he needs me to carry more passengers for him, just one more run and that will be it. They have photos of me with those girls on board, and he says Ole will send them to the authorities, tell them I'm a human trafficker, if I don't do what they say."

He closed his eyes as if the light hurt them. "And do you really think that will bring an end to it?"

"No," she whispered. "I don't think it will ever end."

He opened his eyes again, frowning down at her, but he wasn't angry with her. He was never angry with her. Sometimes she wished he would be.

"You have to tell the police," he said.

"No!" Her stomach contracted at the thought of admitting how utterly stupid she'd been. "No," she said a little more quietly. "I can't, Richard. I just can't."

"Then let me. We've got to, don't you see? These people have to be stopped, and perhaps there's still a chance to save those girls."

CHAPTER 31

Aaron was busy writing a report for the explosion, trying to think of a way to make it sound like protocol rather than a rash action for the pair of them to go inside the building without back-up, when the phone on Asha's desk rang.

"Call for you from PC McGill," the desk sergeant said. "He's the constable who's keeping an eye on Mr White at the hospital."

"Put him through."

The young PC sounded harassed and a little panicky. "Sir, it's about Steve White, you know? The man who was attacked last night at Steele's boatyard?"

"Yes. What's his condition?"

A deep breath. "He was doing well and expected to make a full recovery, but then he had a massive heart attack this morning and they couldn't save him. He died a few minutes ago."

Shit. Fuck. He should have gone down there himself after the ambulance — but the man had been in no fit state to answer questions then either. An unpleasant idea crept in. "Were you there with him the whole time?"

"Yes, sir. I was waiting for someone to relieve me this morning, but no one came. And I didn't sleep, you can ask the nurses on duty. I was awake outside his room the whole time, and I went with him to X-ray and all. I never left him, sir." The lad was gabbling, panicking now.

"It's all right. You did well." *Better than me. I should have sent someone to take over, but I forgot all about it.* "You should go home and get some kip, then come back here and write up a report. You did well, PC McGill. Thank you. None of this is your fault." And now he was repeating himself.

He leaned back in Asha's chair and closed his eyes. They only had Steele's word that there'd been two men in the boatyard last night. What if Richard himself had attacked his yard manager? He needed that CCTV.

His phone went again. "Another call for you, DC Birch. From Mr Steele this time."

"Put him through," Aaron said. His head was spinning with possibilities, and his ears were still ringing from the explosion.

"Detective Constable Birch?" the deep voice of Richard Steele said. "I wonder if it would be possible to talk to you? My sister has got herself into a spot of bother and it might be relevant to your case."

"I can come over and speak with her now if you like." And ask a few probing questions about Steve White while I'm at it.

"No," Steele said sharply. "Sorry, but she's in a bit of a state. I know you'll have to speak to her at some stage, but for now can I give you the gist?"

"All right. Are you at the house or the boatyard?"

"I'm outside the station in my car. I can come in, or you can come out here. I don't mind which."

Aaron sighed. "You should probably come in."

Richard Steele perched uncomfortably on the edge of one of the steel-framed chairs in the interview room. Aaron fiddled with his pen, wishing he had Asha with him.

"Before we begin, I'm afraid I have some bad news for you."

Steele tensed. "Asha?"

"No. Steve White. I just got the call, a few minutes before you phoned. He died this morning in the hospital. I don't have any more information just yet, but I expect there'll be a post-mortem."

Steele put his face in his hands and moaned. "Oh God, no! That poor man. He was so happy yesterday, so full of gratitude that people had turned out to help. I hadn't seen him that happy since Tina left him." He looked up, eyes haunted. "I'll need to call Tina, break the news. But I don't know how to get in touch with her."

"It's all right, sir. We'll deal with that. I'll need to ask you a few more questions about what happened last night, though."

"Yes, of course. Anything."

"You say you saw two men? Can you expand on that?"

Steele didn't answer straight away. He had a distant look, as if he was trying to cast his mind back to the night before. "I was dazzled by the floodlights as I came up the ramp. It was more the impression of movement where there shouldn't have been any. It took my brain a moment to register there was something out of place, but when I shouted, they moved and I saw it was two people. They were away up the hill and out of sight before I got a good look at them. All I'm sure of is that one of them was quite tall and bulky, and I'd say definitely male. Then I heard Steve moan and I forgot about everything else."

That was news to Aaron. "He was conscious when you found him?"

"Sort of. His eyes were open, but he was dazed, slurring his words. He seemed to be saying something about his back, and he'd fallen all twisted, not in a natural position." He swallowed. "I could see it was bad, so I called 999."

"Where was your sister through all this?"

Steele's expression was pained. "Ah. She was still on her boat. She didn't come up to the boatyard until after the ambulance had arrived. About Clara. I still need to tell you what she told me last night. It's even more important now."

"All right. Can you tell me in your own words what your sister said?"

"I'll try. As you know, Clara's been away sailing. She only got home a couple of days ago, and she hasn't been particularly forthcoming about where she's been and what she's been up to. Not until tonight."

He paused, framing his words.

"She was tricked — threatened — by a Norwegian fisherman called Ole into carrying a human cargo between Norway and Ireland," he said. "He told her they were friends of his sisters. It was six very young women who she delivered to a secluded bay on the west coast where they were met by men in a military-style inflatable boat." He gave a short, hard laugh. "She'd never have done it, but Ole threatened me. He showed her a photo of me and said he had someone here watching me, and that if she didn't do as he wanted . . ." He shook his head. "Clara thought that was it, that she'd been foolish, but that it was all over, until earlier tonight."

Aaron hardly dared to breathe.

"We both went down to check our boats. You know? Make sure no ropes were fraying, check for water in the bilges, that sort of thing. I went to my boat and she went to hers. After I was done, I came up here and saw the attack. Clara didn't come up until later, but I didn't notice she was missing at first because I was too busy with Steve."

He stared into the distance, as though the walls of the fusty little room were transparent.

"She said there was a man waiting for her inside her boat. He had her knife, the knife she keeps for emergencies." Steele worked his jaw as if he was grinding his teeth. "It was that same bastard that tried to kill me with the truck, the man you showed me the photo of. The red-haired one."

Aaron's gut contracted. No wonder the poor woman was scared. A close encounter with Aiken had never been pleasant, even before he and Kernaghan went on the run, but if they'd been living rough all these months he probably looked even more unpleasant by now.

"What did he say?"

Steele's face creased. He took a short breath. "He said Ole, the man who tricked Clara into carrying the girls, had another job for her and then that will be it, but we both know that blackmail never stops."

This was Phil Johnston all over again, but with the approach tailored towards a vulnerable young woman instead of a dodgy mechanic. If this was true, it suggested the two cases were related. Whoever was running the drugs could also be involved in the human trafficking.

Richard Steele nodded, as if he was reading Aaron's mind. "I know. She'll never be free of them. That's why I told her we have to work with you on this. It's the only way."

"You're right. What else did he say?"

"He said he'll be in touch. He said he can reach her any time he wants, that he has her number."

The tightness of his voice told Aaron just how much that frightened Richard, even though he appeared calm on the surface.

"She carries a mobile phone, does she?"

"Yes. I got it for her last year. It's one of those heavy-duty, indestructible ones you can just about run a tank over and it'll still work."

Aaron knew the sort. Waterproof and everything. They had a sealed case that might be difficult to get into without causing damage. He'd have to ask the brilliant civilian techie at Lisburn Road, Ken Bishop, to take a look at it. See if he could put a tracker in it and clone it to share the calls and texts.

God, he was tired. This bloody case seemed to have sent tendrils into so many places he felt as if he was being spun around and around so fast, he couldn't get his balance. He'd never felt as disorientated by a case as he had by this one.

"Okay. First things first. I'll need her phone, with her permission, of course, and we need to make sure she's never alone anywhere that bastard can get to her. How secure is your place?"

"Very, but then I thought the yard was secure until the other day. I'll turn the place into Fort Knox if I have to."

"Good. I'll try to get a watch put on it, too. This isn't my territory — I've been brought in from Belfast — but one way or another I'll get them moving and send a patrol to keep an eye."

Steele nodded. "Have you heard anything else about Asha? Inspector Harvey, I mean."

"Not yet. I called, but there was no news except that she'd had a comfortable night."

"Hospital speak for 'we're not telling you a damn thing'," Richard muttered, and Aaron felt his first hint of fellow feeling for the other man.

"I'd also like Clara to meet with our artist, Jilly, to see if we can get a picture of this Norwegian bloke. What did you call him?"

"Ole."

"No surname?"

"She never heard one."

"Well, a description will help, at least. And anything else she can tell us about the place she met these people."

"She keeps a logbook on the boat. There'll be coordinates and places marked on her charts. My sister is a good sailor," he said defensively.

"I'm sure she is," Aaron said. "Thank you for coming in this morning. You can go home to Clara now, unless there's anything more you need to tell me? Could you drop her logbook and phone in as soon as you get the chance?"

"I will, and if anything happens, I'll be in touch," Steele said.

Patterson wasn't in the station, but Aaron finally reached her on her mobile. Voices and laughter sounded in the background of the call.

"DCS Patterson," she said, with a playfulness in her voice that rocked him back on his heels. An image of her seated opposite some man at a table for two flashed through his mind, but the thought of the chief on a date just wasn't going to fly.

"DC Birch here. Sorry to bother you, ma'am."

"Yes, DC Birch. What can I do for you? And when am I going to have to start calling you DS Birch?"

"Soon, ma'am, I hope." If he ever got time to revise in between cases. "I need to bring you up to speed with some new developments, and I might need your help persuading the local crowd to give me some security for a witness I believe might be in danger."

"That sounds intriguing," she said, and Aaron was sure whoever she was with must be listening to her end of the conversation.

He told her what he'd learned from Steele and requested permission to bring Jilly up to Bangor so she could get an artist's impression drawn up for Ole.

"You're on fire today, DC Birch. Go ahead and set it up. But I have one condition."

"Ma'am?"

"I need to be kept informed at every stage. If the witness so much as sneezes, I want to know about it. And you do nothing, you take no action, without speaking to me first. Is that clear?"

"Yes, ma'am. Crystal clear." He wanted to ring off, but the way she'd ended the last sentence made him think she hadn't quite finished with him. "Was there anything else, ma'am?"

"Yes. I'll lend you some bodies from Lisburn Road longer term. It's relatively quiet here at the moment, and it sounds as if you're going to be pretty stretched, especially with DI Harvey in hospital."

That was unusually generous. Perhaps Patterson was feeling the Christmas spirit? He thanked her before she changed her mind, while wishing fervently that one of the bodies might belong to Faith McAvoy.

CHAPTER 32

Asha was woken from a deep and dreamless sleep by a nurse taking her blood pressure and temperature. She went through the usual checklist at waking: arms, legs, all present and correct. As soon as the nurse took the cuff from her arm, she tried for a stretch, being careful not to dislodge her dressings.

There was no pain. That came as a pleasant surprise. And she could hear the background noises of a busy hospital now. Her hearing had come back quite quickly but accompanied by a tinnitus that had prevented her from hearing quieter sounds. Now the tinnitus had faded, and she felt relaxed and refreshed.

By the time the ward round reached her, she'd been to the toilet and brushed her teeth with a horrible hospital toothbrush and some sort of paste that claimed to be for teeth but was probably better suited to cleaning stains from baths. She winced when she saw her face in the mirror, but careful exploration of the bruises with her fingers didn't reveal anything broken.

She'd have liked to have been dressed when the doctors trouped into the room, but her clothes had been cut from her the night before so all she had was a hospital gown. Still, she arrayed herself in the chair by the bed, tucking the thin fabric around herself for the sake of decency.

Appearance counted. If she gave the impression of being strong and healthy and able to function, hopefully she'd have a chance of persuading them to let her out.

Plan B was to phone Aaron and get him to fetch her some clothes so she could do a Richard and discharge herself.

The consultant was an elderly man dressed in a baggy tweed suit, checked shirt and bow tie. He discussed her case with his gaggle of junior doctors as if she was an inanimate object, not a living patient.

"This patient was the victim of an explosion," he said in a voice that made her revise her assessment of his age, "which is something we pride ourselves on dealing well with in Belfast. She took a substantial piece of shrapnel to the back of her left thigh, but she was extremely lucky. Who'd like to tell me which arteries *could* have been severed by a flying piece of metal in that region?"

After he'd given them a detailed account of her surgery that made her stomach want to eject the toast and marmalade she'd had for breakfast, he asked the nurse to fetch the shrapnel he'd removed.

She was back quickly with a clear plastic bag not unlike an evidence bag. It held a bloodstained piece of metal with remnants of green paint still clinging to it.

"Now you've seen the shrapnel, have you any other comments about this injury?"

"Infection?" asked a thin girl with bobbed black hair and glasses. "And maybe toxicity from the paint?"

"Very good." He beamed as if she was a performing dog that he'd trained. "We have the patient on a broad-spectrum antibiotic, and samples of the paint have been sent off for analysis. However, I am confident that no foreign bodies were left in the wound site, and X-rays showed no other metal in her body, which is very lucky indeed."

Damn right, Asha thought.

"Now, would any of you like to assess the patient's condition this morning, considering that she has been out of surgery for less than—" he glanced at his watch — "fourteen hours?"

Asha was examined, questioned and then she listened to a young doctor report that her colour and her CRT, whatever that was, were both surprisingly good considering the amount of blood she'd lost.

"Indeed. A remarkably resilient individual, our patient," he said, and Asha couldn't help but feel a surge of pride before she caught herself on.

"Doctor?" she managed to say as he drew breath to hold forth again to his admiring audience. "Please can you tell me when I'll be allowed to go home?"

He pushed his frameless glasses a little further up his nose. "I'll throw that open to my esteemed colleagues here."

They debated it back and forth, with the common thread being the necessity of keeping her in until her body had recovered from the blood loss. Asha's heart sank.

"Excellent answers," the consultant said. "But consider this. The patient is a police officer, as you know. She's also young, at least relative to my own advanced years." He twinkled at her, and she couldn't help but smile back. "She's exceptionally fit, otherwise healthy, and she will have the support of friends and colleagues, or so I am assured."

By whom? Asha wondered. *Patterson?*

"On that basis, can any of you give me a good reason why she shouldn't be allowed to recuperate in more familiar surroundings, coming in for assessment as an outpatient as and when needed? I'm sure Detective Inspector Harvey will promise to be good, won't you?"

She nodded, fingers crossed in the folds of the robe.

"Very good. I'll write you a discharge letter." He beamed at her again. "Good luck, Detective. I sincerely hope you catch the people that did this. Come back in two days to have the dressings changed for something a little lighter. The nurse will give you an appointment."

* * *

Aaron turned up to collect her with Faith McAvoy in tow. He looked even worse than she did. Fewer cuts and bruises, but he was so pale that his skin appeared translucent.

"Faith helped me find suitable clothes for you," he said, dumping a sports bag on the end of her bed.

She smiled at the young PC, who ducked her head, embarrassed. "Thank you, Faith. Let's see what you brought."

They'd brought her track pants, the sort where the leg unzipped up the side. They must have been digging deep if they'd found those, because she hadn't worn them since training college, as far as she could remember.

Aaron and Faith tactfully left her alone while she dressed. It was a struggle to fasten her bra, because all the ligaments in her shoulders felt as if they'd been jerked to full extension and then twanged back again, but she managed.

Afterwards, she had to sit down on the edge of the bed to catch her breath. She'd never been prone to fainting, so this rushing sound in her ears and the dark walls closing in at the edges of her vision were new to her.

Aaron appeared with a porter and a wheelchair. "Don't give me a hard time," he said. "It's hospital rules."

She scowled, just to keep up the pretence, but she was glad to sink down on to the plastic seat.

"Can we go back to the station, please?" she tried as she fastened her seatbelt.

Aaron ignored her.

When they stopped at her house, the front door was already open with a uniformed constable standing outside. "Has there been a break-in?"

"Only a friendly one. Come in and see," Aaron replied.

He helped her out of the car, keeping a firm grip on her arm as she hopped and hobbled the few steps to her door. The constable nodded a greeting, then stood back to let them pass.

The scent of fresh coffee drifted out from the kitchen along with the sound of voices from the lounge. Asha pushed open the door and let out a squeak of surprise. Lonnie Jacob was just putting down a tray covered in steaming mugs of coffee. Jana Wiśniewska, her favourite Lisburn Road SOCO, was behind her with a plate of sliced sponge sandwich cake, which Asha recognised as from the baker's at the end of her street.

The room blurred and spun, but Aaron's arm stayed strong, and in a moment, she was sinking into her sofa without being aware of crossing the room. Someone pushed a mug of steaming coffee into her hand, then Jana placed a plate of sandwiches at her elbow on a low table that had come from the spare room.

"What's all this?" A welcoming committee like this was absolutely not something you'd expect from the dour, stolid officers of the PSNI.

"DC Birch told us what happened, ma'am," said PC Jim Christie. "About the explosion, and how you got him out of there."

She shook her head. "The boot's on the other foot. DC Birch virtually carried me to safety. If it hadn't been for him, I'd have bled out."

They smiled, but she could see that Aaron had done far too good a PR job on her for them to believe what she was saying. So she returned their smiles and resigned herself to being spoiled. "Thank you."

"Ma'am. We'll be on our way now, but if you need anything fetching from the station, just shout. I left you a TETRA radio on the desk."

"Patterson's given us Faith and PC Orr, who you met on your way in, to help with the case," Aaron said. "Lonnie and Jana were both off duty, so they're here in their own time."

"Yes," Lonnie said. "But now we've seen you're still alive, we can leave with a clear conscience. I can see you're in good hands." She looked Asha in the eye. "But if I hear of you taking any more stupid risks, either of you, there will be repercussions."

Then she smiled, gathered up her capacious handbag, and herded a protesting Jana out of the house in front of her.

"Lonnie is a breath of fresh air," Asha said, sipping the coffee. "Now bring me up to speed. What happened that had you rushing away from the hospital last night?"

He filled her in on the attack on Steve White.

Asha's eyes burned with unshed tears. "I can't believe he's dead. Only yesterday, I was thinking how happy he seemed. Aaron, this has got to stop and we're the ones who need to stop it."

A commotion from the front door heralded the arrival of Superintendent Sewell. He smiled down at her. "I agree. You two know more about Aiken and Kernaghan than anyone else on the force, so I think you have the best chance of cornering them. But, Asha, you're not going to be fit for any heroics for a while, so you'll just have to be the brains while Aaron and the rest of the team run about for you."

"Thank you, sir."

"You're officially resting, of course," Sewell said. "DCS Patterson has been bending my ear, telling me that under no circumstances are you to be allowed into the station until you'd recovered sufficiently. I knew what you'd have to say to that, so instead I've cleared you to access the mainframe remotely. They finished setting it up this morning, so you should be good to go."

Asha laughed, and it felt good.

"Anything you need, just shout," he said. "I'll try to keep DCS Patterson off your back as long as I can."

As the door closed behind him, Aaron let out a breath. "I like your boss, Ash. He's dead on."

"Hmm. I'm lucky. What was that you said about Richard's sister, Aaron?"

Aaron told her what he knew. "I'm going to interview her this afternoon. I'll record it and report back to you." He shook his head. "I wish you could be with me."

She side-eyed him. "You've nothing to worry about. Besides, handling an interview like this will be good on your CV when it comes to promotion."

Faith raised her hand timidly. "Could I go along to take notes? It'd be good for my CV, too."

CHAPTER 33

"Wow!" Faith breathed as she craned her neck to take in the towering building Richard Steele called home. "How the other half live, huh?"

In the open-plan living area, huge windows let in light that had a clarity only found near the coast. Aaron set up the recorder and made the introductions for the tape. Then he asked the first question. "Please can you take us back to where this began?"

Clara started hesitantly, talking quietly and shredding a paper hanky on her lap. She told them about the unpredictable weather and currents around Norway. How her boat had been too close to a lee shore — whatever that was — and her panic when the engine refused to start.

Aaron tried to imagine what it must have been like, out there in a gale with no one nearby to help, especially as their parents had died at sea as well.

Her story was drawn out of her in dribs and drabs by Aaron's gentle questioning. The words stumbled from her lips, her eyes clouded with shame. She must have been putty in the hands of a man like Ole, alone in a foreign land where she couldn't speak or understand the language.

She was tough, though, to have managed that terrible journey from Norway to Ireland single-handed in those conditions. He could imagine how the cold and never-ending watchfulness might sap strength and eat away at judgement.

When Clara talked about finding Aiken waiting for her the night before, her shame changed to anger.

When the statement had been checked and signed, Aaron got up to leave. The lack of home baking and coffee was a shame. He'd been looking forward to more of those cookies, but he supposed it was understandable.

Faith cleared her throat, embarrassed. "Would you mind if I used your toilet?" She looked at Clara for an answer, not Richard.

"Of course. There's one just along here. I'll show you."

Richard walked Aaron down the stairs to the front door and the two men stood in an uncomfortable silence while they waited for Faith. She turned up almost immediately, running down the stairs with her cheeks flushed. Aaron was surprised. He didn't have her pegged as the sort of woman who'd be embarrassed about needing to ask to use the loo. It was quite endearing, actually.

"Well? What did you think?" he asked, when the car doors were closed.

"I think we should have arrested her," Faith said in a hard voice. "All those girls. They'll have been lied to, you know. Promised the world. They were probably told they'd have jobs waiting for them in hotels or retail, but they'll be on their backs with their legs spread until they're too old, or pregnant, and then they'll be thrown out on to the streets to fend for themselves." She took a short, sharp breath. "Sorry. It's just . . ."

Aaron didn't know what to say.

She took another breath, a little deeper this time, and seemed to regain control. "I really am sorry. It's just I've seen it before." She gave him a tight smile. "We should get back. DI Harvey will want to hear this."

Aaron started the engine.

* * *

Asha listened to the recording, then sighed. "So, we have the original drug-smuggling operation, thanks to Patterson's tip-off, and now we have a human-trafficking ring from Norway to worry about." She shook her head. "It's feast or famine. We've had nothing exciting happen in Bangor since I came here, and now this. I blame you, Aaron. You brought trouble with you."

Faith rushed to defend him. "That's just not fair, ma'am. DC Birch is just . . ." Then she dried up as she noticed the amusement in Asha's eyes. "Sorry, ma'am."

"It's all right, Faith. At least it's keeping us busy."

"Anyway, it's all the same case," Aaron said. "Aiken and Kernaghan seem to be a common factor. So, what are we thinking? Two different operations, run by different people but both employing Aiken and Kernaghan, or one operation with multiple strands to it?"

Asha shrugged. "The drugs are no surprise. Both men dealt cocaine for years under the radar, so they'd have learned enough to continue that game on their own, but I never really had either of them pegged as leaders. They *must* be working for someone else. Someone in the force?"

Faith whimpered, a tiny sound. She'd been involved in the last case, too, one of the few people Asha and Aaron had confided in, on the basis that she was too new to the PSNI to have been involved.

"I've been thinking along the same lines," Aaron said.

Asha sighed. "We also need to follow up on this Norwegian lead."

"Aiken told her he'd be in touch on behalf of Ole to tell her when and where she's to go," Aaron said. "Perhaps we can use that to set up a trap."

"Do you think we can rely on Clara Steele to tell us if he gets in touch again?" Faith asked. "I'm just thinking that if he threatened her brother, again, she might be too afraid to tell us." She shivered. "We all know how scary Aiken can be."

"I think she'll tell us," Aaron said. There'd been something in the woman's body language during the interview that suggested resolve. "But we should warn Steele not to let her out of his sight until we're organised. A tracker and a clone phone for starters, maybe."

"I still don't understand why they killed the lorry driver," Asha said. "Or Steve White. It seems likely the same weapon was used for both, although we won't know until the Prof comes back with the results of the second post-mortem. If the lorry driver was part of the team, what had they to gain by killing him, and why steal the truck? Have you heard from the French police on that deep background check I requested on the driver?"

"No, and I should have." Aaron pulled an iPad towards him and tapped in his login details. "I'll chase them . . . Oh, wait. There's an email."

A frown creased his forehead as he scrolled through a long and detailed block of text, then he looked up, a little pale. "You're not going to believe this. It seems our French lorry driver was working undercover." He went back to reading. "The wording is a little hard to follow. I'm not sure if it's saying he worked *for* the French police, or that he was an informer." He handed it to Asha. "What do you think?"

The email appeared to have been written by someone with a slight grasp of the English language and access to Google Translate. She scanned it a second time.

"It sounds as if he might have been arrested then persuaded to inform on his employers. The French must have been on to this for a while."

"Nice of them to share their intelligence with us," Faith said. "How long is it since you asked for information about that driver, Aaron?"

"Boxing Day. Four days ago."

Asha read the email again. "This was sent on the morning of the twenty-seventh."

Aaron shook his head. "But it only appeared in my inbox just now. See the time stamp?"

A cold chill ran down Asha's spine. "Could someone have tampered with it, I wonder? If we'd had that information on the twenty-seventh, we could have warned Serge Durand and he might still be alive."

"*Who* could have done that?"

He frowned. "If we are dealing with someone senior in the PSNI, they may have had their own sources inside the French police. They *could* have leaked the fact that he was undercover to Aiken and Kernaghan, signing Serge Durand's death warrant."

Asha blew out a frustrated sigh. "I hate this. All of it. The suspicion, the looking over your shoulder. I thought we'd seen the last of it, but apparently not." She cast a glance at Faith, who was sitting quietly, staring down at her hands. She was still pale and there were shadows beneath her eyes. Time to move on.

"Aaron, can you contact the Prof and see if he'll take on Steve White's post-mortem, since it's all part of the same case?"

"What about me, ma'am?" Faith asked.

Asha needed an hour or so to give her aching head some time to work on the problem without distractions, but she couldn't say that. "Would you mind chasing Bishop to see if he's managed to get anything off Johnston's phone yet? We really need a lead for whoever is behind this drug smuggling, and that might be our best chance for now."

Faith nodded.

"It's probably best if you beard him in his den, because he doesn't always answer the phone when he's working. Do you have a car?"

"I can run her over there," Aaron said. "Would you mind if we drop by Steele's place to get Clara's phone off her as well so Bishop can put a tracker in it? The Steeles have already agreed to the idea in principle, and Superintendent Sewell says it's okay. I can phone Prof Talbot on the way over there."

"Good thinking." That should keep the pair of them out of her hair for a few hours.

After they'd left, the house seemed very quiet. She'd never noticed the tick of the clock on the mantlepiece before, but then she rarely spent any time in this room, and even then the radio or TV would be on, so she could fall asleep to the sound of canned laughter.

She sank back into the soft armchair and closed her eyes, trying to zone out the ticking that wasn't quite keeping time with the pulsing blood in her ears.

During last year's case, the one that had begun as a historical investigation and turned into something far too current for comfort, she'd had to keep her own counsel. Aiken and Kernaghan had tried to block her and deflect her at every opportunity, but they had in turn been protected by Alistair King.

He had hinted that there was someone else, maybe someone more powerful than him, but she'd not had the chance to question him further. She'd tried to discuss it with Patterson, but the chief was convinced they had all bad apples identified now, and all they needed to do was capture Aiken and Kernaghan.

Asha tried to lay out the facts of both cases in a logical manner, but her head still ached, and her thoughts kept on flitting away before she could pin them down.

She fetched a notepad and biro and started brainstorming.

A rival ordered the hit on King — call the rival "X".

X took over King's drug operation.

What if A & K were working for X all along, as well as for King?

X has been hiding Aiken and Kernaghan.

A and K stole truck and killed Serge. Did X want truck destroyed?

Ole's contact is Aiken. X controls Aiken — and Ole?

So X traffics people as well as drugs.

And then it hit her. Turf wars. The existing group operating here in Northern Ireland, the group that Aiken and Kernaghan were a part of, were trying to take over the French drug-smuggling operation. No, not take it over. Destroy it. So where had Patterson's "tip" come from? It had been the reason they'd started looking into the new boat arriving at Steele's boatyard in the first place.

And why destroy the truck? As a warning? No. Whoever was sitting at the centre of this web, pulling strings — was planning to annihilate the interloper. They wanted to send a message: "no one else trades in this patch."

According to Johnston, this had all kicked off when his employer started to move the business north of the border where Johnston was a familiar figure — and into X's territory.

She took a deep, shuddering breath. Her instincts had been screaming at her for months, but she'd been ignoring them, because if they'd been true, then everything she'd believed in must be put under the microscope. Now, she opened her mind to a possibility that was almost too terrible to contemplate.

Whose tip had brought them to the boatyard in the first place?

Who had channelled resources into last year's operation and pulled strings to bring in armed support from all over the province?

Even Asha had thought it overkill at the time, but not if Patterson was carrying out a coup, taking over King's business. And sending out a message to anyone else in the province that she wouldn't be messed with.

Chief Superintendent Yvonne Patterson was X. She must be. No one else fitted.

If it had been her who'd given the order to kill King, who must have been a thorn in her side, she'd got rid of a competitor while at the same time consolidating her own position as an effective senior officer. If Asha was right, Patterson was a very dangerous woman indeed.

And Patterson now knew, thanks to Aaron, that they'd linked Aiken to the human trafficking crime. Had they put Clara's life in danger?

CHAPTER 34

Ken Bishop was not one bit happy to be interrupted when Aaron and Faith were buzzed into his tiny office in the basement at the Lisburn Road station.

"Phone was a mess," he said. "That chap has the technical ability of a mushroom." The Welsh accent poured into Aaron's ear like golden brandy into a balloon glass. He couldn't help but smile.

"Did you manage to restore any of the texts?"

"Well, I began with a logical acquisition process, and I did find some data that might be useful to you, but he'd deleted a lot of data, so I put it through a file system acquisition protocol, and—"

"English, please, Bishop."

He sounded hurt. "That *was* English, you technophobe oik. I was about to say that it took physical acquisition to pry the last few secrets open, but I think I've got everything you need now."

"What did you find?"

Bishop said stiffly, "Analysing data's your job. I just put everything in a protected folder on the server. I'll WhatsApp you the password." He sounded distracted, as if his mind had moved on to the next challenge, now this one was behind him.

"One more thing. Can you put a tracker in this for me?" Aaron put Clara's bulky smartphone down on the desk. Bishop gave it a glance and nodded. "And clone it, so I can see any messages and calls it receives?"

A derisive snort. Bishop reached into a drawer and pulled out a new, boxed phone. "Give me thirty minutes."

"Thanks," Aaron said, but Bishop had already forgotten him as he tapped keys on a keyboard that was barely visible amid the mess of paperwork on his desk. Aaron's phone pinged a moment later with a WhatsApp alert, and there he found the folder name and password.

"Thanks," he said, and indicated with a tilt of his head to Faith that they should leave.

He set off upstairs to the open-plan office he shared with other DCs and a couple of sergeants, Faith trotting quietly along behind him, but then he thought about the leak of information that might have come from this very station, and he changed his mind and turned right instead of left at the top of the stairs.

Lonnie looked as if she never moved from her computer chair, hunched over her keyboard with her old-fashioned CRT monitor taking up a large part of the desk.

"Hello, Sergeant Jacob," he said. "Mind if we camp out here for a wee while?"

"Be my guest," she said, without looking up. "PC McAvoy, you'll need to bring another chair in from along the corridor unless you want to stand."

Faith cast him a puzzled glance. The elderly sergeant had her back to the door. How had she known Faith was there? He grinned at her and waved a hand to send her on a hunt for a chair.

"Still practicing the old magic, Lonnie?" he asked.

She snorted. "For that, you can fetch the coffee."

He laughed but did as he was told. He and Lonnie were old friends.

When he got back, Faith had found an upright spindle-backed chair from somewhere and was perched on the edge of it, staring blank-faced at her mobile phone.

"Working hard?"

At the sound of his voice, she seemed to wake from a trance. She pocketed her mobile and cleared a space on the cluttered desk for him to put down the coffees. He lowered himself gingerly on to the other chair, a computer swivel chair with a missing castor that always tilted the user sideways when they least expected it.

Before they could get started, the door opened in a rush and Jana came in. The diminutive redhead was one of their scene-of-crime officers, a bundle of sarcasm and a heart of gold. Aaron enjoyed working with her, but he couldn't say the same for Asha. Jana made a habit of pretending to fancy DI Harvey.

At least, he thought it was pretence.

She handed the file she was carrying to Lonnie and turned, a grin splitting her face. "Faith! *Jak się masz?*"

"*Dobrze, a ty?*" Faith replied.

Aaron knew he was staring, but he couldn't help it. "You never told me you speak Russian," he said, keeping his tone light and teasing.

Faith flushed. "It's Polish, not Russian. I don't often get the chance to speak it."

Jana rattled off something else, and Faith replied, a little more subdued this time. She pointed to the computer, and Aaron assumed she was apologising and telling Jana she needed to work, because the little SOCO grinned at them and left. Lonnie barely looked up.

Unsettled, he pulled out the iPad and opened the folder Bishop had set up. There were reams of data, which Bishop had organised into subfolders for images, texts, personal messages via Facebook, etc. and emails.

"Faith, you can use this, and I'll use Sergeant Jacob's spare terminal. I'll do texts, and you can view the images. I'm looking for a deleted image of two men at a service station."

"My mother," she said, avoiding his eyes. "My mother is Polish. I grew up bilingual."

"I didn't know," he said.

"Did you ever ask?" Lonnie murmured, breaking the tension.

He laughed, and wondered how many more surprises Faith had up her sleeve.

Aaron started working his way through the texts. There were a lot of them.

Faith's coffee had gone cold by the time Bishop's half hour was up. They retrieved the phone and the clone and set off for Bangor. Richard Steele was waiting for them at the gate to the boatyard, and he took the original phone back, turning it over to see if anything had changed.

"Bishop says no one will notice the tracker so Clara doesn't need to worry about that side of it," Aaron said.

Steele sighed. "It feels all wrong, putting a tracker in my sister's phone. Once word gets around that she's home, there'll be friends trying to reach her and she's going to feel bad about their calls being tracked and listened to."

"Look at it this way, sir. As long as no one else knows about it, it could save her life." *And yours,* he thought privately.

"All right. I'll tell her to keep quiet about it," he said. "But you'll let me know if you pick anything up, won't you?"

* * *

Asha didn't seem pleased to see them when Aaron rang the doorbell. She wore a scowl that would have curdled milk and barely said hello, which wasn't like her at all.

"When are your pain meds due?" he asked.

She glanced up at him, eyes troubled. "It's not painful. Not really, except a ringing in my ears and a bit of a headache. What have you got there?"

He showed her the cheap phone Bishop had given him. "It's a clone of Clara Steele's mobile, plus he's put a tracker in her phone and there's an app we can use to trace her."

Her face lit up. "Any calls or texts yet?"

He shook his head, but as he handed over the mobile, it vibrated and the screen lit up with a text.

Aaron peered at it then shrugged. "Just some friend of Clara's, suggesting they meet for a coffee."

Asha was frowning over the phone, reading the text. "Harmless enough, I suppose. How do I get on to this tracker app then?"

Aaron showed her what Bishop had shown him. The map allowed for road view or satellite view. He had it on road view for now. "The little blue dot is Clara. She's exactly where she ought to be: at her brother's house."

Asha peered over his shoulder. "Good. We should check it every fifteen minutes." She took it from him and handed it to Faith. "Here's a useful job for you."

"Bishop cracked Johnston's phone," Aaron went on. "He's put everything in a secure folder on the network. Faith and I made a start in Lonnie's office, but I thought we could go through the rest of it here. There's a lot of deleted stuff."

They sat down together at Asha's dining table, logged into the PSNI main server, and opened Bishop's folder. Asha hissed between her teeth as she opened more and more levels of subfolders. "You weren't kidding. He must live his whole life on this phone."

"Yeah," Aaron mumbled, only half-listening. "I wonder how that's working out for him inside a cell. I've already made a start on his texts, and Faith has been looking for that image of him at the service station, where he handed over the first package."

"Okay. I'll check his call history. I have a list of dates he gave us for the times he was ordered to commission boats for these people. If we concentrate on the days around those dates first, that should help to pin down the ones we need."

For a while, the only sound was fingers tapping on keys. Aaron consulted Asha's list of dates. The earliest one was the first time Johnston had been sent down south. There must have been a flurry of activity around then, surely, before the suspect binned that phone. He'd have wanted to appear trustworthy at first to win Johnston's confidence, so he would have used the same number until he had the man well hooked.

There. He'd saved the contact under the name of the boatbuilding company. Aaron let out a breath. "I've got the first number used to contact him, the one claiming to be a rep from the boatbuilding company." He scribbled it on a page of his notebook and pushed it across the desk to Asha.

"Thanks." More finger tapping. "I have him. His first phone call. This is a French international code, isn't it? The call lasted nearly three minutes."

"Interesting. Either he was pretending to be calling from France and went to the trouble of buying a SIM from over there, or it's someone working there who's behind all this, or maybe the boatbuilders themselves are a part of this operation. We should pass this to Interpol."

"Maybe." She didn't sound convinced.

"Asha? Is something bothering you?"

Her expression was unreadable. "What makes you think that?"

"I don't know. You don't seem yourself. Did something happen after Faith and I left?"

She sighed and her lips tightened for a moment. "Nothing happened. I think maybe it's just this headache. It's slowing down my thinking." But she didn't seem quite able to meet his eyes.

He forced a smile. "Okay. I'm here if you need anything."

"Mm. Thanks." She was back to her laptop screen. Aaron studied her profile for a few seconds. A slow blush darkened her cheeks, but she stared resolutely at the text as it scrolled past. He returned to his work.

Gradually, they accumulated a list of numbers that seemed to be associated with the man who'd recruited Johnston and sent him his instructions. There were seven different phone numbers, four of which were from French service providers, two with Irish area codes and one — Aaron breathed a little faster — had a UK area code, so it could be from Northern Ireland. Maybe that would give them a lead to whoever was running this end of the operation?

CHAPTER 35

Asha couldn't share her suspicions with Aaron or Faith until she had concrete evidence to back them up, but the weight of her anxiety pressed down on her as they worked together.

Aaron huffed out a breath and leaned back in his upright dining-room chair. "If Bishop can trace this UK number, maybe we'll have a lead to the whereabouts of at least one member of this operation."

"Good for you. Go for it." Aaron would make a great sergeant if he'd just do the damn exams. She was shocked to find it was after five already. "On second thoughts, that can wait until tomorrow. I don't know about you, but I'm bushed. Want to share a carry-out or do you have plans for the evening?"

He glanced at Faith, who gave a tiny nod. "We were thinking of heading back into Belfast, if that's okay? Faith gets off duty at six and we thought we might eat out tonight."

A tiny stab of jealousy surprised her. She swallowed. "That sounds lovely. Where are you thinking of?"

"There's a new place opened just around the corner from me. Thai food. Thought we might give it a try."

The house felt empty again once they'd left. She ordered in pizza and sat at her laptop, looking through the files from Johnston's phone until her head began to nod. The stairs seemed too big a challenge, so she rooted out a sleeping bag from her Duke of Edinburgh days and tried to get comfortable on the sofa with the injured leg propped up. One more day, then she could get rid of this dratted dressing and start to get back to normal life.

* * *

She thought she'd never manage to sleep in such an uncomfortable position, but she woke before her alarm at half past six with a stiff neck and cramp inside the bandage. That got her to her feet, hopping around and cursing.

She hobbled through to the bathroom to bathe, what her mother called a birdbath, and brush her teeth. She longed for a shower to freshen up, but there was no chance until the dressing came off.

Coffee with toast and marmalade lifted her dark mood a little. She made a second mug and carried it carefully into the dining room where she picked up the files from Johnston's phone at the same place she'd left off the night before.

Aaron arrived at nine, bright-eyed and looking extremely pleased with himself. He had a paper bag with him, slightly greasy.

"I take it the Thai place was a success?"

He rolled his eyes. "Mm. So good. I bought us some Danish pastries from the garage on the main road. They're still warm. More coffee? Faith's on her way."

"I'm good for caffeine, but if you got one of those wee almond-paste ones . . .?" The pastries tasted as delicious as they sounded, and the sugar rush made her feel that if there was a way to the centre of this maze of facts, she and Aaron would find it.

Faith arrived just in time to snatch the last pastry from Aaron before he could bolt it down. Her cheeks were pink from the fresh air.

"I've found the photo from the service station," she said, putting a hand to her mouth to catch the flaky pastry crumbs.

"It shows Johnston's face quite clearly, but only the back of the head of his contact, and he's even wearing a baseball cap to hide his hair colour."

The photo had been taken from quite high up, maybe from the cab of a truck. Not that that got them anywhere, but Asha stored the information away anyway just in case it became relevant later.

Faith checked the cloned phone and choked on her pastry. "She's gone!"

"What do you mean?"

"Clara Steele. The little blue dot isn't at the house any more." She dropped the pastry on the table and started zooming out on the screen, looking for the dot. "I can't believe this! I've been checking it every fifteen minutes all night, and it's never moved."

"Maybe she's gone for a walk to clear her head," Aaron suggested. He took the phone from Faith. "There's a *centre target* command somewhere . . . here!" He frowned. "That can't be right. According to this, she's on the main road to Newtownards and travelling fast."

"Shit!" Asha dialled Clara's number. No answer. She called Richard's number instead, drumming her fingers on the table as she waited for him to answer.

"Asha?" His voice was warm and welcoming, and it gave her a feeling of reassurance. "How are you? I've been worried about you."

She didn't mince her words. "Where's Clara?"

There was a moment of hesitation. "She's here in the house. She was a bit emotional after the interview and didn't sleep well last night, so she said she'd go and lie down on her bed for an hour or so. Do you need to talk to her?"

"Yes please, if you don't mind."

She could hear his feet on the wooden stairs, fast-moving, possibly taking two at a time, then the click of his shoes on the downstairs corridor. A knock and his voice, a little muffled as he held the phone away from him.

"Clara? Are you awake? I have Asha on the phone for you."

Silence.

"Clara, I'm coming in, okay?" He was beginning to sound anxious, maybe picking it up from Asha.

A door creaked. If she'd been less worried, she might have smiled at the thought of a creaky hinge in his state-of-the-art house, but instead she held her breath, listening hard.

"Clara?" Definitely tense. "She's not here, Asha. I'll get her to call you when I find her, if you like?"

"No, Richard. Don't ring off. Keep me connected while you search for her." She put her hand over the microphone and mouthed at Aaron, "Get a uniform from Newtownards out on that road. Unmarked car. Direct them where to go from the app."

She listened again as Richard ran from room to room in his huge house, his breath coming in shorter and shorter gasps as anxiety wore away at his composure. "I can't find her, Asha. I've been outside, all around the grounds. My car's still in the garage, so she's either on foot or she's got a lift from someone. I'm heading back in now to look at the CCTV."

"The CCTV will be useful," she said, trying to stay calm for his sake as much as her own, "but we're looking at her icon on the app now, and it's halfway to Newtownards. Don't worry, Richard. We'll find her."

"I can be in Newtownards in under twenty minutes."

"No. I need you to stay put, keep the gates locked, and don't let anyone in unless it's me or Aaron. *No one else*, do you hear? And get me that CCTV."

"I'll get it to you as fast as I can," he said in a tight voice.

She sent a questioning look at Aaron. "Report."

"I have two unmarked cars with plain clothes converging on her, one from Ards, one from here. The first car should be in visual range within the next few minutes. They wanted to know what sort of car she drives?"

"She's not in Richard's car, and she doesn't have one of her own, so if she's travelling that fast, someone must have given her a lift."

"I'm sorry," Faith said. "I should have seen it sooner."

"Can't be helped."

Aaron turned his attention back to the phone he still held to his ear.

"No. Keep your distance for now, but try to see if anyone gets off when it stops. You're looking for an IC1 female in her late twenties. Slim, athletic build, long, dark hair."

He looked up at Asha again. "A Translink bus, heading to Newtownards. I have a car tailing it from a good distance, and I told him to stay back for now. Once we have the second car on them, they can overtake and try to see if she's on board."

"Good. How far out is the second car?"

"Couple of minutes."

Asha's phone rang at the same moment as Aaron started speaking into his and giving orders.

"Richard? Anything?"

"Yes. She left the house nearly twenty minutes ago, on foot. There was no sign of anyone meeting her, and I watched her walk along the lane until she was out of sight. She was heading towards the main road." He sounded determined, now. "What's the news from your end?"

"We have two cars on her." She glanced at Aaron, who nodded confirmation. "She's on a bus. We're waiting for visual confirmation."

"I know you're doing your best, but I feel so helpless here."

She wanted to reassure him, but there was nothing she could say to comfort him now that wouldn't be a lie. "If I think of anything you can do to help, I'll let you know."

"Thank you for that," he said, and the bitterness in his voice made her flinch.

"I'll be in touch," she said inadequately.

Aaron was talking quietly into the phone. When he noticed she'd finished her call, he put his hand over the mic. "Dispatch are relaying reports to me. The first car passed the bus when it stopped to let a schoolboy off, and they said there was a young woman that could have been Clara, but it was hard to see because she was sitting on the left-hand side, away from our officers. They're going to stop further on, on the outskirts of town, and let the bus overtake them again. They'll try to get a photo as it passes, but I wouldn't hold out much hope."

No. She looked through the window at the drizzly weather outside. The roads would be wet, and salty after the ice. The bus windows would be filthy, and it would be moving fast. Still, it was a chance, at least.

The tension in the room mounted as they waited to hear from the car. Asha's frustration rose with it. She should be out there doing something, not stuck here with one leg like a fat, white sausage.

Her laptop and Aaron's both pinged at the exact same moment. An incoming email from the station with an attachment and the short message: *Is this her?*

She opened it with shaking fingers and then groaned as the image loaded. The image was slightly blurred by the rain running down the bus windows, but clear enough to show a young woman, staring out across the head of the photographer. She had long, dark hair and was roughly the right age, but it wasn't Clara Steele.

"Shit," she breathed. "She must have planted the phone on another woman. I should have thought of that. Aiken's too slippery to be caught that easily. But if she's meeting Aiken, how did he get a message to her?"

Aaron groaned.

"What?"

"That text. The one I said was from a friend?" He held out his hand to Faith for the phone. "Let's see it again."

Hey, Little Clara. So happy to hear you're back in the country. I'll maybe pop round tomorrow morning to say hi. G x

G for George, Aiken's first name. It was obscure enough to look innocent at first glance, but here was Clara, sneaking out of the house when she knew she was supposed to stay put, and then planting her phone on someone else.

Asha called Richard again. He answered on the first ring.

"Any news?"

"Not yet," she lied. "Richard, has Clara said anything to you about messages from a friend? Maybe making plans for meeting someone?"

He didn't answer immediately. Then he took an audible breath. "No, but she was very quiet at breakfast. Why?"

"Was she definitely alone when she left?"

"Yes. And no cars passed after that in either direction. I checked."

So, she'd probably got as far as the bus stop then. Maybe she'd got on the bus, dumped the phone, then jumped off at the next stop. Or any random stop between there and where they'd picked up her signal.

"Okay. Leave it with us. We'll find her, Richard." She crossed her fingers as she rang off. "We have to find her, Aaron. It could be our one chance to follow Aiken, and we can't blow it."

"I should call Patterson. She could have an experienced team out here in no time."

"No!" She'd been too sharp. "There *is* no time. We need to check all the cameras we have access to, see if we can spot her getting on or off the bus. And get the patrol to pull the bus over and see if it has a working camera onboard. We *have* to find her!"

CHAPTER 36

"They've pulled over the bus," Aaron said, "but there's no working CCTV onboard. We don't know if she ever got on it, never mind where she might have got off."

"Anything from other CCTV?" But she knew the answer before he shook his head. Any cameras would be on private houses, and it would take forever to track those down. She hobbled up and down her small dining room, then stopped and glared out of the window at the rain sheeting down, blurring what little view she had.

"We've lost her." It came out as a wail that she'd have called back if she could. How would she tell Richard?

"Why would she just go off like this without telling us, or at least telling her brother?"

Faith swallowed hard and said in a small voice, "Because he'll have threatened to kill her brother if she didn't do exactly as she was told."

"Very possible," Aaron said, "but how could he have communicated with her? You were there when I interviewed her. I'd swear she told us everything in her statement, wouldn't you? If Aiken had given her detailed instructions when he cornered her in her boat, I think we'd have seen some signs of evasion, and he hasn't had any chance to speak with her since, or contact her. We'd have known if he had."

Faith licked her lips. "He sent her a message. A note. With full instructions, and—"

Asha's skin prickled with a premonition. "Faith? What have you done?"

PC McAvoy froze like a rabbit in the headlights, eyes wide. The silence lengthened.

"No!" Aaron's face was pale. "No," he repeated quietly. "When you said you needed the toilet?"

Faith nodded, her shoulders slumped in misery. "I'm sorry. I had no choice."

Anger burned deep inside Asha. "*No choice?* How long have you been working for them, PC McAvoy? I hope they paid you well, because this is the end of your career in the PSNI."

"You don't understand. You couldn't . . ." She stopped. "I can waste time trying to make you understand, or I can tell you where to find her. I read the note before I handed it over."

"And?" Aaron's voice was even. Too even. *He must be in shock,* Asha thought. *I'm in shock, too, but it's making me want to kill this woman who's been in all our counsels, listening to everything we say. Passing it on.*

Faith took her phone out. "I photographed it." She opened the phone and flicked through to the image she wanted, then handed it over. Asha sucked in a breath.

The piece of paper had been folded over many times, but the handwritten note only covered the bottom half. The top section was a photo, printed on plain paper. It showed Serge Durand lying naked in the hotel bathroom, and standing over him with a long, heavy bat in his hand was a tall man in an ill-fitting balaclava. The pair of piggy eyes behind the mask looked horribly familiar. Kernaghan.

The note was written in George Aiken's distinctive hand, familiar to Asha from the reports and files of his she'd read when they were first trying to track him down.

This is what will happen to your brother if you don't do exactly what I say. Except he won't have it so easy. We'll take our time with him.
They'll have your phone tracked, so when you get a text from G telling you when, the first thing you need to do is get rid of it. Put it on someone else. In a pocket or car. Make sure it's a stranger.
Once you've lost the phone, walk to the end of your lane, Donaghadee direction, and wait at the junction with the main road. Stay out of sight. A green van will pick you up at 09.30.

Asha's hand trembled as she held the phone. "You knew all this, and you let it happen?"

Faith McAvoy eyes were wide and swimming with tears. "I'm so sorry, ma'am. Patterson had my mother. She's been really ill, dying. I should have come to you sooner, but I was afraid for her." She took a shuddering breath. "But . . . my mother's dead. I only heard yesterday, when I was in Belfast."

Aaron moved as if to comfort Faith, then stopped. "I don't believe it," he said in a flat voice. "Patterson?"

Asha felt a surge of sympathy for him. She hardened her heart. "Yes, Patterson. We'll come back to that later. Faith, do you know anything about this green van? A registration number, make, model? Anything at all?"

"No. They used to have a red van, but I don't know about a green one."

"What make was the red one?" Aaron asked, his voice hoarse.

"A Fiat," she said without hesitation.

"Number plate?"

She shook her head. "It might have begun with PEZ, but I can't be sure, and I have no idea what the numbers were."

"What size?" He pulled up images on the computer for comparison until they had it narrowed down to a rough make and model, then got on the phone, putting out an alert for a green Fiat Ducato with possible PEZ plate.

But why did they want Clara Steele? Ole might have seen her as an opportunity, a cheap way to save himself an unpleasant sea trip in winter. But once she'd completed that task, why would they need her again? Her heart sank. They wouldn't, surely? But she was the only one who could identify Ole, wasn't she?

Richard. He'd do anything to keep his sister safe, and everything Aiken and Kernaghan had done had been about money. Easy money.

"They want her as a hostage," Asha whispered.

She dialled Richard's number, eyes tight shut as she listened to it ringing out, unanswered. She was about to give up when his voice came on, breathing hard.

"Any news?"

Relief made her weak. "Nothing concrete yet. Anything your end?"

"Nothing."

"I'm coming over there, Richard. Don't open the gate or the door until you can see it's me on the cameras, no matter who else arrives. You understand?"

"Okay." Puzzled but willing to trust her.

She ended the call and looked around for her coat. Aaron gave her a flat look. "You're not driving yourself."

"Then Faith can drive me," she said. Aaron placed his back to the door, barring her way.

"I don't think so. I'll drive you and—"

"And what? Leave Faith here on her own? So she can warn her friends?" Faith made a tiny sound of protest, but Asha ignored her. "*You* need to coordinate this search, Aaron. Faith can drive me, and we can have a nice chat on the way. Get a good family liaison briefed and sent over to Steele's place, someone with no association with Patterson, and a tech team to monitor the house phones and Steele's mobile."

He wasn't happy, but he stepped aside to let them pass.

Faith looked tiny in the driver's seat of the big four-wheel drive. She had to move the seat up to see over the steering wheel.

"To Mr Steele's house?" she asked meekly.

Asha nodded. "While you drive, you can tell me how and when you became involved in all this."

"I know this might be hard to believe, but I'm glad it's over." Faith darted a look at Asha. "I've been so unhappy."

"Oh, it's not over, my girl," Asha said, feeling old. "Not by a long way. Now, from the beginning. I want a summary of the salient points first, then I can dive in for detail later. Who recruited you?" As if she needed to ask, but she did need to hear the words from McAvoy's own lips.

"DCS Patterson recruited me, but I was only a child then and I didn't have a choice—"

"When did she recruit you? How?"

"My mum was one of her girls, and—"

Another jigsaw puzzle piece dropped into place. "Okay. When you say, 'one of her girls'?"

"Patterson owns the place my mother was put to work in after she was shipped in from Eastern Europe when she was fourteen. She had me when she was sixteen. I don't know who my dad was."

"How much of this does Aaron know?"

"Nothing. He's asked me about my family, but he's easily distracted, and I'm good at evasion." She blinked as tears filled her eyes again. "I've hated lying to him."

"He trusted you. *I* trusted you." She took a deep breath. "So, your mum was a victim of human trafficking, and now you're working for the people behind it, helping them to bring *more* girls into the country?"

Faith nodded miserably. "I didn't know, at first. Growing up, I knew Patterson owned all the houses and that she was police, but I just thought she had a soft spot for me and was doing her best to help me make something of my life. She was *doing the rounds*, as she called it. Checking on the houses. She took an interest in me. Told me I was too good for that life. That she had something better in mind for me."

Asha felt sick. She didn't really need to ask, but she did anyway. "What was going on in the houses?"

"Do you want me to spell it out or draw you a picture? They were brothels. Whorehouses," McAvoy snapped.

A flash of spirit. Maybe that was what Patterson had seen in the girl. "What age were you then?"

"Ten. Mother — that's not my mum, but the woman who ran the place. She made us call her Mother — she got me to help her with the books sometimes. I've always had a good head for numbers."

A roil of nausea distracted Asha for a moment, but she thought about the crimes Aiken and Kernaghan had committed and went on. "What did Patterson want from you?"

"She helped me to get into grammar school: pulled some strings, I expect." McAvoy shook her head. "That was weird. I didn't fit in at all, because all the other kids had proper homes and families and I couldn't exactly bring them back to the brothel to visit. I was miles behind them all at first, but I worked hard and caught up. I wasn't there to make friends, so I just threw myself into the lessons." She flicked her hair back in a self-conscious gesture, part pride, part embarrassment. "I did well in my exams." Her face shadowed. "But Patterson said that wasn't enough. I needed to learn how to make people like me, for the job she had in mind."

"And did you?"

"Yes." Contemptuous. "I grew up in a brothel. If there's one thing you learn from example, it's how to make people like you. By the time I left, I had a network of friends. Not one of them knows where I came from, but I know all about them."

Asha controlled her breathing. She'd trusted this woman, confided in he, treated her as a friend as well as a colleague. Now she had to reassess everything that had happened and see it through a different lens.

"I assume it was on her orders that you joined the police."

"Yep. The headmaster of the grammar school acted as referee and the PSNI was delighted to get me. Not university educated, but Catholic, black, female and bright, in pretty much that order of importance. Good for their equal opportunities stats, see?"

Asha did see. The PSNI was still trying to redeem itself after decades of discrimination. It just hadn't quite worked out how yet.

"And you've been working alongside Aiken and Kernaghan all this time?"

"No!" The word exploded out of her. "No. I don't know if they even know I'm working for Patterson. She calls me her secret weapon, her eyes and ears. Until yesterday, all I had to do was report back to her."

"How?"

McAvoy fished a phone out of her pocket and handed it to Asha. It looked like an old-fashioned mobile crossed with a walkie-talkie. "It's a satellite phone. Supposed to be harder to track and to listen in to."

"And your relationship with Aaron?"

"That wasn't supposed to happen," Faith said miserably. "She doesn't know about it." She pulled a face. "Or at least, I don't think she knows, but she might have other eyes and ears watching me."

Asha wanted to believe her, but it was hard. The woman had made a career of being believable while lying to those close to her. She sighed. "What am I going to do with you?"

"Use me."

A double agent. How Le Carré. It did open up possibilities, but they'd have to keep her on a tight leash.

"Ma'am, I don't expect you to believe me. God knows, *I* wouldn't believe me, but I'm sickened by what's been going on. When she first put me forward for the PSNI, I was so excited. I thought I'd finally be able to do something to right the wrongs done to people like my mum and all the other women I grew up with. Then the pressure began, just a little at a time, and now I'm getting sucked into something so nasty I can't sleep at night for worrying about it." She stopped for breath, chest heaving. "So, use me. Don't tell me anything you don't want to get back to Patterson, but use me somehow. I *want* to get out of this net she's got wrapped around me."

Asha took a moment to answer, weighing the options. It could work. "All right. Go on reporting, at least for now. And I'll be with you when you report."

Faith McAvoy nodded, eyes shining. "I won't disappoint you, ma'am."

Oh, you already have.

CHAPTER 37

When that young police constable, McAvoy, had pressed a note into her hand, Clara had been bemused but not at all wary. A finger to the lips begged her silence, then the woman was gone.

It wasn't until she'd locked herself in the bathroom that Clara unfolded the note and saw the picture.

She'd dropped it as if it was on fire, but it had lain like a scar on the white floor tiles, dragging her eyes back to it. She knew who it was, because the photo of the dead lorry driver had been on the news. Murdered. Why not use the word? Why would they send her that?

So she'd picked it up gingerly between finger and thumb and opened up the last fold. The writing was in a flowing hand, quite old-fashioned, with even letters. It would have been attractive if the meaning hadn't been so mind-numbingly awful.

This is what will happen to your brother—

For a full minute, she could read no further, but after a few deep breaths, she forced herself onwards.

However many times she read it, she couldn't comprehend its meaning. She could only see the image of Richard lying naked with the back of his head stoved in, just like the man in the photo. And the note said his would not be so easy a death.

Now, alone in a darkened room, surrounded by the groaning timbers of an old house and the stink of decay, she shivered and wondered if she'd been right to follow the instructions. She'd panicked when the text came through, signed G, but had carried out the orders to the last detail. She'd even found a woman who looked a bit like her and managed to drop her mobile phone in her coat pocket as she brushed past. It had felt, then, as if she had no choice; now she saw that as long as she'd been free, they had stood a chance. Richard would do anything, even put himself in danger, if he thought it would help her.

A board creaked out in the hall. There had been two men in the green van: one driving, the one who'd been lying in wait for her in *Snow Goose*, and one in the back. He'd opened the door from the inside, and she'd climbed in willingly, wanting to get it over with, whatever *it* was.

She'd assumed they would want her to use her boat to move more girls, but they hadn't asked anything of her. Every time she tried to speak, she'd been silenced by a look, and once by a casual backhander from the man in the back.

She hadn't seen him before, but she'd seen his picture. Couldn't remember the name. He was a rogue PSNI officer on the run, like the red-haired man, Aiken, she remembered that much.

She licked her lips now, tasting coppery blood from the split lip he'd given her. It had jolted her back into sanity, and triggered her fight reflex, but she'd kept her eyes lowered, pretending to be cowed. She had to wait for the right time. She needed an opportunity to catch one of them on his own when she had a weapon in her hand.

But the opportunity never came. They'd driven miles, taking lefts and rights, and lefts again until she was all turned around inside her head, as she was no doubt meant to be. She had no clue where they were taking her.

When the van finally stopped, she continued to act as if the stuffing was knocked out of her. She kept her head down and waited to be told before she moved. Even then, she stayed sitting on the cold metal floor until the big, dark-haired man hauled her to her feet roughly, banging her head on the steel roof.

He yanked her through the door, and she almost fell. Would have fallen except that he pulled her up sharply, twisting her arm. She let herself go limp again as if she'd ceased to care what happened to her, but she hugged the pain to herself, fuel to drive her to escape.

They were outside a huge old house, like, really old, maybe Victorian. The lower windows were boarded up, and the walls were dark green with slime and moss. Bits of broken roof tile were scattered around on the ground, and she could smell the damp from here.

The dark-haired man pushed her roughly towards the front of the house. She tried to look about her without making it obvious. Everything was totally overgrown, but there was a rusty red gate covered with ivy and weeds in a gap in the blowsy hedge. It looked barely able to hold itself up, so she'd need to be careful if she decided to climb it on her way out.

Then the front door creaked open as Aiken unlocked it, and she was shoved up the stone steps. She fell, skinning both knees on the stone before she was hauled to her feet again. More pain to fuel the fire.

They took her into a ground-floor room. From the glimpse she got of the decaying grand staircase, upstairs wasn't an option. She expected the room to be as derelict as the rest of the house, but it was dry and there was a weak electric bulb hanging from the ceiling.

The room showed signs of residence: a two-ring primus stove was set up in one corner, surrounded by pans that hadn't been cleaned out. Empty soup tins lay discarded on the bare floorboards and there were mouse droppings scattered everywhere. Some of them looked too big to be mouse. Clara shivered. If there was one thing she hated, it was rats.

"Stay here," Aiken said. "And don't try anything, 'cos we'll be right the other side of that door. And Kerny would really enjoy hurting you, so don't give him the excuse, right?"

Kerny. That was the name. *Kernaghan.* He glowered at her, the light bulb casting shadows across his face that made him appear even more sinister than the features nature had given him.

The terrified look she gave him didn't take any acting at all as she retreated to the furthest corner of the room. She sat on the floor, knees drawn up to her chest, and hid her face in her hands.

Kernaghan snorted. "She'll be no trouble."

Aiken hissed something that Clara didn't quite catch, and the big man flushed, an unpleasant expression on his face.

Then they left her there. The door had a rusty iron handle with a keyhole beneath it. Clara heard the key turn in the lock. At least she was alone.

Once the sound of their feet had moved away, she scurried over to the door and stuck her ear to the blistered wood.

". . . her here until tomorrow night at least. We just need everyone looking away from the . . ."

Then another door closed and the voices were shut off.

It didn't take long to check every corner of the room for a potential escape route. The window was her only hope, and that was boarded up. Her spirits lifted when she realised it was boarded from the inside, and a faint draught of cold air suggested there was little or no glass behind the wood, but it was nailed firmly in place, and she had no tools to draw the nails even if the heads hadn't been driven deep into the soft wood.

The floorboards were in surprisingly good condition, with only a few mouse-chewed holes. No way out downwards. She eyed the window again. If she could only lift a couple of the nails, the ones nearest the corner, maybe she could find something to lever it out and create a gap big enough to squeeze through?

She tried the tin lids first, but all she achieved was a deep cut at the base of her thumb from the sharp edge and a groove across the surface of the wood. She sucked at the cut and cursed.

After trying almost everything she could find, she finally lit on the idea of folding a lid to make it stronger and give her a blunt edge to hold.

She attacked the first nail with optimism, because this one was right in the corner and it didn't have its head as buried as some of the others. Her makeshift claw hammer bent at her first attempt.

She almost gave up then, huddled back in her corner, but when she licked her lips and tasted that blood, it rekindled her determination.

She held her breath, listening for footsteps. Was that the front door creaking? The wind had got up and the old house moaned more than ever. It meant she couldn't be certain she'd heard someone leave the house, but it also meant she wouldn't be heard as she tried to break through the boarded-up window.

She scrambled to her feet and took up her bent tool again. It was twisted beyond usefulness, but there had to be something she could use.

She tried to put her eye to the crack along the side of the window board. Earlier, there'd been daylight in that crack; now it was black. Had so much time passed? Richard would be sick with worry. She tried to work out the time and decided it must be after six. Her stomach gurgled agreement. She hadn't eaten since coffee and toast at breakfast time, and she'd been too sick with guilt and anxiety to eat much then.

There was nothing edible in this room. Even the empty tins had been licked and nibbled clean, but more importantly, there was no water in here.

As soon as the thought occurred to her, she tried to swallow and found her mouth dry. A flash of panic. They'd left her here to die. Her weakened body would feed the rats when she was no longer strong enough to fight them off.

She caught the fear and bottled it, as she'd learned to do when she was at sea and the weather turned dangerous. Take one step at a time and think it through.

Why would they want to kill her by neglect when they could have killed her easily at any time since they'd had her.

So, they needed her alive, at least for now. But no water? Maybe that meant they weren't planning to keep her here very long. How long could the human body go without water? Days? Weeks? She wracked her memory. She'd been taught this, years ago on a sea survival course.

Three days? She was pretty sure she'd heard the coach say three days, or less if it was a hot climate.

That didn't sound too bad. She could cope with being kept here for three days, couldn't she?

Unless they didn't care whether she lived or died as long as Richard thought she was alive and would pay to keep her that way.

A sound broke into her thoughts. The key turned in the lock and Kernaghan stuck his head inside, scowling. He had a tray in one hand, which he put on the floor, then he turned, left the room, and locked the door once more. She listened to his footsteps retreating.

She eyed the tray. A small loaf of brown bread, and a plastic bottle of water. Perhaps somebody did want her alive, after all.

CHAPTER 38

Richard met them at the front door. He'd run his hands through his hair so often that it stood on end, but he seemed oblivious. "Any news?"

"We have a lead we're following," Asha said. "We know where she was picked up and have a description of the vehicle."

"Picked up?" He sounded vague, as if he was sleep-deprived and not thinking straight. "By the bus? What happened to the tracker?"

Asha braced herself. "She didn't catch a bus. She planted her phone on another woman to mislead us and then met somebody. It's possible Clara may have been taken as a hostage. You're a very wealthy man, Mr Steele. They might be wanting to ransom her."

He sagged against the door post, his face draining of any remaining colour. Between them, she and Faith managed to get him up the stairs and into the family room. Faith, without needing to be told, busied herself with the kettle and rummaged around for biscuits in the cupboards. Richard sat with his face in his hands. Every so often, his shoulders heaved with a sob.

"Who?"

Asha hesitated, and he clocked the hesitation, drawing his own conclusions. She hadn't thought he could get any paler, but he did. "Those two bastards? The ones that killed Steve?"

He clutched at his chest, and she thought he might be having a heart attack, but he just wrapped his arms around himself and rocked like a child. She wanted to sit down next to him and wrap her arms around him, holding him close, but she had to stay professional, for both their sakes.

Faith put a mug of steaming, dark coffee down in front of him and a plate of chocolate biscuits. He didn't seem to notice.

A buzzer sounded and Asha jumped.

"That's the gate." Richard leaped to his feet and strode to the screen on the kitchen wall. It was a police car, and a woman stood at the gate, looking up into the camera. Claudia Fox, one of their family liaisons. Asha was glad it was her, because the older woman had years of experience, helping bereaved families and families of missing children. She couldn't have wished for a better person to help Richard through this. Also, she was Bangor born and bred, and therefore unlikely to have come under Patterson's influence.

"She's one of ours. How do I let her in?"

He pressed a button and the gates began to swing open, then he went back to his seat, rocking again. Asha thought her own heart would burst, watching his misery. *This is why we're not supposed to get close to people in a case.*

She sent Faith downstairs to let Claudia and the team in. She had two civilian techies from Bangor with her. They didn't bother introducing themselves but set about tracing the phone line to where it came into the building. Claudia, a motherly woman in her sixties with raven-black hair dressed in a beehive, sat down opposite Richard.

"Mr Steele? I'm Claudia Fox. I'll be staying here with you until we get Clara back home. My job is to make sure you're safe, and that you remain fully informed about everything that is going on during this operation. I'll also help to protect your privacy, especially in terms of press curiosity. Is there anything you need right now?"

He raised haunted eyes to her face. "I need to know that Clara is safe, and why they took her." He turned to Asha. "Is it because she gave you that statement? Is that why they took her? Because she knows too much?"

"It's really too early to tell. I'm sorry." The words tasted like ashes in her mouth. Platitudes that had been drummed into her through her training. Make no promises you can't keep. Don't speculate in front of the family.

"Now I'm here," Claudia said, "Detective Inspector Harvey and PC McAvoy can return to work. I promise I'll stay in close touch, so as soon as they find anything out, anything at all, I can pass it on to you."

He nodded, then he put a hand out to Asha. She took it in hers, and it trembled in her grasp.

"I know you'll find her," he said.

* * *

"Oh God, that was awful," Asha said as they drove away from the house. "That poor man."

Faith said nothing, concentrating on her driving. Her lips were clamped tight as if she wanted to say something but couldn't. She must have felt Asha's eyes on her because a slow flush spread up her neck and on to her cheeks. Asha let the silence stretch.

"I do feel sorry for him," she said at last. "But the sister deserves all she gets. She took those girls, even when she guessed what was going on."

The spite in her voice shocked Asha. "Are you sure you're in the best position to cast slurs like that, PC McAvoy?"

"I didn't know that's what they were doing. Not until I heard Clara Steele's story." She blinked quickly. "That's when I knew I had to come clean."

Asha was saved from having to reply by her phone ringing. It was Aaron.

"The super called in a favour and borrowed the helicopter, Ash. We've found the van. It's parked at a derelict house about fifteen miles down the coast from Steele's place. We sent an unmarked car to do a drive-by and they confirmed the registration plates. PEZ."

"Send the location to my phone."

Aaron didn't answer immediately. Then he cleared his throat. "Superintendent Sewell would like to know why you're not in your house, and why you're not resting."

"He's standing right there, isn't he?"

"Yep."

"Tell him I'm on my way back to my house now."

"Okay." Those two syllables reeked of disbelief.

"PC McAvoy? Take me back to my house, please," she said for the sake of anyone listening.

* * *

Sewell was waiting for her at her front door. He helped her out of the passenger seat and lent her an arm that she was glad to lean on as she hobbled into the house.

"What's been going on?" she asked.

"We have a perimeter set up around the house, but no sign of movement so far. If this is a hostage situation, we can't take any risks, so they're to stay well out of sight and off the police bands." He glanced at Faith, who had followed them in and was now standing just inside the door, shifting from foot to foot. "Have you anything new to tell me?"

"Yes, sir. PC McAvoy, would you please wait in the kitchen?"

"You can help DC Birch," Sewell added. "He's trying to find out who owns the place."

Faith went meekly enough, but she shot Asha a frightened look as she left, closing the door behind her.

"Well?"

"It seems PC McAvoy was recruited at a very young age by one of our senior officers, who happened to have a hand in human trafficking and drug smuggling, and groomed for a role as eyes and ears in the force for this senior officer."

Sewell closed his eyes as if he was in pain. "And do we have a name for the senior officer? Please tell me it was Alistair King."

"Afraid not, sir. This was since his time. PC McAvoy was recruited by DCS Patterson."

Asha filled him in with the rest of Faith's story. "Now Patterson no longer has a hold over her, she says she wants to help. It seems as if she was okay with snitching our every move until human trafficking was confirmed, although it seems a bit odd that she didn't put two and two together earlier than this, what with her mum and all."

"What happened to change PC McAvoy's mind?"

"She got word that her mother had died."

Sewell had visibly aged. There were lines around his mouth she hadn't noticed before. "Everyone has a tipping point," he said. "Do we think we can take her at face value now? That she won't turn on us the minute we take eyes off her?"

Asha bit her bottom lip. She sighed. "I am absolutely furious that she's been working for Patterson all this time, making complete fools of us all. Would Steve White and that poor French lorry driver still be alive now if she had been straight? Serge Durand had a young family, I'm told." She took a deep breath. "When she first confessed, I wanted to lock her up and throw away the key, but I've had time to cool down a little now. She had a pretty awful childhood, from the sound of it, and Patterson's groomed her ever since she was wee. She was shaping up to be a good officer, notwithstanding the leg-up she's received from the chief. We can't trust her fully, sir, but maybe we could make use of her for a bit of controlled leakage of information?"

"What have you in mind?"

"Well, I was thinking that if she let slip that we were following up on a sighting of Clara Steele getting into a car, say a silver hatchback, on the road to Belfast, that might give us some breathing space while we decide how to take a peek inside that house on the Ards Peninsula. Get them looking the other way."

He nodded. "All right."

"Sir?"

"Hm?"

"You're not acting very surprised. About the chief, sir."

"No." He shook his head. "I was talking to ACC Miller the other day. She was very interested in DCS Patterson's role in the pursuit and capture of Alistair King last year. It got me to thinking."

Asha laughed. "Harriet Miller. I should have guessed." When he looked puzzled, she added, "She's my mum's best friend. Seriously clever woman, and the reason I joined the PSNI in the first place. We always joke that my mum is a witch, but if that's the case, Harriet Miller is the leader of the coven. She has a sixth sense for people."

He laughed. "Okay. Try a limited leak of information and let's see what happens, shall we?" He opened the door and raised his voice. "Aaron? Could you and PC McAvoy join us in here, please?"

Faith sent a short text via the satellite phone to Patterson. She said this was the way she got in touch in between her regular scheduled times.

Sewell sent her back to the kitchen to continue the search with Aaron for the owners of the house on the Ards Peninsula. He had her satellite phone in his hand, in case there was a reply.

"I'd like a closer look at that house," he said. "We need evidence of Clara Steele being held there, or of Aiken and his friend staying there. This has to be fully covert, or we could put that young woman's life at risk."

Asha glanced at her watch. "It'll be dark soon, sir."

"Yes. I think we need one officer to go in with caution. The team I have watching the place said there's no sign of CCTV cameras or other security measures."

Aaron spoke from the open kitchen door. "No luck at all, sir. I can find nothing in Land Registry about the place, and none of the searches are turning up any results since it was sold to a mystery buyer at auction in the early eighties."

Sewell pulled a face. "It shouldn't be this hard to track down ownership of a building, even a derelict one."

"Someone hiding their tracks, sir?" Aaron said.

"Possibly, and in this country it could be political. Organised crime on a sectarian basis. They're really good at covering their tracks."

"With your permission, sir, I'd like to be the one to reconnoitre the property."

Sewell smiled. "Good. Just the man for the job." Then he turned to Asha. "When's this one joining our team?"

"When he gets off his arse and takes his sergeant's exams, sir?"

CHAPTER 39

Aaron was already wearing dark clothes, but he changed his leather shoes for a pair of trainers he kept in his car boot.

"They're white," Asha said flatly. "You'll show up like a beacon." She went into the kitchen and rummaged in a cupboard, emerging with shoe polish. "You could darken them with this?"

Aaron shuddered. "Do you have any idea how much these cost? They're Gucci."

"Gucci knock-offs, I think you mean," Sewell said. "I've seen those in St George's Market for a score."

"Not knock-offs, sir!" Aaron stared down at them glumly. They'd cost him over £400, and he'd hardly worn them. But there was a young woman whose life might be in danger. He sighed. "Give me the polish."

Sewell patted him on the shoulder. "What size are you, son? I have my gym bag in the car boot, and my trainers are black."

A few minutes later, Aaron was wriggling his toes inside a pair of trainers that were slightly small for his size ten feet, but they were well worn and still had a bit more stretch left in them. He tried not to think about Sewell sweating in the gym.

Asha had the satellite view of the property up on the big screen, zoomed in as far it could go without losing detail.

Sewell pointed to a position to one side of the house. "This is where the van is parked. There are tall hedges surrounding the place, and the main gate doesn't look as if it's been opened in years, but there's a farm track that approaches the main building from the rear, off the Cloughey Road." He traced a pale line along several field boundaries.

"We think they must have come in that way. But the patrol says the hedge at the front is thin in places and a determined officer could push his way through."

Aaron remembered pushing his way through a similar hedge when he was trying to give Asha back-up in a previous case. It had left his leather jacket in shreds. "Yes, sir. Determined officer. Got it."

"The team are here." Sewell pointed again. "No sign of life yet, apparently, but they'll call if they see anything."

Aaron flexed his shoulders. "Okay, sir. I'll go now. It'll be dark enough by the time I get there."

He turned to go but was stopped by Asha's hand on his arm. Her dark eyes were troubled. "Take care, Aaron, won't you? You know how dangerous those two can be."

He smiled reassurance. "This is just a recce. I promise, Ash. Sneak in, have a look, retreat and call in the cavalry if necessary."

"No heroics?"

"Promise."

* * *

Promise. That word echoed in his head now as he crept along the hedge to where the two officers had told him the hedge was thinnest. Maybe it had looked thin in daylight, but now, with not even moonlight to help him, it seemed a formidable barrier.

Still, he was here to scout, so he needed to get through, and the rusty, lopsided wrought-iron gate was no use at all.

It looked as if it'd collapse into a pile of shrieking metal fragments if a bird landed on it.

He took a deep breath, pulled up the collar of his thick woollen jacket, and started to push his way through the hedge.

He emerged the other side, cursing under his breath. His hands and cheeks stung with dozens of tiny scrapes. Why did it always have to be a thorn hedge?

The house was surrounded by long grass, dead and crunchy underfoot as the frost began to bite. The satellite images had shown him the ghost of a pathway, running diagonally across what must have once been a nice garden to the house. He felt his way toward it, glad when his feet skidded on a stone slab. It must have been paved once, but years of neglect had covered it in weeds. At least they were quieter underfoot, even if they were slimy.

There were no lights on in the house that he could see. He touched the rough brickwork, then felt his way along to the nearest window. It was too high for him to see in, but the old building had been designed with a decorative row of stone around its base, and that layer stuck out slightly from the brickwork. It was barely more than a toe-hold, but with care he thought he might be able to lever himself high enough to get a glimpse through the window.

He grasped the sill as firmly as he could, but it was slimy with moss and his grip wasn't secure. One foot on the ledge and he hoisted himself up, glad the trainers were a size too small and not a size too large.

He only managed a couple of seconds before his hands slipped and he fell back down, but it was enough to show him two things. One was that the window was boarded up from the inside, and the second was that a faint strip of light showed at the very edge, where the MDF hadn't been cut quite straight. Someone was home.

Once he knew the house was occupied, he abandoned any further attempts to look in windows. He'd been lucky that time, and his fall had made no noise, but if he'd landed on a clump of dead thistles or a fallen branch, he could have alerted the inhabitants to his presence.

Priorities. He edged around the house to where the van was supposed to be, near a corrugated metal shed. He smelled old diesel oil before he touched the cold metal of its bonnet. Without light, there was no way to determine whether it had been resprayed or not. He ran his fingers over the edges of each panel of the bodywork, trying to feel if there might be a change in texture suggesting two different paints.

This was useless. He had no idea.

A long look back at the house showed several darkened windows on this side, where a wary ex-peeler might be sitting to watch for movement.

Damn it. Unless he could see the van, this was a waste of time. He tried the back door, expecting it to be locked, but it opened easily and with only the faintest of creaks.

No light came on inside, which was a blessing. He felt inside the double doors. The one he'd opened was lined with soft plastic, but the other one was bare metal as if the lining had been ripped away.

An image flashed into his mind, of a woman held captive in the back of a moving van last summer. A woman who had managed to break free and survived. That van had been red; this one was, according to the team, green.

He stuck his head around the side. Still no sign of life from the house. He held up his phone on the camera setting, shielding it as best he could with his hand, and pointed it at the van door. The flash was blinding, wrecking his night vision even in that fraction of a second, and the door lining, after all that, was green.

He checked the image on his phone anyway. Had it all been green? Was there a touch of red behind one of the reinforcing spars? It could have been rust, of course.

He zoomed in. There it was: a line of red paint beneath a strip of green metal where it would have been hard to get the spray nozzle.

He pocketed his phone and closed his eyes, willing the bright after-images to fade so he could see his way back through the overgrown site.

A soft sound alerted him. A door closing? It was all the warning he needed. He swished through the long grass, but he didn't slow until he had the flimsy shed between him and the van. Then he stood with his back to it, feeling the heat sucking from his body and into the cold metal. Someone was coming, and they weren't trying to be quiet.

One person? He thought so, but couldn't be sure. It was difficult to control his breathing, and his pounding heart must surely sound like a Lambeg drum in the silence of the night.

A twig snapped and someone stumbled, cursing. Then the wall of the shed moved as if a heavy body had pushed against it. If this was someone doing the security rounds, they were being pretty clumsy about it. Harsh breathing came closer and Aaron braced himself to move if the intruder came his way.

Instead, he heard a sharp rasp and a light appeared, silhouetting the edge of the shed. It went out almost immediately, but was followed by the aroma of cheap cigarettes. Someone breathed out a long sigh that turned into a hacking cough, shaking the flimsy shed wall.

"Fuckin' A," growled a voice. "'Mind the lassie,' he says. 'Don't take your eyes off've her,' he says. 'I've business to attend to.' Dickhead."

That was Kernaghan, all right, but more breathless and unfit than before, if that was possible.

He waited for the man to say something else, but it seemed he was done. The glowing butt landed in the grass at Aaron's feet and sat there like a baleful red eye, staring up at him.

If Kerny came around here looking for it, he was done for. He fingered the Glock at his belt, but if he fired it now, he'd alert anyone still inside the house and that couldn't end well for Clara Steele. Reluctantly, he pulled his hand away and hefted the Maglite instead, but then he heard the other man retreating back towards the house, still muttering.

Once he was certain he'd really gone, Aaron reached out a foot and put it down firmly on the fag-end, extinguishing it in the frosty grass. His armpits were soaking with sweat.

He made his way back to the hedge and pushed through. An arm came out of the darkness and helped him, hauling him through the last bit. He straightened and brushed himself down.

"Kernaghan is there with the missing woman." Honesty made him add: "At least I assume it's her he's muttering about. And it is the right van. It used to be red."

As the message was relayed back to Sewell and Asha, Aaron knew he should feel elated that they'd found Clara, but he didn't. He just felt a heavy dread deep in his gut.

CHAPTER 40

Sewell gave Asha a grim smile. "The van used to be red."

Asha closed her eyes. "It probably has some repairs to the back door, too. A woman was abducted in a red van in a case last year. She ripped the back door panel apart to escape. We can check that later, to add to the chain of evidence and connect the two cases."

"I think we have enough to take this up a level, don't you?"

"Sir?"

"I think a phone call to ACC Miller might be in order."

"Skipping the chain of command, sir?"

"Until we know for certain that Patterson's behind all this . . ." He put up a hand to stop her interrupting. "We only have PC McAvoy's word for it so far, and a gut feeling. That isn't enough to proceed against a serving senior officer with an unblemished career behind her. So until we have confirmation, I think we need to go straight to the top."

"What do you want me to do, sir?"

"I should be telling you to rest, but I know you won't, so instead, I'm suggesting that you call ACC Miller. You have a family connection, and we might need all the leverage we can get to persuade her to give us the go-ahead on a covert operation. And I think we'll move ourselves back to the station. I don't see that the chief has the right to dictate to you where you spend your recovery time, especially not now."

Harriet Miller had always been distant and aloof to the young Asha, and once her friend's daughter decided on a career in the PSNI, she'd become positively frosty. Miller hated nepotism with a vengeance and would have chopped off her own right arm with a blunt axe before she'd show favouritism.

"I'm not sure the ACC is such a good idea, sir."

"Really?" He seemed surprised. "It seems like an excellent idea to me. Do you have her number, or will I look it up for you?"

Cornered. "I have her mobile number, sir."

It was only as she hit call that she remembered it was Tuesday, and Harriet Miller always spent Tuesday nights with Asha's mother and a select few influential female friends. They drank brandy, played bridge and talked about current affairs. Her father had a theory that the real political decisions of this tiny province were made during those bridge evenings, not in the marbled halls of Stormont. The fact that it was also New Year's Eve would be unlikely to change their schedule.

The phone continued to ring. She considered ending the call and telling Sewell there'd been no reply, but that would be a craven act. And then the ACC answered.

"Asha? What do you want?" The words: "don't you know I'm busy?" hung unsaid in the ether.

"I'm very sorry to bother you, ACC Miller," she said stiffly. Hopefully by not calling her "Aunt Harriet" she'd get the message across that this was serious. "We have an abducted young woman and a firm lead on two of the cases we've been working: a drug ring and a human-trafficking operation. We've located the place the young woman is being held, and Superintendent Sewell asked me to contact you to seek permission to gather a task force."

There. It was said, and she'd managed to palm some of the responsibility on to the super, too.

She could imagine Aunt Harriet's face, giving nothing away as she thought through the ramifications of what she already knew and added it to the new information. Asha thought she recognised her mother's low voice in the background.

"Ladies, I'm afraid I might need to leave you for a while," ACC Miller said. "Work calls."

A cacophony of voices uttered complaints, then her mother's voice cut through them all. "Of course, Harriet. We understand. I'll pour your coffee into a non-spill mug so you can drink it on your way."

Then the voices faded and crockery clinked. Her mother said, very clearly, "Please tell Asha to take care when you see her. She's running out of new hospitals to survey."

"A hospital will be the least of her worries if she's dragged me away from my bridge without a very good reason."

Asha winced. Two witches.

Then the ACC must have left the house because there was a rustling, the sound of a car engine, and the tone of the call changed. ACC Miller had put her on speaker.

"Now, DI Harvey. Tell me everything while I drive."

Asha put her phone on speaker and nodded to Sewell, almost forgetting that this was her mother's friend as she carefully laid out the history of the cases, including Faith's background and revelations, and her own suspicions of DCS Patterson. She ended by telling her about the derelict property and Aaron's report about Kernaghan. Miller listened without interrupting until she'd finished.

"You said you want to put together a task force. What are you hoping to achieve?"

"From what DC Birch overheard, it seems they have Clara Steele inside that house. We'd hope to liberate her and arrest Kernaghan at the same time."

"On what charge?"

Asha was taken by surprise by the question. She looked to Sewell for help.

He shrugged. "Take your pick. We're still looking for DNA evidence to place him at the scene of Steve White's fatal attack, and in Serge Durand's hotel room, but I think we have plenty to hold him, ma'am, if not from this case, then from last year's fiasco."

"And if we find him guarding Clara Steele, we'll have him on an abduction charge as well, ma'am," Asha added.

"Hmm." Miller didn't sound convinced. "It seems to me that most of the evidence you have from this case points to Aiken rather than Kernaghan. You have a positive ID on him from Richard Steele, who is still alive as far as you know?" She made it sound as if Asha and Sewell were personally responsible for the other deaths.

"Yes, ma'am, and we have a liaison with him. He's going nowhere."

"I'd really like to wait and see if Aiken returns before sending in a team to the property."

"But Clara—"

"Yes, Inspector. I know. Clara Steele." She huffed a sigh. "I'll order drone air cover with an infra-red camera. That should tell us how many people are in the house, and we can watch for Aiken returning as well. I'm on my way to Bangor station now, but I'll ring off and organise some back-up for you. I assume your resources are stretched as it is, Superintendent Sewell?"

"Yes, ma'am. But we're coping. I have a first-class team here."

"I'm sure you do," she responded in a dry voice, and then rang off.

Asha's palms were damp with sweat, and she put the mobile back in her pocket with a hand that shook a little. "Well, we've set the ball rolling now, sir."

"I think putting the cat in among the pigeons is a better analogy," he said. "We'd better let Aaron know what's happening, then head to the station. I want to be set up before the ACC arrives."

ACC Miller must have driven like a demon, because her outwardly unprepossessing grey Peugeot car drew up in the car park at Bangor PSNI station in well under the hour and a half it usually took Asha to drive from her parents' house in Rostrevor.

Her little office felt even smaller when the tall, dignified figure of the ACC strode in. She wore a red dress and lipstick. Her hair was coiffured and her nails buffed to perfection. Her eyes were like chips of granite.

Asha stepped forward to take her coat, a grey wool affair with a fur collar, but Harriet Miller flashed her a scornful glance. "Sit, girl, before you fall down. What on earth possessed you to continue working with a serious injury? You should hope your mother never finds out what you get up to."

Then she was back to being ACC Miller again. "I have a drone sitting above the property in surveillance mode. The operator reports two possible heat sources inside the building and no more. No sign of Aiken returning as yet."

Aaron had reported that there was no sign of life once more at the property. Where had Aiken disappeared to?

"We checked in with the team keeping an eye on Richard Steele," Asha said. "Nothing there, but the liaison, Claudia, says he's pacing like a caged lion. It's getting increasingly difficult to keep him from leaving the house to go looking for his sister himself."

ACC Miller twitched an eyebrow but said nothing.

Sewell shifted in his seat. "Ma'am?"

"Yes?"

"I'm worried about the condition of the hostage. Shouldn't we be going in after her?"

Miller pulled a face. "I think we may have to. I've organised an experienced team to meet your DC Birch. They should be nearly there by now. Once they've had the chance to assess the situation, we'll make a decision."

Good old Aunt Harriet. She'd planned all along to send people in after Clara Steele, despite her apparent reluctance.

A little while later, Asha's phone rang.

"Aaron, I'm putting you on speaker," she said. "There's myself, Superintendent Sewell, and ACC Miller here."

"There's an armed team here on standby," Aaron replied. "They've scouted the area and they think there are a couple of viable approaches they can use. I have their commander here."

There was a rustle as the phone was handed over, then another voice came on, with a thick Strabane accent. "ACC Miller, this is Willetts. We have two possible means of entry to the house, and I propose splitting my team and sending them into both. If there's only one man in there who's armed, we should be able to apprehend him with minimal risk to the hostage. We're waiting to hear from the overhead surveillance when he separates from the woman, assuming she's going to stay put in one place while he moves around."

"Very good. You have permission to proceed."

Then they waited. It seemed to Asha that the time stretched into hours, but the clock on the wall gave her the lie. It was barely half an hour before Aaron called to say that they were about to go in.

"I'm staying here as a line of communication," he said. "Especially as we're not able to—"

The sound of an explosion ripped through the room.

"Aaron!" Asha called. "Aaron, answer me!"

Silence. The line was dead.

A wail of grief broke the sudden silence. Asha hadn't noticed Faith standing in the doorway. Tears sheeted down the young officer's cheeks as she sank down in a boneless heap, sobbing Aaron's name.

Harriet Miller's face was pale, lips set, and it dawned on Asha that the older woman was as traumatised by the explosion as any of them. Then she snatched a radio from the table and called up the drone operator. "This is ACC Miller. What's happening on the ground?"

"An explosion of some sort, ma'am. It's sent all our equipment haywire. We're trying to get a clearer image of what's happened, but we're wary of going in too low in case there are further explosions."

"Keep me informed," ACC Miller snapped. "Asha, try DC Birch's phone again. Keep trying it."

In a daze, Asha did as she was told. Sweat trickled down her back. That sound, the terrible rending of the air as the explosion hit, had knocked the wind out of her as if she'd been lifted by the shock wave again.

She tried Aaron's mobile, but it just gave an engaged tone. She went through the motions with little guidance from her numbed mind, redialling again and again. The ACC was busy on her own phone, mobilising the emergency services and sending them to the property.

When her desk phone rang, Asha didn't react; it was Harriet Miller who lifted it and answered.

"Asha. You need to take this," she said. There was a look in her eye that Asha couldn't interpret. She dropped her mobile on the table and took the handset.

"Hello?"

"Ash! It's Aaron. I'm okay. I've been trying to get through to your mobile, but it's ringing engaged—"

Asha put him on speaker. "Can you repeat that please, Aaron? Someone here very much wants to hear it."

Faith made a small sound and uncurled from her position on the floor.

"I'm okay," Aaron said. "There was an explosion, and the house went up, but I'm fine."

"Stay where you are," Harriet Miller said, "and get ready to direct the emergency services. Stay on the line so you can keep us up to date."

* * *

Clara was sleeping fitfully, dreaming of Richard striding up and down and running his hands through his hair, as he did when he was upset. She was dragged back to full, heart-pounding wakefulness by an explosion that rocked the house, leaving her confused and disorientated. A flicker of orange beneath the door sent her heart racing even faster. Fire!

She rubbed her eyes to clear the stinging dust and tears, but her hands were grey with powder and only made things worse, and her head pounded from the noise. Think, woman! During a fire, you were supposed to stay low where there'd be more air, but this was different. Dust and debris filled the room from floor to ceiling. It was easier to breathe, standing. She couldn't see very far, but the cloud wasn't quite as thick at this level.

The paint on the inside of the locked door was beginning to blister, and the heat in the room was rising. Maybe the explosion had jolted the lock open or something?

Half a bottle of water remained from the ration she'd been given, so she whipped off an antimacassar from the back of an old, moth-eaten armchair and poured some of the water on to it until the cloth was soaked. Then she wrapped it around her face, covering her nose and mouth. She tried not to think of mouse droppings.

It was instantly easier to breathe. Another cloth acted as a glove while she tried the round doorknob, but the door remained immovable. She tried both pulling and pushing, just in case, but it was definitely locked. The rushing in her ears might be panic, but the roaring and popping of old wood burning was real enough. Then a new sound caught her attention. Someone else was coughing violently, and he was heading this way.

The door rattled, and she stepped back just in time as it was thrown open, bouncing back until it almost hit her.

The big man staggered in, his clothing smoking, and headed straight towards the corner where she'd been sitting. Apparently he was blinded by smoke, but he'd soon see that the corner was empty and then he'd be back, looking for her.

Quicker than thought, Clara was through the door. She slammed it behind her and turned the key in the lock.

The smoke was worse out in the hallway, and flames danced above her on the rotten staircase.

She ran blindly in the direction of the door she'd been brought in through, locating it by feel. Her eyes burned and stung, but this door was unlocked. She sobbed as it opened to her hand and swung wide to let in a gush of cold winter air.

CHAPTER 41

ACC Miller had told Aaron to stay where he was, but she didn't know where he was, not exactly. He'd followed the teams as they moved in, keeping a safe distance behind. There was plenty of cover nearby if he needed to go to ground.

He kept the line open as ordered but began to move stealthily towards the window he'd tried to look in before. From that corner of the house, he'd be able to reach the gate to direct the emergency services, and he'd also be able to help any injured team members trying to get back to their rendezvous point.

The fire burned noisily, a background roar of flames punctuated by occasional crackles almost as loud as gunfire. Ancient wooden beams exploding in the extreme heat.

Then there was real gunfire. He threw himself down, instinct taking over, but as he lay in the long grass, cursing a thistle that had managed to stab him through his shirt, just beneath his stab vest, he realised this was no ordinary gunfire. The sounds were staccato, a loud crackling explosion followed by individual shots.

Had the flames reached a cache of ammunition?

Then another sound made him freeze. There was a squeal like nails on a blackboard, and a corner of light showed at the base of the boarding. Was Clara trying to escape?

Another screech of protesting nails and the boarding was ripped away until the whole window showed as a rectangle of flickering light. The window above him creaked as someone raised the sash from inside. Fluent cursing in a harsh whisper as it stuck.

Kernaghan? Impossible to tell over the noise of the fire.

Aaron eased himself into a crouch and edged sideways until he was just to one side of the window. He loosened the Glock in its holster and silently ran through his training. Even though he rarely carried a handgun these days, he was familiar with the weapon and still attended the compulsory training. The chill of the hard polymer grip in his hand was reassuring.

The window sash gave one last protesting shriek and lost its battle. A moment later the ground shook as a heavy figure landed, maybe five feet from Aaron. He was silhouetted against the orange light of the flames, tall, heavy-set. It had to be Kernaghan.

He'd swear he'd made no sound as he raised the Glock, finger on the trigger, but some instinct brought Kernaghan snapping around to face him. Before Aaron could even pull the trigger, never mind shout a warning, Kernaghan's arm swung in a short arc and something hit Aaron across the shoulder, at the base of his neck. Pain lanced down his spine and up into his skull, and the gun dangled from his numbed fingers as his arm dropped uselessly to his side.

Then the big man was on him in a short charge that would have made a rhino proud.

The breath whooshed out of Aaron as he fell, Kernaghan on top of him. The gun was trapped somewhere between them, his finger mashed against the trigger guard. He tried to get a knee up to kick the other man in the balls, but his legs were pinned.

Now an arm came across his throat, pressing down, and breathing became the only thing that mattered. His throat rasped and his vision sparked. He had to move fast, before he lost consciousness.

With a heave and a twist, he managed to budge Kernaghan's body, only for a fraction of a second and no more than a few inches, but the brief respite had shifted the gun. He couldn't tell which way it was pointing, whether at Kernaghan's gut or his own, but the trigger was free now, and his finger had room to move.

As his vision began to fade, that finger twitched and the trigger moved past the first safety position. He made another attempt to throw the big man off him, but his strength was draining away with the air in his lungs.

Kernaghan was a killer. If he'd ever doubted it, the expression in those steely eyes staring into his swept those doubts away. If he pulled the trigger the rest of the way, he might shoot himself, but he was wearing a stab vest. A stab vest that wasn't designed to stop gunfire at point-blank range. If he did nothing, he'd be dead anyway. Kernaghan wasn't going to stop when he lost consciousness; he'd finish the job and enjoy it.

Afterwards, he didn't know if it had been a conscious decision or a muscle spasm as the life faded from him, but the impact of the bullet shuddered through both their bodies. Everything went dark.

* * *

The sound of his own breath whistling was the first thing he became aware of, barely enough to keep him alive. He struggled to help it, heaving his chest, sucking at the life-giving air.

He'd heard an old street fighter say that the first full breath after being strangled was like a mountain waterfall after a drought. He wished he could tell the old man that he'd nailed it. Cold night air flooded into him, and his wits gradually returned.

Kernaghan still lay like a dead weight on top of him, but not dead enough. Foul, stinking breath washed over Aaron, smelling like an unflushed toilet after a curry party.

His strength returned, and he tried once more. This time, Kernaghan's body slid sideways and off him far enough for him to wriggle out from under. He knelt on the cold ground and patted himself down. He was sticky with blood that was already coagulating into lumps, but he felt no pain, except some bruised ribs that felt as if he'd been punched.

The Glock still dangled from his right hand. He holstered it and swallowed. He'd never shot a man before.

The squeaky, tinny voice finally penetrated his consciousness. As he dropped to one knee to check the big man for weapons and tried to decide if he should cuff him or not, he put the mobile to his ear.

"I'm here."

"Oh, thank God." Asha. "What the hell's going on, Aaron?"

"I've got Kernaghan, but he's been shot." He tried to work moisture back into his dry mouth. Training. Prioritise. "I need an ambulance here fast, and a team to secure him. I don't think he's going anywhere."

"Is he still alive?"

"Still breathing."

She spoke to someone in the background, then came back to him. "There's an ambulance on its way, and we're sending some of the team to you now. And Clara Steele is safe. She managed to get out and one of the teams found her."

Aaron fished the Maglite out of his pocket and tried the switch, not expecting it to work, but the beam flashed out for a brief moment before shutting down. Damn. He still had it to the law-enforcement setting. He clicked the switch again and the powerful beam shot out, turning the shadowy scene into a set from a war movie.

Kernaghan lay half on his side, one hand clutched to his belly. He hadn't been wearing a vest, and Aaron's bullet had entered his body a few inches below the ribs. Another splash of blood shone in the torchlight at the back of his chest. The bullet must have gone straight through, but what damage would it have caused as it ripped through vital organs on its path of destruction?

Kernaghan's eyes were half open, still glaring at him. His other hand opened and closed convulsively and his lips moved, but Aaron wasn't going to put his face close enough to hear what was being said.

Then there were flashing lights in the lane and someone was shouting his name.

"Over here!"

He stepped back to let the professionals do their job. The next half hour passed in a blur as they worked on the injured man before somehow getting him on to a stretcher. Aaron helped with that part, as did every able body around. Kernaghan weighed about as much as a young killer whale.

The medical party moved towards the lane, and Aaron was left alone in the darkness. He shone his torch around one last time before heading back to report. There'd be an investigation, of course. There always was after a police shooting, and he fully expected to be relieved of active duty until the investigation reached its conclusions, but for now no one was paying him any attention.

Just as he was turning away, the light caught the edge of a shape, almost hidden by the long grass. He swung the beam back around. It was a slim metal object, perhaps sixty centimetres long. A closer look revealed that it was thicker at one end than the other, not unlike a baseball bat but in dull, black metal instead of wood.

He remembered the pathologist's report regarding the injuries to Serge Durand and Steve White. A heavy, blunt object. A shiver rippled through him as he realised how lucky he'd been. He photographed it in situ with his phone camera from a few angles, including a wider shot to show where it lay in relation to the window Kernaghan had jumped from.

"DC Birch?" It was a uniformed officer Aaron didn't recognise. "I was sent over to secure the area." His eyes followed the direction of Aaron's torch beam. "Found something?"

"I think this could possibly be a murder weapon, so we need to preserve the scene. Can you call for someone to tape off the area and get a SOC team in here?"

The young officer radioed in the request and the reply came back promptly. A SOC team was on its way. The constable had blue tape with him, so Aaron helped him to string it around the area, with a generous margin in case anything else had been dropped during his struggle with Kernaghan.

The officer's radio squawked again. He replied, shooting a look at Aaron.

"They want you back at the station, sir. There's a car waiting for you in the lane."

Aaron nodded, too tired and too sore to speak. The distance to the gate, which someone had wrenched open and pinned back against the hedge, seemed longer than he remembered, and his feet dragged through the long grass.

The lane was filled with cars, their headlights dazzling him. Helicopter rotors spun overhead, high enough that there was little downdraught, but low enough that he could see the underside of the police aircraft with its spotlight highlighting an area to the west of the house.

Blackened roof beams reached towards the night sky, appearing and disappearing in a cloud of smoke and steam as fire appliances soaked the area with high-powered hoses. He realised with a lurch of shame that he'd quite forgotten about the second team, the ones who'd gone round the back of the house. Had they been caught up in the explosion?

"Sir? This way, sir." He was gently herded along the lane between parked and seemingly abandoned vehicles. An ambulance stood with its doors open, flooding light out on to the muddy verge. Two men sat inside, both conscious but dazed-looking. Their clothes were blackened and smoking, and one had a raw oozing burn on his temple that had singed away most of the hair on that side of his head. A paramedic was applying a burn dressing.

Aaron stopped and stuck his head inside. "You from the west team?"

The one with the burn nodded, then winced. He swallowed and tried to speak, but no words came.

"Everyone get out?"

A tired smile and a not-quite-nod gave him the answer, and he took a deep breath of relief.

CHAPTER 42

When Aaron walked into the incident room, Asha's heart leaped. He was filthy, covered in blood, and his left hand held his right arm across his body as if it needed a sling.

Before she could speak, Faith McAvoy was across the room. She flung her arms around him and buried her face in his filthy coat.

"Hey! Steady now." He pushed her away, but gently.

She backed away, brushing self-consciously at the blood she'd picked up from hugging him. "I'm sorry. Are you hurt?"

He shrugged. "How's Clara Steele? Any news?"

"Shaken but mostly unhurt," Asha said. "Claudia Fox, the family liaison, is bringing Richard up to the hospital to see her. We thought it best if she went for a check-up."

"And the two teams?"

"They were very lucky. The west team spotted the trip-wire but the initial investigation suggests the explosion may have been triggered from inside the house."

"Kernaghan, maybe. Any word on Aiken?"

"Nothing," Harriet Miller said. Asha had almost forgotten she was there, she'd been so quiet. "And he's not in the part of the house that survived. We won't know for a couple of days if he was in the part of the house that burned, but it seems unlikely. I think he's too cunning to get caught in his own trap."

Aaron nodded. "And what about Kernaghan? Will he pull through?"

Harriet Miller answered again. "He's going into surgery as we speak. I have an officer on duty at the hospital just in case he says anything, but he lost a lot of blood." She paused, a tiny crease between those perfectly made-up brows. "There'll be an investigation, DC Birch, but for now, can you tell me roughly what happened?"

He took them through the events that had led up to the gun firing. Asha sat down, weak with relief. Her own trouser leg was sticky with blood that had leaked through the dressing, but everyone was too busy to notice.

"So you didn't make a conscious decision to pull the trigger?"

"No, ma'am." His face twisted in a wry smile that made creases in the dirt covering his skin. "I couldn't tell which way the damn thing was pointing. If I pulled the trigger, it was a 50:50 chance I'd shoot myself instead of him. I think it must have been a muscle spasm as I lost consciousness, ma'am."

She sighed. "Very well. Make sure you tell it the same way during the investigation, and you should be all right."

Faith stirred. She'd retreated to the edge of a desk in the far corner of the room, out of Harriet Miller's line of sight. She took a breath, but Asha got in before her. That young woman was in enough trouble already without compounding it by springing to Aaron's defence.

"I'd very much like to know where Aiken is, ma'am. Why wasn't he in the house with Kernaghan? I don't like not knowing what he's up to."

"I agree, DI Harvey. I'd like you to head over to the hospital and see if Clara Steele is fit to be questioned. Maybe she knows something that could help us. I'll organise a uniform to drive you."

"Yes, ma'am." Her heart gave a little flutter. Richard would be at the hospital.

* * *

He was, but he looked haggard, sitting on a chair in a small waiting area with Claudia Fox, the liaison. Asha had a moment or two to collect herself before Claudia noticed her.

"Asha! Glad you could make it."

"Claudia. Richard. Any news about Clara?"

Claudia answered for him. "She has some superficial injuries" — Richard's hand clenched into a fist where it lay on his lap — "and she's tired and a bit shocked, of course, but the doctor says she's going to be just fine."

"That's great," Asha mumbled. Richard's emotions were naked in his eyes. It made it hard to think clearly.

Claudia stood and straightened her jacket. "I think I'll go and get a coffee and some chocolate from the machine on the next floor. Anyone want anything? No?"

Asha hobbled over to the empty chair beside him and lowered herself on to it. He took her hand in his and turned it over, frowning at the dried blood in the creases of her palm. "What's this?"

"Oh. Nothing."

He searched her face. "You're pale. Has your wound reopened? Have you seen a doctor?"

"No." She shook her head. "Well, yes, but that was . . ." When was it? So much had happened. She'd been due to go for a dressing change.

He stood up, letting go of her hand, and her skin felt chilled in its absence. "Nurse! Can you get a doctor to check DI Harvey? Urgently."

Such was the power of his personality, the diminutive Indian nurse left her station almost at a trot and disappeared in search of a doctor.

Asha tried to speak, but no sound emerged. She cleared her throat and tried again. "You shouldn't give me sympathy, not after what's happened to Clara." Tears pricked at the backs of her eyes.

"Clara's in good hands, but you've been running yourself ragged trying to find her, and no one's been looking after you." He rubbed the back of her hand with strong fingers and she swallowed down a sob. This was ridiculous. She never cried.

The nurse returned with a junior doctor in tow, his shirt and tie limp and a faint stain on the knee of his chinos.

Richard stood up, letting go of her hand. "Ah, Doctor. Detective Inspector Harvey here was involved in an explosion recently and she was wounded. Instead of resting, she's been on her feet and now the wound is bleeding again. Please could you have a look at it?"

Asha was fairly sure that ordinarily in this sort of situation, the junior doctor would recommend she go down to A&E, but one look at Richard's face seemed to convince him that he'd be wasting his breath. He straightened his tired shoulders and hunched over a computer terminal.

"If you give your details to me, I'll find your records."

Asha obediently gave the doctor her name and date of birth, aware of Richard listening in as he confirmed her address. She wondered if he'd notice that her birthday was imminent.

She followed the doctor into a small room lined with shelves and drawers, furnished with an examination couch and various wheeled instrument trolleys.

With the nurse present, Asha pulled down her trackpants as far as her upper thigh, where dried blood had welded the cloth to the blood-soaked bandage beneath. When she tugged, something tore and a hot gush of fresh blood flowed, soaking through the already blackened dressing.

"Whoa," the doctor said. "That's more than a slight bleed."

It took him and two nurses more than half an hour to stop the bleeding, while Asha lay on her front, trying not to cry out as they carefully teased apart the blood-soaked bandages to get to the wound.

"Some of your sutures have ripped out," he said. "We can sew you back up, Detective, but you're going to have to be more careful. You're very, very lucky the damage isn't worse. Please treat this as a serious warning and try to stay off your feet for at least a week, preferably two."

"Yes, Doctor," she said meekly. Anything to get herself out of this claustrophobic room that stank of antiseptic and cleaning chemicals.

Finally, they were done, and the nurse helped her to her feet, handing her the trackpants. "I'm afraid these are pretty wrecked. I can ask around and see if anyone has any spare trousers they can lend you?"

"Honestly, don't bother," Asha said, "I can roll this leg all the way to the top and tuck it in, and the other leg is fine."

The nurse held up the trousers and looked dubiously at the rusty patches in the right leg. "If you're sure?"

"I'm sure. I don't think this new bandage will fit into the trouser leg anyway, not fastened."

The nurse smiled. "Possibly not. It's based on what we call a Robert Jones bandage, don't ask me why, but it's designed to stop the leg bending. It's usually used for fractures, but the doctor thought it might slow you down a bit and stop you from opening the wound again."

Asha rubbed the thickly layered material. The surface was so hard that she could tap it like a drum with her fingernails. "Yes, I can't exactly see myself running after a suspect with this one. How long must I keep it on?"

She consulted the doctor's scrawled notes. "A week, and then you're to report to your GP to get it removed. He's sending them a letter."

"Thank you," Asha remembered to say as she hobbled out of the room. This new, stiff, fat leg was going to take some getting used to. She had to swing it wide as she walked because the padding was so thick.

Richard was no longer where she'd left him. The two seats were empty, and she noticed with a small stab of guilt that the one she'd been sitting on had a dark stain on it. More work for the worn-out hospital cleaners.

A door down the corridor swung open and Richard stuck his head out.

"Clara needs to talk to you."

CHAPTER 43

The hospital room was quiet, clean, and impersonal. Clara lay on the white sheets, embracing their coolness. Every part of her body ached, and a persistent hammer was driving inside her skull. The doctors had said it was the after-effects of smoke inhalation, and that it would ease with time as long as she took it easy. The machine at her bedside beeped regularly, measuring her pulse and her oxygen levels, which were apparently surprisingly good for someone who'd survived a fire.

She was finally alone, all the doctors and nurses having moved on, satisfied that she was stable enough for now, but there would no doubt be a police officer on guard outside this private room.

There must be something useful she could tell the police. Something to stop her kidnappers and the man they worked for.

The door opened, and Richard peered in. A lump rose in her throat. He looked terrible.

"They said I can come and spend a bit of time with you," he whispered, "but I'm not to let you talk too much."

She smiled and patted the bed. She didn't feel much like talking, but there were things that needed to be said.

"I'm sorry." It came out as a hoarse rasp, but he understood. He took her hand in his and cradled it like an injured bird.

"You've nothing to be sorry about. You're safe now, and that's all that matters. Everything else can wait."

"Catch them?" she asked. She'd need to ration her words if she was to get the vital information across.

"I think they said they've picked up one of them, but the other might have been caught in the explosion."

"Which one?" she mouthed.

"They caught the big fella, Kernaghan, but the other one, the little ginger one, is still missing."

The overheard words came back to her again.

"Police . . ." She struggled, then added, "Need to tell . . . Important."

"There's a constable just down the corridor?"

"No. More senior."

"Okay. DI Harvey is here." He flushed slightly. "Asha. She's being seen by a doctor because her wound opened up again, but I can get her in here as soon as they've finished with her?"

Clara nodded gratefully. Yes. Asha was just the person. She'd understand the importance of what Clara had to tell.

He returned a few minutes later with Asha Harvey, hobbled somewhat by a heavy dressing that stretched from upper thigh to ankle. The detective cursed as she almost lost her balance. Richard caught her with a firm hand beneath her elbow, and she flashed him a warm smile as she slipped into the chair by Clara's bed.

"I'm so glad you're okay," she said to Clara.

Clara flushed, but this was too important for guilt to stop her from talking. "I overheard . . ." Her voice broke and she swallowed painfully. "Useful," she croaked.

Asha's face brightened. "From Aiken and Kernaghan?"

She nodded to save words. "Till . . . tomorrow night. Need to . . . keep everyone looking." Another swallow. "Away from . . ."

"Tomorrow night," Asha mused. "And they needed everyone looking away from . . . what?"

"Didn't hear." Clara made another effort. "Aiken went out . . . soon after . . . left Kernaghan." Her voice was getting a little stronger, but her throat itched abominably.

Asha's face closed as she retreated into deep thought. Richard shot her a concerned look, but Clara shook her head and smiled at him. "Thinking," she mouthed.

Then the young detective seemed to shake herself. "Will you excuse me for a moment? I need to make a phone call." She hobbled out of the room faster than she'd entered.

"Don't talk," Richard said. "Just nod or shake your head."

She nodded, trying to smile with her eyes.

"Did they hurt you?"

She shrugged and indicated a strike to her head, holding up a finger to indicate "once". That backhander had been enough to knock the fight out of her. The hammering picked up its beat a little. "No food," she said. Whispering helped.

He grinned. "So, torture, then?"

"So sorry," she said again. "So stupid."

He moved closer and put his arm around her. "We all do stupid things from time to time. That's how we learn and grow."

Tears pricked her eyes. That's what their mother used to say to them when they were wee. She swallowed and buried her face in his shirt collar. He smelled of sweat and fear, and she sobbed for what she'd put him through.

* * *

"Where are you?" Yvonne hated the vulnerability in her voice, yet that was one of the reasons she loved Ole so much. He made her feel feminine, and with that came vulnerability.

He had to shout over the noise of the engines. "Almost there. Are you sure the way is clear?"

"Certain. One of my little birds messaged to tell me they're looking in the wrong place completely. They're chasing phantoms miles from the boatyard. It's safe, my love."

"I don't like using this place you told me about. It's had too much attention already."

"I know, but I've organised such an excellent diversion. No one will have time to look that way until we're clear. It's easy access, and there'll be no one there. In this weather, it's really your only option apart from Bangor, and that's far too public. We're keeping the local police very busy elsewhere, I promise you."

"I trust you, Vonnie. We'll be there in less than half an hour. Will you be meeting me?"

She smiled, even though he couldn't see her. "I'll be there."

"Be careful," he said, then the connection ended, and Yvonne Patterson looked down at the rectangle of plastic in her hand. Her mouth was dry, but the hand that held the satellite phone was steady.

The corridors were empty as she walked briskly along them, taking the stairs in preference to the lift that always smelled of stale urine and vomit. She couldn't bear him to smell that on her.

Outside, the night sky was clearing but clouds scudded across, blotting out the half-moon periodically. She'd have preferred a moonless night for this adventure, but then the tides wouldn't have served, or so Ole assured her.

There were few cars in the car park. She slid into the silver Mercedes and let the engine run for a moment to clear the misted windscreen before driving out through the barrier and into the streets of Belfast.

A flash of multicoloured light illuminated the sky, then another and another and she remembered it was New Year's Eve. A new year, a new life. She would be glad to see the back of this dreary city with its miserable people. Alistair King had known what he was doing, building his own private paradise far from here. But rural isolation wouldn't suit her. She liked having people around her.

A picturesque town at the edge of a fjord? That, she could work with. And Ole was thinking of standing for mayor next year. He'd been popular as an alderman and stood a good chance of being elected, despite his slightly shady past. With her at his side, he'd be unbeatable.

As she passed drunken merrymakers at the City Hall, she was almost tempted to call it in. They were staggering in loose groups across the road in front of cars. A bottle flew through the air and bounced off her windscreen to shatter on the pavement in a foam of beer.

Then she remembered this city was no longer her problem.

It was a good thought.

CHAPTER 44

"Ma'am, it's DI Harvey. I've just been in to see Clara Steele."

"Is she all right?" The ACC sounded distracted, but Asha persevered.

"Yes, ma'am. She's shaken but thinking clearly." Asha filled her in. "And she's pretty sure Aiken left the property shortly after."

"So you think this whole operation, the kidnapping and the explosion, were just a big distraction?"

"I don't know about the explosion, ma'am. That seems a bit like overkill, so maybe it was a mistake, but I do think the kidnapping was a distraction, yes. And it worked beautifully." The last sentence came out more bitterly than she'd intended. "I'd give my right arm to find out where Aiken disappeared to."

"As would I," Miller said.

"Do we still have that helicopter available, ma'am?"

"We do. What are you thinking?"

"This entire affair has centred around the Steeles, especially the boatyard and marina."

"You think they're involved?"

"No!" Asha said firmly. "Richard Steele has been worried sick about his sister, and I can't see him letting harm come to his yard manager, plus he was injured himself when the truck was stolen, and could easily have been killed. It's too elaborate to be a smokescreen, ma'am. I think we can clear him, and probably Clara, too."

She could almost hear the cogs going around in the ACC's head. "You think the distraction is to keep us looking away from the boatyard and marina?"

"I do. Can you get the helicopter to take a look? The place will be closed up with Richard here at the hospital and Steve White dead."

"I'll do that." There was muffled speech. "But I want you back here, at Bangor police station as soon as you can."

"Yes, ma'am. On my way." ACC Miller ended the call before Asha remembered that she didn't have the use of a car, and even if she did, she'd be unable to drive it with this great, clumsy bandage.

She wondered if she dared to ask the uniformed constable who was on duty outside Clara's room, but when she turned, Richard was standing not six feet from her, a quizzical look on his face.

"Thank you," he said.

Asha felt the blush rising inexorably up her neck. "What for?" It came out far too stiff and formal.

"For vouching for me to your superior. I'm glad you trust me enough to do that, even if—"

"Even if what?"

He smiled, genuinely amused now. "Even if I can't seem to persuade you to have dinner with me."

She opened her mouth, then closed it again. He laughed aloud. "When this is all over, maybe I'll try again," he said, then looked pointedly at her leg. "But in the meantime, I think you need a driver. Am I right?"

* * *

ACC Miller got the helicopter back out and requested a high flight over the boatyard. The crew reported no visible activity, although there was a car parked on the road a few hundred yards from the entrance and the possibility of several faint heat sources inside the building. Nothing definite. Their main concern was a trawler not far offshore that wasn't showing up on the AIS system. It appeared to be on a direct course for the boatyard. The ACC decided it was enough to warrant sending a team in for a closer look.

She had initially refused to let Aaron go to the boatyard with the armed team. "You've done enough, DC Birch. Besides, Professional Standards and the Policing Board are going to be all over you like a rash after Kernaghan's shooting. I can't take any chances with you."

"But, ma'am—"

"But nothing."

Then the commander of the tactical squad spoke up. "If not DC Birch, have you anyone else who knows the place well?"

ACC Miller had looked at Aaron, who shrugged. "Only DI Harvey, and she's injured. Otherwise, it's just civilians."

Faith cleared her throat. "Sergeant Casey and PC Christie would know the boatyard, sir. They helped rebuild the place after Aiken demolished it, remember?"

"Good. That's settled. Radio Sergeant Casey, Constable, and tell him to report back here immediately."

Aaron listened in to the briefing given by the commander. He still hadn't given up on the idea of joining them.

"Ma'am?" Faith said in a small voice. "I can't raise either the sergeant or PC Christie on radio or on their mobiles. I've checked, and they are on duty. Their last check-in was nearly half an hour ago, and they were patrolling the coast road from Donaghadee back towards Bangor."

Aaron had a bad feeling about this. "Ma'am. They're both local men, born and bred. That road would take them right past the boatyard and if they saw any sign of activity, they might have stopped for a look." He shut up, feeling that the ACC wasn't a woman to be driven into an action before she'd thought it through.

Harriet Miller made an impatient noise. "Is there *anyone* in this godforsaken backwater who obeys orders?"

Aaron opened his mouth to speak.

"Not one word, DC Birch. You're as bad as the rest of them."

Superintendent Sewell stood up and stretched. "I think we should send Aaron," he said. "He's sensible, he's up to date with his firearms training, and didn't I read somewhere that you'd applied for the ARU at one time?"

"Yes, sir, but then I made detective," Aaron said. He held his breath, waiting for the ACC to make up her mind.

She huffed out a breath. "Very well. It seems you'll get your way, Birch. Go and get changed and book out a ballistics vest and shield."

"Yes, ma'am!" If Tom and Jim had got themselves into trouble, he wanted to be there to help.

* * *

The black Jaguar was deceptively spacious inside, with plenty of room for her and the Robert Jones bandage. It was the first time she'd been in a car with Richard driving, and she was pleasantly surprised. With a car like this, she'd expected fast acceleration and late braking with bonnet dips at every red light, but instead she found herself relaxing.

"So, you think my sister's kidnapping was a diversion?" he asked out of the blue. "They took her to draw the police's attention away from my boatyard? But why?"

"Hmm. I think they did, but I wonder if Aiken and Kernaghan might also have thought about ransoming her, maybe against orders. Patterson will have wanted her dead, because she can identify this Norwegian man. I expect that bomb was meant to put an end to her, once they'd finished whatever they're planning for tonight." She was getting sleepy after all the alarms and excursions of the night, and the car engine was so quiet it barely registered in her mind.

She must have dozed off, because she woke with a start as the car hit a pothole.

"Happy New Year," he said, sounding amused.

She blinked and looked around. It was still full dark, but at this time of year the sun wouldn't rise until after seven o'clock. She glanced at her watch — only a quarter past two. How had they packed so much into one brief night?

"Where are we?"

He didn't answer, but when the sign for a coastal holiday village flashed past, she knew. "Richard! You're supposed to be taking me to the station. What the hell are you thinking?"

He drew a deep breath. "I'm sorry. I'll take you back there shortly, but I need to see if there's anything going on at the boatyard first."

"No!" She struggled to sit up. "This is beyond stupid. Have you any idea how dangerous this is? Take us back to the station right now!"

His fingers clenched a little more tightly on the steering wheel, but that was the only indication that he'd heard her. The car, if anything, accelerated slightly. In a couple of minutes, they'd be passing the entrance to the boatyard.

He allowed the car to slow at the top of the hill that wound down to the boatyard entrance.

"At least keep going at the same speed," she hissed at him "Don't you dare stop, Richard. I mean it."

As the gate flashed past they saw it was standing wide open.

Richard cursed fluently and let the car slow even more.

"No! Keep going. We mustn't be seen, Richard."

Reluctantly, or so it seemed to her, he pushed the big car onwards. They climbed the hill and kept going along the coast road that would eventually take them to Donaghadee.

"Wait!" Asha had seen something that caught her eye. "Stop the car."

"Make your mind up," he said through gritted teeth. But he brought the Jag to a gentle stop, engine purring.

"Just back there. A car. I think it might be Sergeant Casey and PC Christie. What on earth are they doing here?"

"I can turn just up ahead in a driveway. Want me to go back?"

Asha bit her lip, undecided. She had a responsibility to keep herself, and especially a civilian like Richard, well away from any danger, but then Tom Casey and Jim Christie might be in danger themselves. Tom was supposed to be winding down towards retirement. He was a relic of the days when a policeman would only have to stand under a lamp-post, rising up and down on to his toes, hands clasped behind his back, for the most violent pub brawl to fizzle out and the antagonists to slink away before they could be collared. Sewell had told her more than once that he was worried the old sergeant thought himself invincible.

"Yes. Go back." It hurt to say it. "Lights off and drive slowly until I tell you to stop."

He did as she said, then stopped the car across the farm gateway Tom Casey had used to hide the unmarked car he'd been driving. The car was empty.

"Shit." She pulled out her mobile and dialled Harriet Miller's line direct.

"Asha? I expected you back by now."

"Yes, ma'am. Sorry. Mr Steele had other ideas." She began to explain where they were, and about the empty police car. The ACC latched on immediately.

"Damnit! Why does no one ever do what they're told these days? I have an armed team going in there at any moment, and I need you as far away from there as possible. Do you hear me—"

A blast of automatic gunfire interrupted. Asha swore. "Did you hear that, ma'am? It was very close."

"I did. Get back here, right now. I already have a team in place, and I don't want you or any civilians anywhere near."

"Yes, ma'am." She ended the call and turned to Richard. "Drive. Back to the station, Richard. I mean it, No detours!"

This time he didn't argue. The big car lived up to its namesake, carrying them silently through the night until the lights of Bangor came into view. He pulled into the police station car park and Asha scrambled out, almost falling on her face as her fat leg caught on the sill. He was there immediately, helping her with an arm around her waist. She was too distracted to rebuff him, accepting his help all the way to the incident room.

ACC Miller had set up whiteboards as screens to show the views from several different video feeds. The main one seemed to be from a drone or helicopter. It showed a black background with more than a dozen pale blobs moving around. Heat sources. Another screen showed the feed from a body camera: a group of men in the dark uniform and body armour of the PSNI's armed response unit.

It took Asha a moment to orientate herself, but when the man carrying the body camera turned, she recognised a landmark, a patch of scrubby whin bushes hugging the remains of a piece of rusting farm equipment, not far from the road she'd driven along with Richard a short while before.

The cameraman turned the other way, and the faces of his team swam into view, almost unrecognisable with their helmets and eye protectors. But one face stood out from the group, because she knew it so well.

ACC Miller made an impatient noise and gave Richard a look that would have cowed a lesser man. "I can't have civilians in here during an operation. I need you to leave, Mr Steele. Now." She gestured to one of the uniformed PCs. "Please escort Mr Steele out of the building and make sure he leaves the premises."

Richard searched Asha's face.

"She's right, Richard. You should go."

He gave a lopsided smile and turned on his heel.

"Good," ACC Miller said. "To bring you up to date, DI Harvey, we're moving into a mobile incident unit. You can come with us, but only if you promise not do anything strenuous."

Asha controlled her features. "Thank you, ma'am."

* * *

Now she sat in the back seat of the lead car, sandwiched between ACC Miller and Superintendent Sewell. She suspected it was mostly so her mother's friend could keep an eye on her.

The officer in the passenger seat turned to speak to them. "Just received a message from the ARU, ma'am. Contact confirmed. No sign of Horseshoe yet but they have Pipistrelle under observation, driving towards the area in a silver Mercedes saloon. There's activity in the marina and they're moving in to investigate now. Any orders for them, ma'am?"

"No. Tell them to proceed as planned. But we'll need to set up roadblocks to make sure no one escapes the scene this way. See to it."

"Yes, ma'am."

"Pipistrelle and Horseshoe?" Asha asked.

Sewell gave a strained smile. "P for Patterson, H for Hansen, which is what the Norwegian police believe Ole's surname to be. He matches Clara's description, so it seems likely."

Harriet Miller said nothing, but a twitch at the corner of her mouth made Asha certain that the ACC had chosen the name of a bat for Patterson's code word.

CHAPTER 45

Aaron stood on a freezing clifftop, trying to find respite from the icy wind behind a clump of whin bushes and reconsidering his life choices.

A whisper came back along the line of men. "No sign of gunfire now, but the drone reports activity near the water's edge. Apparently, there's a boat with a very hot engine down there, too. Seems likely it's the trawler the helicopter pilot reported."

"What about our two lost officers?" he asked.

"No sign yet, but it seems likely they engaged with whoever's down there, and shots were exchanged. We'll look for them as soon as we secure the area."

They retreated down the hill, moving stealthily, but these were police officers, however highly trained, not the SAS, and Aaron hoped whoever they were up against didn't have military experience and more firepower.

It was a miserable muddy slog, feet sliding with every step and their bodies so close together that he couldn't have seen the ground even if there'd been enough light. It seemed to take forever, but they were finally on the edge of the concrete approach road to the boatyard.

Either the wind had dropped or they were more sheltered down here, but it was quiet now, so a stone rolling beneath a careless boot would be easily heard from the yard. And the clouds had cleared so the half-moon cast a faint grey light over everything.

They split into two groups as planned. Aaron went with the commander, following the fence around to the right, towards the marina buildings. The other group peeled off left to where the rows of boats on stands would give them cover.

They made it almost all the way to the prefabricated building before they saw any movement, and then it was just a tiny red spot that marked someone smoking a cigarette.

The group froze. They were exposed here, with pale concrete on one side and short grass on the other, alongside the chain-link fence. Aaron tried to breathe quietly, but with his pulse hammering in his ears, it was hard to believe no one else could hear it.

Then a shadow detached itself from the group and slunk forward. Aaron lost the man almost immediately as he moved into the dappled shadows of the bushes behind the building. The waiting was agony, but the red light disappeared and, straining his ears, he thought there might have been a muffled grunt.

They moved forward again, and at last they were under the cover of the triangular block of shadow cast by the marina office.

There was no light from inside. Aaron, who was close to a window that he thought must belong to Steele's office, dared a peek through. It looked empty and undisturbed, but there was a momentary flash of light beneath the connecting door into the social area.

He touched the sleeve of the commander and whispered what he'd seen.

One man was sent inside to check it out. The door creaked a little, then there was a scuffle and a shout, cut off sharply, followed by a thump. The wall next to him shook to an impact, and then it was over.

They moved inside. Aaron's eyes, adjusted to the darkness, made out three people on the floor. One of the unit was fitting handcuffs to an unconscious man with no attempt at gentleness, but what drew his attention was the other two, one of them making furious sounds around a gag. Aaron dropped down next to Sergeant Casey and put a finger to his lips before undoing the gag.

"Are you okay, Tom?"

"I'm fine, lad, but I don't know about Jim here. He took a bullet."

The other officers were already attending to Jim. Aaron caught a glimpse of a pale face, eyes closed, but there was something wrong with the shape of the face. He realised half of it was dark with blood that had sheeted down from a head wound and turned black, disguising the edges of Jim's usually cheerful, plump features. His heart thumped painfully.

Tom was whispering again. "Get me out of these restraints and give me a fucking gun. I'm fit enough to keep up with you lot."

The commander leaned down and put a hand on the sergeant's shoulder. "You've done enough, Sergeant. I need you to stay here and look after Jim until the medics get here. Can you do that for me?"

Tom Casey pressed his lips together, then he looked towards his colleague and nodded. "I suppose you're right. If I hadn't been so damned stupid, Jim would still be up there in the car with the heater on, sipping coffee from a flask. I've done enough damage for one night. I'll stay here."

"Good man." The commander stood up. "Any news from the other team?"

"No, sir," said another officer. "They missed their last contact."

Aaron tensed. There hadn't been any exchange of gunfire, so perhaps it just meant they were close to the suspects and couldn't risk making a sound.

When they rounded the outside of the marina building, Aaron could see pinpoints of light moving around in the direction of the ramp down to the marina.

Then the order came back along the line to go to ground, and they all dropped into the shadows. Aaron touched the Glock at his hip to reassure himself. An engine approached from the landward side, and a car swept in, headlights on main beam. He flattened himself even more but had the sense not to move as the twin rays of light swept over him and away. It was movement that caught the eye at night, more than shape or even colour. It must have made it through before the ACC had managed to get a roadblock in place.

The silver Mercedes pulled up about thirty metres from his position and the driver's door opened, lighting up the courtesy lamp inside. His breath caught as he recognised the tall figure getting out, her trouser suit crumpled from sitting and her mop of blonde hair glinting in the light. The man nearest him drew in his breath and swore quietly.

They'd been told in the briefing that they might see one or more senior officers on the ground but that anyone in the vicinity of the boatyard, with the exception of those present in the incident room, should be treated as suspects. Aaron didn't think it had occurred to his fellow officer that the suspect might be quite so high ranking.

A man rushed up to Yvonne Patterson from the ramp, and she opened her arms, clearly expecting a warm welcome, but he reached past her into the car, dowsing the lights and closing the driver's door. Then he turned and hugged her. With the engine silenced, Aaron could hear every word as if he was beside them.

"Ole. At last. It's felt like a lifetime." Patterson's voice was softer than he'd ever heard it before, but totally recognisable. The man in front of him, who was even closer to the couple — for that's clearly what they were — turned and looked questioningly at Aaron. He nodded and mouthed, "Patterson," although he wasn't sure if the man would see enough to read his lips. His own night vision had fled after being assaulted by her headlights.

"You need to be more careful, *min kjære*. You are too bold."

Patterson laughed, a sexy, throaty laugh that Aaron would never have believed possible. "It's all right, my love. They are chasing their tails, looking for Clara Steele miles in the wrong direction. The distraction is working perfectly, and no one is giving a thought to this place. And your little messenger will be dead by morning, so there'll be no one to identify you."

They kissed, and Aaron's stomach turned over. To suspect his boss was bad enough, but to have her turn up here and prove her guilt was far worse.

"You arrived just in time," Ole said. "Come. Meet your new girls."

So, that was Clara's tormentor, the trafficker. Aaron hadn't managed to get a good look at him in the dark, but his English was near perfect with only the slightest trace of an accent. The two of them walked towards the marina, arms around each other's waists. At a word from the commander, the group followed, but at a safe distance.

They paused at the head of the ramp. Patterson asked a question and he laughed in response, then goosed her. She giggled. Giggled!

Close behind him, someone made a disgusted noise. He turned around to tell the officer to keep the noise down and met a pair of familiar dark eyes.

"What the hell?" he hissed.

Faith flinched, then her eyes went back to the couple, who were now kissing. Her mouth twisted and her eyes hardened.

"What the fuck are you doing here?" When this was over, if they both walked away, he was going to give her such a bollocking.

"I can help," Faith hissed.

Aaron shook his head. He was so angry he could barely speak. "Stay put, be quiet, and pray you don't get arrested after all you've done."

The hurt in her eyes stabbed him, but he kept his face stern.

Then the shuffle of feet came their way, coming from the direction of the ramp, and he turned his back on her. He couldn't let her distract him from the task in hand.

A group of four or five girls stopped right next to them, chattering to each other in high young voices that reminded him of the schoolgirls who flooded past the station in Belfast every afternoon on their way to the bus stop. Whatever language they were speaking, Aaron couldn't understand a word.

Faith tugged at his sleeve, but he shrugged her off. This was no time for discussion.

Another tug, more determined, then he felt her breath on the back of his neck as she whispered in his ear.

"They're speaking Polish. Their dialect's unusual — they might be from Lithuania or Belarus, but I think they'll understand me."

The commander spun around and glared as his eye fell on Faith. "What the hell's she doing here? She's supposed to be under supervision."

Faith didn't back down, but she bit her lip. "I can help, sir. They're speaking Polish, and I'm fluent," she whispered.

The commander threw her a speculative look. "What are they saying?"

"They're talking about the wonderful new life they're going to have," she said. "Oh, and they're wondering if they'll ever get the smell of fish out of their hair."

"So if we round them up, you can communicate with them?"

"Yes, sir." She flashed a triumphant glance at Aaron as if to say, "I told you I could be useful!"

"All right. New plan. Once all the women are off the boat and up here in the yard, we move in to separate them from the traffickers. You." He pointed to Faith. "You will reassure them and guide them to the marina building. You can go with her," he said to Aaron.

Aaron nodded. "We need to detain the chief and that Norwegian—"

"We will."

More girls gathered in a loose group in the middle of the boatyard, and their captors — if that was the right word, because they seemed to be coming off the boat willingly enough — were mostly still on the jetty.

One of the men with the girls offered cigarettes around, and a light. The girls appeared relaxed and happy, as if they were out on a family picnic.

At a signal from the commander, most of the squad melted away into the darkness, leaving Aaron, Faith and four more men together. This was going to be tricky. They had to separate the last two men from the group of women. Aaron wondered how they'd manage it.

He was still wondering when gunfire broke out down on the jetties.

The girls screamed and huddled even closer together. Some had their arms around each other, and a few were crying. The men with them hesitated, undecided, then they cast a glance at the girls and must have decided they were going nowhere. They ran towards the ramp, leaving the group unguarded.

"Now!" said the sergeant in charge of their small group. "You'd better be as good as you claim, Constable, or we'll have all hell breaking loose."

Faith shot him a scornful look and rose to her feet. If she'd ever had a gun, she'd left it behind her as she walked towards the milling group, talking in a calm manner but loud enough that most of them would be able to hear her over the commotion.

Aaron couldn't understand what she was saying, but the girls nearest to her were listening, still frightened, eyes like dark shadows in the moonlight.

Faith called back. "Aaron? Can you join me?"

He stood up slowly, making sure his Glock was holstered and safe. He raised his hands out from his sides so they could see he had no weapon and walked towards Faith. She chattered again in fluent Polish. He picked up a word that sounded like *purleetsia*, which he took to mean "police".

Dark eyes turned towards him, and the girls exchanged worried questions. Faith talked again at length, and they began to calm down.

"We need to get them moving," Aaron said through gritted teeth.

"I know. I'm trying, but they're scared, and they don't understand why the police would be interested in them. They think all this is above board." She spoke bitterly, and one or two of the girls looked towards the ramp and the sound of sporadic gunfire.

Faith spoke up. She waved her arms around, her passion clear. Tears glinted in her eyes, and the girls began to look shocked.

"What are you telling them?"

She ignored him. At last she had their full attention, even the waverers, and she started to lead them away towards the buildings.

They were halfway there when the sergeant's radio crackled into life. He and his men had remained hidden, leaving Faith and Aaron to try diplomacy first, so the sudden sound from an unexpected direction startled the girls. They scattered, some running clumsily in high heels, others fleet on bare feet or in flat shoes. In a heartbeat, the situation had gone from good to awful.

At least none of them had run towards the ramp, Aaron thought. The sergeant stood up — there was no longer any point in concealment — and shouted at Aaron. "Hostiles incoming! Get under cover."

His words were drowned out by the roar of a powerful engine as a white van raced down the access road and through the gates.

One of the girls was hit a glancing blow by the van as it skidded to a halt. She was flung sideways and lay where she'd fallen, limbs awkwardly splayed.

The driver's door opened and gunfire ripped across the boatyard, apparently indiscriminately. Aaron dived for the ground and rolled. He freed his handgun and looked about for a target. The shooter was using the van doors as a shield, so Aaron couldn't see what he was aiming at, but he sent a couple of bullets into the closest door and was rewarded with a yelp.

Faith was nowhere near him. He raised his head to see better, but there was no sign.

A bullet ricocheted off the ground not two feet from his hand, showering him with concrete chips and dust. He dropped back down, but just as he did, he spotted her. She was at the other side of the boatyard, in among the girls, tugging and pulling them towards the marina building.

She was going to get herself killed.

He rolled over until he had a boat between him and the van, and then got to his feet and ran, bent double, towards the back of the building.

Faith had maybe half a dozen of the girls with her. She pushed them inside, holding the door for them, then turned to follow them in. She hadn't seen him. He had no breath to shout, and anyway, he didn't want to draw attention. His last sprint carried him to her as she was letting the door close behind her.

Some instinct made her turn, and her eyes widened as the shot resounded.

Aaron's momentum took him crashing into Faith and they fell together into the darkened room. Girls were screaming again, but he had no time to see if they were all right. He levered himself off her still body and began to undo her body armour so he could see how much damage had been done.

His fingers struggled with the fastenings, stupid and numb with panic. He was breathing too fast and too loudly, and his vision was blurred by tears. "Faith! Faith, speak to me. Where are you hurt?"

Something hit him across the back of the neck, close to where he'd been hit before. He collapsed forward on to Faith and rolled, cursing and ready to lash out.

It was one of the trafficked girls. She'd hit him with a chair. She still held it in front of her like a weapon. Then her chin trembled and she dropped the chair with a clatter before running to the safety of her friends.

He bent over Faith again. Her eyes were open and fixed on his. He patted her body, feeling for sticky blood.

She whimpered and her body convulsed. He was frantic. "I need a medic. Where are the medics?" Until it dawned on him that the convulsions were laughter.

"Your face," she wheezed. "You thought I was dead."

"You bloody deserve to be dead," he said. The tension was oozing out of him. She was going to be okay. "Why didn't you speak?"

"Have you ever been shot in the chest with a ballistics vest on? I couldn't breathe." She pushed him away and held out her hand. "Here. Help me up."

They leaned on each other, and her warmth beneath the uniform sent a surge of love through him.

"All very romantic," said a dry voice, "but no one's sent us any medics."

He'd completely forgotten about Sergeant Tom Casey and Jim Christie. He swallowed down the guilt. "Is Jim—?"

"I'll live to walk another beat," replied a weak voice.

"Aye. It takes more than a bullet to get through a skull as thick as yours," said his sergeant.

CHAPTER 46

"Did you see who the shooter was?" Faith asked, sobering up.

"No, but I think I winged him."

"It was Aiken," she said. They moved over to the window, trying to see what was going on.

The Norwegians had fallen back to the trawler and taken cover behind its steel bulwarks. From there, they would be able to fire down on the squad without much risk of being hit themselves, which made it a stalemate. Until the ship started her engines with a deep-throated rumble.

"They're going to get away," Faith groaned. "Please tell me we have a patrol boat out there?"

"The ACC said there were none near enough to be useful."

The team on the jetties was pinned down, unable to prevent the boat leaving. The ship began to reverse. It was very wide for the small marina, and the skipper had to shuffle forwards and backwards to get her turned.

But at least the team Aaron had been with seemed to have got the shooter under control now. Aiken was spitting and trying to throw his diminutive weight around, even though his hands were cuffed behind his back. There were enough officers all around him for Aaron to be fairly certain he wouldn't escape.

Another car appeared at the gate of the boatyard, disgorging Superintendent Sewell and Asha. She hobbled down towards them and Aaron went out to meet her.

"I thought you were supposed to be resting?"

She ignored his comment. "That trawler is going to get away, and Patterson with it," she snarled, then stomped past him towards the ramp, her heavy bandage making her swing her leg with each stride. Sewell appeared at his shoulder.

"At least I managed to make her wear a vest," he said. He was also bulky in a ballistics vest, but neither of them were wearing helmets. He followed in Asha's wake, stopping alongside her at the top of the ramp.

Aaron thought back to the first day he'd visited this boatyard, and Fred Mills had been telling him all about the system they had for closing the lock gate across the entrance in case of bad weather and big spring tides. There'd been a control room for the mechanism that moved the gate up and down.

With a quick glance at Asha and Sewell, he ran around the building. The controls had looked simple enough when Mills had shown him them, basically just a button for up and one for down. The big trawler was still trying to make its turn and struggling in the tight space. He had a few minutes to get the thing working, with luck.

When he pressed the button to raise the gate, machinery whirred and lights flashed on the control panel, but Mills hadn't warned him about the warning klaxon that sounded out across the yard. It was as loud as an air-raid siren.

The men on the trawler finally noticed him and started taking pot shots. A bullet ricocheted from the corner of the shed and he flinched. That had been way too close for comfort, and he was exposed here. He ducked and ran for cover behind the building, chest heaving. Had he done enough? Would the gate keep going up now he'd released the button? Would the trawler still be able to get through? He wished he knew more about boats.

The vessel had completed her turn now and was driving towards the entrance, water churning at her stern. His heart sank. The way still looked clear. Ole and Patterson were going to get away.

Then the big boat reached the gap and she stopped dead in the water with a shuddering groan of rending metal. Her engines still strained to push her forward, but the gate must have been high enough to stop her, because she was going nowhere.

Then the water stopped churning and the boat stopped shuddering. With its engines in neutral, the trawler began to drift back towards the jetty.

CHAPTER 47

When had the sun risen? Aaron rubbed his gritty eyes and walked over to join Asha and Sewell on the ramp. Morning light brought with it the sort of flat calm and hazy sunshine that promised a clear winter's day, but Aaron had no time to waste on it. "What's happening now?"

"Patterson's up to something," Asha said. "I don't trust her."

"How is Jim Christie?" Sewell asked.

"Both him and Sergeant Casey are away safely in an ambulance. Jim has a head wound, and the paramedic said it had bled profusely, but she could find no evidence of a fractured skull. Still, they're not taking any chances. He's to get an MRI."

Sewell snorted. "Hard-headed bugger. He'll be fine. And Tom?"

"They dragged him off for a check-up as well. They've taken some of the injured trafficking victims to the hospital, too. That girl who was hit by the van looked to be in a bad way."

The armed response team had taken up defensive positions, as much as was possible on the exposed jetties, covering the trawler as it reversed slowly back towards them. Some were on the breakwater, where they'd have a line of fire down into the trawler.

Patterson appeared to be alone on the deck now, but Ole's shadow could be seen in the wheelhouse, steering the boat, and his men wouldn't be far away.

As soon as she was close enough to talk without shouting, Patterson turned a red, furious face to the commander of the ARU, who'd taken cover behind the workboat and his ballistics shield.

"What the hell do you think you're doing?" she spat. "You have seriously damaged an ongoing undercover operation with your clumsy interference. Tell your team to lower their guns. It's high time this fiasco ends."

Sewell stepped forward and seemed about to engage with her, when a voice stopped him in his tracks.

"Good morning, Yvonne," ACC Miller said from the top of the ramp, in a clear voice that carried on the still air. "Still trying to bullshit your way out of trouble?"

Patterson paled, but she wasn't giving in that easily. "I see you've allowed your blind love for the Harvey family to overrule your judgement, Harriet. I hope you don't believe a word DI Harvey says. She's resented me for years. Jealousy, I believe."

Asha smiled grimly and said nothing.

"I don't have time to engage in an exchange of insults, Chief Superintendent Patterson. Kindly ask your men to lay down their guns and walk into view with their hands behind their heads."

"*My* men?" Patterson injected scorn into those two words. "What the hell do you think is going on here? I responded to a tip-off from one of my confidential informants that an organised crime gang was planning to use this marina as a port of entry — with the knowledge of the owner — and came down here to investigate just as your team of heroes started shooting at everything that moved. I ran for cover and was taken hostage."

Aaron whispered to Asha, "You'd almost think she believes her own lies."

The rumble of engines in the distance made them all turn around. Two armoured vehicles drew up in the compound and more officers from the ARU jumped out, fully prepared with shields and weapons. *Even Patterson must be able to see that the game was up, surely?*

ACC Miller smiled. "If that's the case, Yvonne, you should let us rescue you." Aaron noticed the ACC had taken the time to put on a ballistics vest.

Asha stepped up to stand next to her ACC. "Yvonne Patterson, I'm arresting you on charges of trafficking for sexual exploitation, dealing class A substances, conspiracy to murder, and—"

Patterson dropped all pretence at civility, swearing like a fishwife. She had both hands clasped on the steel gunwales of the trawler, leaning over the side as if she wanted to leap ashore and attack Asha.

"What the fuck would you know? You were born with a silver spoon in your stupid mouth. I came from fucking nothing. I had to make my own way in life!"

Asha hesitated for only a moment before continuing to read the woman her rights in a clear voice.

"Good lass," ACC Miller said without moving her lips. "Keep her attention on you."

Asha dragged things out as much as she could, but eventually she'd said all the official words. She took a breath. "And what is more, Ms Patterson, there are likely to be further charges added in the near future, including keeping a brothel and controlling prostitution for gain—"

Members of the new armed unit were taking up their positions along the breakwater, overlooking the boat. No one seemed to have noticed them yet, so the distraction was working.

Patterson screamed and tried to wrench a gun from one of the trawler's crew who'd all moved closer to listen. He dodged out of her way and brought up the rifle to bear on her.

"No, no, no!" muttered the ACC. "I want her brought to trial."

Before he could pull the trigger, his chest bloomed with a dark stain. He looked down, confused, then his knees buckled and he collapsed out of sight of the group on the jetty. Ole Hansen calmly replaced the spent cartridge in the shotgun he held.

Gunfire broke out all over the boat, muzzle flashes and screams shattering the momentary calm. At the same time, the armed response team on the jetties moved in.

Aaron sprinted for the nearest finger pontoon and launched himself at the tall side of the trawler, which was a little over a metre away. He managed to get his arms hooked over the steel bulwarks, then swung his leg until his foot hooked the edge.

He hadn't realised how exhausted he was until he tried to haul himself the rest of the way. It took all his strength to climb over, and instead of landing on his feet as he'd intended, he fell, landing heavily on his side.

Feet clattered towards him. He tried to bring his gun up, but Patterson was too quick for him. She lashed out with her foot. Pain flared up his hand, and his fingers refused to close on the Glock's comforting grip.

She brought her foot back for another swing. He was still too winded to dodge so he tried to curl, to protect his head with his arms, but she kicked him in the gut instead. He retched, bile burning his throat, and tried to push himself to his feet before she could come at him again. What was she wearing? Steel toecaps? One more kick would finish him.

And here it came. He grabbed her foot before it made contact and twisted it sharply, using her own momentum against her.

He didn't quite manage to pitch her over — he was in too weak a position for that — but he did throw her off balance. He took the opportunity to stagger to his feet, head spinning and air whistling as he tried to draw a full breath.

Then he was on her.

She spun with him, teetered as if she was going to fall, then put a hand out to the wall of the wheelhouse to steady herself.

His right hand throbbed, which he took to be a sign that the nerves had recovered. He grabbed her right wrist and hauled it up behind her back, praying his grip would hold, then slammed her against the wall.

He managed to holster the Glock, clumsily with his left hand, and grab the cuffs from his belt. He got one secured to her right wrist, but then she heaved her body away from the wall. God, she was strong! It took all his strength to hold her, and the snap of the cuffs was the best sound in the world at that moment.

Not that he was about to relax. Even with her wrists secured behind her back, Yvonne Patterson was dangerous.

A movement behind him brought him around and reaching for the gun again, but it was an ARU officer in dark coveralls and a ballistic vest who greeted him. It was only now that he realised the gunfire had ended.

The part of the face visible beneath the helmet and eye protection grinned at him. "Need any help, sir?"

"No, thank you," Aaron wheezed. "Everything's under control. What's going on in the rest of the boat?"

"We have it secure, sir. The crew have been disarmed and we're lining them up ready to get them off."

"Did you find the captain? Tall, light-coloured sweater, designer stubble."

The officer shrugged. "I think we got everyone. Want to come and see?"

"Okay." Patterson took advantage of his distraction to lash out backwards, catching him on the shin with one of her heavy shoes. His eyes stung and he blinked away tears of pain but didn't release his hold on her. "Maybe I do need a bit of help with this one. She doesn't know when she's beaten."

On the aft deck, a dozen handcuffed men stood in a line, looking defeated. Aaron scanned the row, but he wasn't convinced any of them was Ole. He hadn't got a good look at the man's face, and it had been dark, but there'd been a presence about the Norwegian skipper, and an upright posture that none of these men exhibited.

He turned towards the marina and raised his voice to attract the ACC's attention. "I think Ole might still be at large!"

Harriet Miller flashed him an irritated look and snapped out orders to the original team, who had converged on her now the action seemed to be over.

Aaron searched the dock for Asha but couldn't see her anywhere. His heart skipped a beat.

CHAPTER 48

Asha only realised she'd been holding her breath when Aaron finally had Patterson subdued and cuffed, then she gasped for air as if it had been her kicked in the gut.

ACC Miller shot her a look, irritation warring with concern on her harsh features. "For God's sake, Asha, go and sit down before you fall down. It's all over now, and I won't have my officers running themselves into the ground." The question of how she'd face Asha's mother if she took any long-term harm from today's events hung unsaid in the air between them.

Richard took Asha's arm and turned her away. "The boss lady is right, Asha. Could you spare me a minute, do you think?"

"Where did you spring from?"

"I was watching from up on the headland, and I had the same idea as Aaron about the lock gate, but he beat me to it."

"Well, I think I can probably spare you two minutes," she said, trying to keep her face serious.

He laughed, and she found herself responding. His presence lightened her mood. "What do you want me for?"

He paused for half a beat too long, and her cheeks flamed in the cold morning. Then he grinned and said, as if he hadn't heard her, "I need to check my boat didn't take any damage in the gunfight. Want to come? I could put the kettle on and make you a drink."

Asha glanced back. Harriet Miller was in her element, giving out orders and covering every eventuality. She wasn't needed here; in fact, she'd been ordered to go away and rest, hadn't she? "All right. I'd like that."

He slowed his pace to match her painful hobble. That stupid Robert Jones bandage weighed her down with every stride.

Cloud lay serenely in her usual berth, her creamy hull and gleaming woodwork like something from a lifestyle magazine. Richard unclipped a little gate in the railings and reached up for a small stool that he placed on the jetty as a step. She'd been wondering how on earth she'd manage to climb on board with a leg that couldn't bend.

The deck was wide, the wood oiled to a soft golden hue. She followed Richard to the back of the boat to the doors of the deep cockpit. He fiddled with a lock on a miniature set of wooden doors and swung them open. "Would you prefer to go first or second?"

Asha stuck her head inside. Wooden steps led down to a U-shaped seating area and a navigation table surrounded by electronic screens. Further inside the boat were more steps, and she caught a glimpse of a tidy little kitchen area with a gleaming stainless-steel stove and marbled work surfaces. Even in the dim light, the richness of the interior was impressive.

"Maybe you should go first," she said, hanging back to let him through.

He made light work of the steps, then turned to offer her his hand, but at that moment, the boat lurched a little and Asha was thrown off balance. She grabbed the edge of the cabin roof to steady herself.

It must have been a stray wave, she thought, but her instincts were screaming at her. Instead of taking his hand, she straightened up and looked around the boat, as much of it as she could see from here.

There was nothing. It looked clean and tidy and ready to sail the world. She was tired, that was all. Off balance and jumping at shadows. Then the sun glinted off the deck, just a brief reflection as the boat bobbed on the waves.

Her eyes were drawn to the spot. Neither wood nor plastic reflected like that, so what was it? Two steps took her closer to the far side of the boat. A pool of water on the teak deck had caught the light. If she tried, she could convince herself that it was shaped like a human foot.

"Asha?" Richard called, an edge of anxiety to his voice.

"Coming," she replied, but instead of returning to the cabin door, she leaned forward a little more, to look around the side of the raised cabin wall.

A figure reared up in front of her, bellowing with rage. Ole Hansen towered over her even in his stockinged feet. His eyes were wild and furious as those of an angry bull, and his hair was matted with weed and seawater.

Asha didn't have time to think. She lowered her head and ran at him like a battering ram — at least, that was the intention, but her bandage-encased foot caught on a deck fitting and she tripped, hitting him in the midriff with her shoulder.

For a moment they stood there, the Norwegian fisherman windmilling his arms for balance and Asha clinging to his soaking wool sweater to stop herself from toppling overboard.

Then he grabbed hold of the edge of the cabin roof and swung his free hand at her. She only had time to see the glint of a knife before it bit home with a dull thud.

Aaron had said that being stabbed hadn't hurt at first. He'd thought he'd been punched until he collapsed, bleeding, but this felt like nothing at all.

They both looked down at the same moment, and Asha saw that Ole's knife was embedded in her upper left thigh. The trackpants had unrolled themselves and covered the bandage, so he couldn't have known that she was effectively wearing armour. If he'd struck true, that would have been her femoral artery and she'd have been bleeding out all over the deck, but as it was, he stood baffled, unable to understand why she hadn't fallen.

She took advantage of his confusion and charged him a second time. This time she got her shoulder under his armpit. He was bigger than her, and stronger. It shouldn't have worked. She should have bounced off him, but instead his wet socks slipped on the polished wooden side deck, and he fell backwards, coming up hard against the railings.

Asha gave him another shove to help him on his way and he dropped, but at the last moment, he hooked an arm over the side of the boat, dangling there.

He'd be back up in a second, a man like that.

Asha drew back her foot, the left one, and kicked him in the face with as much force as she could muster. She caught him on the angle of his jaw, jerking his head back. The fury in his eyes turned to panic, then they glazed over. The arm that was on the deck slackened and he slid back into the water with barely a splash.

The whole thing must have taken a few seconds because Richard was only just at her side. He grabbed hold of her before the momentum of her kick could carry her over the railings after the fisherman.

Together, they leaned over the side. The white sweater formed a pale blob beneath the surface of the water, and it wasn't coming back up again.

"We should try to save him," Asha said.

"Why? That's the bastard who tricked my sister, isn't it?"

"Well. We need his evidence for the trial. And I expect we already have an international incident on our hands. Let's not make it worse by murdering Norwegian citizens."

He gave her a strained smile. "Fair enough, but just for the record? I'd rather let him drown."

Between them, they managed to hook his clothing with a boathook. Ole Hansen floated like a speared fish, and Asha thought she must have killed him, but when his body bumped against the hull of the boat, he jerked and started coughing and spluttering.

She left Richard to keep him afloat, but held at boathook's length so he couldn't climb aboard again, and shouted for help. The ARU team came running, and between them they managed to land the dazed fisherman on to the jetty.

All the fight seemed to have gone out of him. He barely struggled as the cuffs clicked on to his wrists. Asha was relieved to hear him cursing fluently as he was marched away to the boatyard for processing.

Asha, following them up the ramp with her injured leg dragging, leaned heavily on Richard's arm. She dragged her gaze away from Ole Hansen and swept it over the boatyard. So much destruction. So much fear and heartache, and for what?

Aaron was helping Faith McAvoy lead a lot of frightened young women out of the marina office towards a police van. Her heart sank for that young officer. A few days ago, she'd had a promising future ahead of her, but now what? Certainly not a career in the police, not after her involvement with Patterson, not to mention Aiken and Kernaghan, but she had proved herself these past few hours. Her quick thinking might well have saved lives, because those poor frightened girls wouldn't have gone with anyone else while shots were being fired all around them.

She tilted her head to look up at Richard. Would his sister prove as resilient as Faith? A lot would be resting on her in court. There'd be difficult times ahead for Clara, and she couldn't even begin to imagine how that might impact any relationship she might be tentatively building with this man.

Her head was still buzzing as they passed near a patrol car with its rear door open. She glanced across to see Patterson in the back seat, handcuffed and bruised. Those hard eyes bored into Asha as if committing every detail of her face to memory.

Asha shivered. "Take me home, Richard."

But before they could turn to leave, Patterson's lips moved soundlessly.

"I'll be coming for you."

THE END

ACKNOWLEDGEMENTS

I would like to thank several people for supporting me through a very difficult time while I was writing this book, not least my publisher, Joffe Books, and in particular Emma Grundy Haigh, who was wonderfully understanding when this novel took far longer than it should have to see the light of day. Also the editing team, especially Sam Matthews. She's an absolute star and I'm very lucky to have her.

I'd also like to thank Ann McMaster (who was single-handedly responsible for keeping me going to the end of the novel with her positivity and encouragement), Vickie Hanna from Bangor Marina, and my husband, Fraser, for reading early versions and giving me such useful feedback. I should also thank all the staff at Bangor Marina, as well as John Harkness from BJ Marine for being so helpful and answering all the daft questions I ask in the name of accuracy.

Lastly, I'd like to thank Maureen, not only for dog-sitting, which allows us to go sailing so often, but also for passing on her own love of sailing and the sea to both of us.

ALSO BY KERRY BUCHANAN

HARVEY & BIRCH
Book 1: KNIFE EDGE
Book 2: SMALL BONES
Book 3: DEADLY SHORES

Thank you for reading this book.

If you enjoyed it please leave feedback on Amazon or Goodreads, and if there is anything we missed or you have a question about, then please get in touch. We appreciate you choosing our book.

Founded in 2014 in Shoreditch, London, we at Joffe Books pride ourselves on our history of innovative publishing. We were thrilled to be shortlisted for Independent Publisher of the Year at the British Book Awards.

www.joffebooks.com

We're very grateful to eagle-eyed readers who take the time to contact us. Please send any errors you find to corrections@joffebooks.com. We'll get them fixed ASAP.

Printed in Great Britain
by Amazon

79338297R10174